Killer Calories

Nancy Good

ISBN: 978-1-62420-445-6

Credits
Cover Design: Design by Ms G
Editor: Sherry Derr-Wille

Dedication

For Lena

New York City

My feet pounded the pavement. Four blocks to go to finish three miles. By this hour, lights were off in most stores. Midnight was not my preferred running time, but you gotta do what you gotta do.

"Hey bitch," an angry voice yelled in my ear as a heavy weight crashed into me. I landed hard, sprawled flat on the pavement. Knees throbbing, palms scraped and...damn, this was gonna mess up my time.

"Mind your own business," the voice screamed. I raised my head a few inches from the pavement just as a large hooded figure turned the corner. His fist pumped the air.

"Screw you," I yelled to the now empty sidewalk, sounding far tougher than I felt.

"Are you all right?" A white-haired gentleman with a kind face bent down. He held a shopping bag of groceries in one hand as he helped me up with the other.

"Just bruises, I hope." I tested my legs. "Did you see that guy?"

"I saw what he did. Might have been a woman though, that kind of run. Couldn't see a face. Came from the corner over there." He pointed down the block. "Whoever it was aimed for you like a torpedo. Slammed right into you. Lunatics are all over. I wouldn't run at night if I were you."

"Thanks," I said, surprised he thought this was some random loony. The phrase, "mind your own business," had been blasted with my name all over it. I was almost proud. I'd gone from being boring to thriller-worthy in a really short time. I guess this meant I was getting close to the truth.

I shuffled painfully back to the apartment looking like a police decoy trying to lure a mugger except I didn't have a weapon. A seedy guy eyed me hungrily.

"Not on your life," I screamed and sprinted the rest of the way faster than I'd ever run.

Chapter One

Never eat ingredients you can't pronounce. Except quinoa. You should eat quinoa.

Unknown

His lips met mine, warm, accepting, passionate. The glorious kiss touched every part…

"What happened to the crème fraiche? Are you still asleep?" Hurricane Daniel stomped through the bedroom, roaring through my dream.

"Nice wake-up call." I jumped out of bed, grabbed a sweater from the closet and the jeans thrown over a chair last night. I splashed water on my face, but my lips still felt that kiss.

Whose lips were those anyway? Dreams were too vague. They should come with screen credits.

I stuck my head into our daughter Chloe's room to check on her progress, and continued to the kitchen, also known as the war zone.

"It's gone. This is a disaster."

Daniel was in desperate search mode with his head in the fridge searching for heavy clotted cream. The only catastrophe was that this stuff existed. I saw the container from five feet away.

"Here it is. Disaster relief." I gingerly picked it up. "You do know this has eleven grams of fat and two grams of protein in two tablespoons, right?"

"That's why it tastes good. Spare me the lecture."

Daniel dropped down into a carved chair at the oak table. He dumped the entire container of solid white gook on strawberries.

My husband should have been born an English Lord of the Manor in a different century. Every morning a groaning sideboard laden with clotted cream, goose egg delicacies, and large slabs of freshly made bread would greet him. Instead, he lived with me, an overly zealous health nut, in an old apartment on Manhattan's Upper West Side.

The downstairs buzzer signaled the school bus. Chloe raced out of the bathroom, past the kitchen yelling "bye," and down the stairs, where I saw her off on the bus. She had breakfast at Huntley Private School, which was like dining at The Plaza. Daniel's mother footed the bill for the outrageous tuition at the school, her alma mater.

Three more times up and down the four flights to our apartment brought my step count to twelve hundred. I was feeling pretty good about myself until a new neighbor, all bones, ran up beside me.

"Race you to the roof," he yelled, zooming past to the sixteenth floor.

"Knock yourself out," I gasped.

This is a really competitive city. I walked in the back door to our kitchen.

"Who does he think he's kidding? Three stars? I've eaten there twenty times. The chicken's like straw and the fettuccine alfredo is glue. His Prozac's making him giddy." Daniel was reading a rival food critic's review in the New York Times.

"Doesn't all fettuccine alfredo taste like glue?" I sniped.

Daniel looked up. "It's a good thing I have taste buds for both of us."

"And a stomach to match," I stared at his paunch. This was usual breakfast jousting.

Maybe the weight gain was an occupational hazard. Daniel was a nationally known food writer. We were the odd couple, like Oscar and Felix. I cooked vegetables. He made anything just off the hoof, like oxtail stew or tripe.

Why was this odd couple together? Wouldn't I have been happier with a bike-riding pescatarian and he with a Rachel Ray? The short answer was it had a lot to do with orgasms. Orgasms were more important than food years ago. Orgasms and a guy who could support himself. Daniel worked on both counts. Money still mattered, but sex? Twenty-five-year-olds should not make big decisions.

Daniel picked up his bowl and walked over to me. Holding the bowl with one hand, he kissed the back of my neck. "How about we go back to bed and I'll stop eating?"

"You know I'd love to." Probably the most popular white lie said by women to their men. I stared into his brown eyes trying to bore into me seductively. "But I teach this morning and have fencing."

He nodded and went back to his clotted cream. Sure, I could have skipped the gym, but a beard that dripped white gook was not a turn on. I grabbed a goat yogurt, eight grams of protein, four grams of fat, and went into the foyer to pack up supplies for the class. Jars of jelly beans, flowers in vases, stuffed animals.

This gig was the latest in a long list of embarrassing jobs I'd had in the last nine years. *Creative writing for toddlers*. The very name made me twitch. Helene, the deceitful Association President, called it writing, and parents believed her. I'd been an editor at a magazine, and sold a screenplay years ago. This job was the very lowest point in my resume, but I needed the money.

It was now seven forty-five. I had to be at the playground by nine ten. That left one hour for *en gardes*, ripostes and lunging. Aggression and your butt get worked at the same time.

"Daniel," I called, with one foot out the door. "I'm leaving. I signed up for a screenplay writing workshop for six weeks on Tuesday nights. We'll need a sitter."

"What? No," he yelled to the closing door.

I went down the stairs. Daniel didn't get why I needed a course. "Just write," he said. As if creating a screenplay was the same as describing lobster bisque.

~ * ~

Outside. I relished the fresh air and a delicious sense of freedom. Indian summer had arrived. Late September's cooling Canadian breezes eased out New York's oppressive summer. Now I would see my crush, my secret fantasy, Ralph.

Looking up, the sun was visible through a thin screen of haze, and a quarter moon left over from last night's sky. Around the moon was a reddish halo. What was that old poem? "Red sky at night, sailors delight. Red sky in the morning, sailors take warning." A shiver went through me. Maybe the reddish halo was a bad omen. Or could it be I was getting sick? Damn, I forgot to take my ten vitamins running out like that. I popped two vitamin C's.

At the gym I wrestled my too-thick auburn hair into a lumpy pony tail and threw on a T- shirt and leggings. Marta, our group's Russian coach, ran through *en gardes* and lunges till sweat poured down my face. Let's just say we didn't look like the Three Musketeers.

Class ended. I showered, dressed and left for the park. Eight fifty-five.

"Have a good day." Blanca nodded to me.

Blanca was the newest of the club receptionists, a middle-aged blonde with dark roots and an olive complexion, and after only two weeks, a history of lateness. Since there was no one at the desk when I arrived, she'd been late again. I gave her one more week before she joined the long list of fired employees.

On the way to the park, I relaxed by listening to a ten-minute meditation.

"*I love myself unconditionally.* Breathe. *I try to be positive in all interactions.* Breathe." My next interaction was with Ralph, the playground caretaker. Maybe it was his kindness, maybe it was his incredible physique, but my thoughts about Ralph were embarrassingly more than positive.

~ * ~

I arrived at Riverside Drive and 91st Street, the park entrance to the playground and the cute red brick building that housed the classes for kids. Riverside Park was Central Park's less famous Manhattan cousin, but it boasted miles of views of the Hudson River.

Old beech and oak trees in leafy foliage made a dark heavy curtain on the steep hill leading down to the playground. It would be noon before the sun would light up the park this far west so I couldn't see Ralph around the swings.

Riverside Park was eerily empty. City people don't like quiet empty spaces. Drop us on a mountain top in Maine and we'll see muggers behind every tree. Quiet is bad and people mean safety. Today it was so silent I could hear my heart pound.

Fortunately, I had my secret weapon. I patted the illegal Mace in my pocket and felt reassured. Still, I walked quickly down the hill to the playground.

The gate was closed. This was odd. Ralph always left it wide open. I pushed on the gate and it easily swung clear of the lock. This meant he was here, but where?

"Hey Ralph, save me a donut," I called out, a standing joke between us.

The last thing I'd eat before starving would be a donut. My dire warnings about the perils of sugar were well known but not appreciated.

Ralph did not respond. I headed toward the class building. Where was he? This was too many changes. I never liked change unless I caused it.

From here on everything happened so fast. Jars of jelly beans, flowers, vases shattered into pieces as they hit the ground. Why did that happen? What klutz let them fall? Part of my brain thought all the rolling colors were pretty. The other didn't understand how they got there. There was so much broken glass. I looked again and understood what my eyes and hands saw before my mind caught up.

Feet. Ominous, quiet feet in work boots stuck out past some bushes next to the storage building. Dead feet. I shivered. My hands, free now, reached into my pocket. I grabbed the Mace, and sprayed everything in front of me. I covered my face as I walked as close as I dared to the boots.

"Ralph. Where are you? What the heck's going on?"

Something moved. Maybe twenty feet away. In the woods beyond the building, near a hole in the wire fence. That hole should have been fixed years ago. You could get in when the front gate was locked, if you knew it was there. I was far away, but I swear I saw a glint of an eye watching me. I stared, determined to see into the thick woods. The eye disappeared, but definitely something moved this time. It was too big to be a squirrel. No deer lived in Manhattan. A coyote was spotted in the Bronx. Coyote or a killer in New York City? My bet was on a murderer.

No crazed psycho was going to take me down at only 4,790 steps. I turned and ran fast around the holly bushes, around the path where it merged into the larger walkway, and up the hill. My legs really moved, but my sneaker caught on the edge of the uneven pavement. When I fell my knee slammed against the concrete upraised edge of the flower bed. Pain raced up my leg.

I needed help. A jogger ran past on the nearby promenade. "Stop, please," I shouted.

His head turned in my direction but he kept going. I had to get control of myself. I took a deep breath and stood up. The knee hurt badly when I put weight on it, dizziness overwhelmed me.

After the second breath, I thought the man lying there might not be dead. Maybe Ralph went to get help. I didn't get close enough to see a face. It could be a homeless guy on drugs. That happened everywhere, why not here? A flush of embarrassment made my neck feel like an oven was on somewhere. Maybe Ralph had a heart attack and I just left him. Or he could be in a diabetic coma after all that sugar.

Whoever it was, someone was in trouble and I ran away. I shouldn't bring in the cops without knowing. We could all get fired. But what about the glint of an eye in the leaves, maybe someone in the woods just waited for my return? I wasn't brave, living without any caffeine or sugar. Childbirth was the only brave moment in my life, but if I could have hired someone to go through it for me, I would have.

Damn, my knee hurt. I spotted a large branch on the ground and picked it up. I automatically assumed the *en garde* position.

"What are you doing?"

My feet shifted and I lunged in the direction of the voice.

"Hey, cut that out." Louisa ducked nicely before I could impale her with the stick. Just as well that my aim was off and my lunge was too weak.

She squinted at me. "You look awful." Louisa was my assistant teacher and my friend, who was supposed to wear glasses. "You're crying?"

I didn't feel the tears till now. "Oh Louisa, I'm so glad to see you. Something's wrong. Come on." I limped back to the playground. We arrived there and saw the jagged shards of glass and jelly beans.

"What happened?" Louisa looked confused.

"Call me butterfingers. Over here."

I pulled her like a kid who tried to get mom to look at the store window. We were close enough now and saw the entire body. We knew immediately who it was. Louisa screamed. The scream was a solid ten. It filled the playground with its shock and horror.

"Shh."

What was I saying shush for? Like we'd wake him? I held Louisa's arm. Ralph did not stir. I peered carefully into the woods. All was quiet. Whoever, or whatever had been there was gone. It was Ralph. Wonderful Ralph was lying there.

"What's happened to him? Melanie, it's something bad. Let's get the police. This is not for us." Louisa pulled at my arm.

I couldn't move. Ralph lay motionless on the ground: his still form bluntly confronted us. I started sobbing. Louisa's eyes filled with tears too. "Oh there, there, *pobrecita*," she said, "little one" in Spanish. My father in his casket flashed before me. I shivered.

"We have to see if he's alive or not." I was stalling. We both knew the answer. Ralph's face told us the truth. His eyes stared; his mouth unnaturally gaped open.

"*Mama mia*, I don't want to touch him," gasped Louisa. She crossed herself.

"I don't either, but we have to." I knelt by Ralph's heart. Between the pain in my leg and the sight before me, nausea made me gag. I've always felt sick seeing blood, but it wasn't just the terrible way Ralph looked. There was an awful smell. Bile came up in my throat. I looked away and took a gulp of fresher air. I turned back holding my breath. "Louisa, can you do this with me?" She reached out a trembling hand and together we picked up his wrist. It felt like meat left out on a warm day— clammy, slightly warm. There was no pulse. I couldn't bring myself to

7

listen for a heartbeat.

"Ralph, Ralph," I called into his ear.

I'd never been this close to his face before. I fought back an urge to stroke his cheek.

"Melanie, he's gone. We've got to call the police," Louisa said softly.

"Yes, yes you're right."

I was relieved she was there to stop me from shaking him. *Wake up, goddammit. Please don't be dead. Wake up so this will just be a bad dream and disappear.*

"We have to call the police," Louisa said again, but louder this time.

"Okay. I'll go. Watch out for kids coming. Keep everyone out of here."

If I didn't get away from his body, I'd throw up all over the crime scene. This looked like a murder, not a death from an accident or natural causes.

I used the branch as a cane and limped around the storage room. I got to the entrance of the larger classroom building. The door was open. I peered inside, cautiously flicked on the lights. I ran to the bathroom and lost the contents of my stomach. Disgusting. Purple cutouts of dinosaurs watched me.

I dropped into a tiny chair, tried to breathe, and dialed 911 for the first time in my life. "Police, help," I yelled when a woman answered. "A man's been killed." Not just a man–Ralph, my friend, my secret fantasy.

"Hold on, miss," a bored voice responded. "How do you know?"

"How do I know? Do I have to pass a medical exam? There's blood all over, no pulse, get me the police this minute." My screaming helped. In moments I gave the location of the playground to a Sergeant Murphy.

I grabbed a blanket we kept for picnics. Back outside, children's voices wafted down the hill. Louisa and I laid the blanket over Ralph's body. "The police are coming. Stay here. I've got to stop the kids."

Up the pathway two members of my class were in sight. Nicole Bender, with her son Jason and his friend Cody in tow. Nicole was trying to act as if it was easy to totter down a steep hill wearing three-inch heels. Nicole, a parent with an exaggerated sense of entitlement who I loathed, gave me the sense each week that I had not lived up to her expectations as a teacher or a fashionista.

The children looked puzzled by my walking stick. "The playground is closed this morning. There's been a problem. The class has been canceled."

Nicole's outraged expression was almost amusing. Absolutely nothing in life was ever as important as what she wanted this very minute. I gave her my still-being-worked-on contemptuous look.

"What do you mean there's been a problem? What am I supposed to do with the boys?" she snarled, teeth bared. "I have an appointment. You'll just have to keep them until I get back."

She folded her arms across her clinging white low-cut shirt. I had waited for this moment. This was the invitation I needed.

"I'm not one of your housekeepers, bitch." Bitch was mumbled because of the kids, but it still felt good. "The kids can't be here. Try being a mother for a change, or a human being," I yelled.

Too bad she didn't hear me. The sound of wailing sirens pierced the morning quiet. Even Nicole kept her mouth shut as we watched five police cars from three different directions speed down the paths, across the promenade and past the walkway lined with cherry trees covered with rotting fruit.

Like Nascar choreography, all the cars squealed to a stop at precisely the same time. I walked toward them feeling guilty, as I usually did around police. They'd blame me, and before I could explain I'd have handcuffs on and be locked in a jail cell for the rest of my life. Which terrified me, but was tempting. I might get to finish a screenplay.

Chapter Two

Keep Calm and Carry On and Eat Well
M. Deming

Maybe it was being over thirty, but these cops looked like they were too young to even drive or worse, carry guns. I put my hands in the air and closed my eyes. If I was going to get shot, I didn't want to watch. I swayed, off balance. Teenage cops, Ralph dead, blood everywhere. Did someone put a Molly in my goat yogurt?

"You can put your hands down and open your eyes." The blond cop's badge read Officer Crandall.

"It's the guns, you know. This is my first time." What a dumb thing to say. I felt my cheeks turn red.

Nicole, of course, was a woman who would not be shy in front of the KGB. She jumped between me and Crandall as if she'd strike me. I stepped back.

"I cannot believe you called the police over a little accident." She punched out each word and pointed a finger at my chin, the other hand on her hips, maybe to keep her balance on the hill with those heels, or to stick her chest in his face. She did an interesting and probably difficult maneuver, turning and fearlessly pinning Crandall with an outraged gaze. Her back was arched, chest out. Crandall worked hard at not looking down her blouse. He stared straight ahead.

"What she did has to be reported. I hope you're writing this up," Nicole said in an imperious tone.

Was it her nose in the air, or her biting 'you're my slave look' that made me want to break one of her heels over her head?

"Yes, ma'am. That's why we're here."

Who said NYC cops aren't polite?

"Well, good. I don't know if it's a misdemeanor or a felony, but she's preventing these children from being educated." The ruby nails pointed again at me, the evil queen from Sleeping Beauty.

Crandall shook his head, sighed, and moved aside. He asked her to step with him away from the boys.

"We were called about a possible homicide. Do you want your kids to see a murder victim?"

His mouth assumed a slightly amused expression which made him older, or wiser, than I imagined he was.

For a nanosecond her eyes got wider, there was a slight jerk of her head. Perhaps Nicole was flustered for the first time in her life. No, not this time. Her true bitch came back.

"Well, I never...kids, come with me. This will turn out to be a hoax. She called you for nothing. She's probably unprepared as usual. Just an excuse not to do her job."

This almost forced me to grab hold of the long streaked blonde hair which was definitely extensions. The only reason I didn't was the children had gotten enough of a show today.

She clicked back up the hill with effort, each enraged step echoed in the trees. 9/11 must have been a major scheduling disaster for her. I wondered if there was a special place in hell reserved for parents who didn't care about the lives of others if it affected their childcare plans. For one glorious moment, I enjoyed watching her struggle up the hill. Then I was back with the awful truth about Ralph.

The cops hurried down to the playground and I limped along behind. Louisa was already in a conversation with the other cop in Spanish. She always knew who was Spanish-speaking without the usual "do you speak my language?" thing. Amazing radar.

I hid in the classroom, put my leg up, and fished in my backpack for Arnica Montana 30 cc. Never leave home without it. In this city where you can trip in a pothole running for a bus, or get hit by an elbow or a backpack on crowded subways, arnica's essential.

"I have a few questions." Crandall's voice startled me.

He leaned against the door frame, looking like a recruitment poster for the police academy, or one of those calendars of scantily clad men in uniform.

"We know Ralph's last name was Duvet. Was he married? We need to notify next of kin."

"I don't know. He lived somewhere in the Bronx." There went a shooting pain in my left temple. Ralph might have had six kids and a wife somewhere. "Call Helene Springer. She's the playground president and has all the records." I gave him her number.

He reached her and got off fast. Helene had that effect on people.

"Did you see anyone on your way into the park?"

Definitely alone walking to work, definitely had that illegal Mace still in my pocket.

Crandall waited uncomfortably, shifting his feet back and forth like a third grader.

"No, there wasn't anyone, except a jogger on the promenade who wouldn't stop when I called for help. Maybe Louisa saw someone. She was five minutes behind me."

Crandall seemed disappointed at my lack of information. He went outside where the sound of voices was building.

Suddenly it hit me. I could have to answer a lot of questions in interrogation rooms with small spaces, a locked door, no windows and a one-way mirror. Scenes from *Law and Order SVU* raced through my head. My stomach twisted in a knot. I needed California poppy. The liquid herbal remedy, not opium. Twenty-five drops in water to calm down. Valerian would be perfect, the herbal form of valium. Who would carry remedies for murder when they came to teach toddlers?

"Hey, Melanie." Louisa walked in looking shell-shocked. She flopped down next to me.

"The cops asked me some questions. I told them what happened. I only saw one jogger. He was on another path."

"Dark hair? Stocky?" Louisa nodded. "Must be the same guy I saw just after I tripped." I massaged my knee.

"So, I'm leaving. I wanted to check in with you first. How are you doing?" Her face was still as ashen as mine must be.

"I'm just torturing myself. Will the cops think I did it? You know, kill the messenger. I was the first one here. I called it in."

Louisa looked at the ceiling and crossed herself. "You shouldn't even say something like that. They just ask what you saw, what you did. What you knew about Ralph. That's it. Don't think like that."

"You're right, you're right. Bad habit." Like it was easy to stop thinking.

"You did good. Go home and lie down. That's what I'm doing. I think this place will be closed for a while."

"You were a lot braver than I was. Did you ever notice anything off about Ralph? Why someone would kill him?"

"I don't know. Ralph was a ladies' man."

She smiled at me like she knew I had a crush on him.

"Would that get him killed?"

"Where I come from, men kill each other. Drunken fights, someone looked at their girlfriend. Usually drugs and alcohol and a party."

I had known Louisa for years. "I had no idea."

"Nobody related to me, don't worry. I'd kill the guy myself if he did something like that. It happens more in my world." Louisa suddenly took out her phone and checked text messages like she wanted to change the topic.

"Why don't you go home? I'll be fine."

She looked exhausted and relieved to get the boss's permission to leave. I forget I'm her boss. We hugged like two people who had just survived a plane crash. Louisa left.

So, a boyfriend or husband who had it in for Ralph? He messed around with the wrong woman? It didn't feel right, but it was better than thinking I'd be locked up.

I had a bad habit of considering every possible negative outcome. Terrorist bombs, tsunamis, subway collisions, bridge collapses. I had wasted a lot of time worrying about all of these when it's always a tragedy you'd never imagine that hits you without warning.

I had to get out of here. Outside an ambulance had arrived, orange tape was up around the playground. A man and a woman in business suits examined Ralph. The man was maybe forty-five, medium height, big shoulders, stocky. If he wasn't a detective, he should play one on TV. His female counterpart had on a no-nonsense blue suit, short dark feathered hair, a full sallow face with a determined look. Those two were so engrossed with Ralph, they'd never notice if I left. I stepped outside and started tiptoeing away. The female blue suit walked right over. So much for leaving.

"I'm Janet Brown, Detective, NYPD." We shook hands. I hoped she didn't notice how sweaty my palms were, a sure sign of guilt.

"You're the teacher who found the victim?" I nodded. A little rush of relief ran through me. Maybe I didn't fit her killer profile. White, late thirties, struggling middle class, old J Crew sweater with no blood stains. Not apparently on substances. In therapy for fifteen years, like everyone on the Upper West Side.

"Hey Janet, take a look at this," her colleague called from the huddle around Ralph. His matter-of-factness was unnerving.

"Stick around so we can talk." Detective Brown walked away.

How could she chase after a perpetrator wearing a straight skirt like that? Damn, I was stuck here. Uneasiness swamped me like a sudden case of sea sickness. I went back inside and dialed Food Lovers, Inc. Daniel worked at this magazine about rich food for rich people.

"Hello."

"Daniel. It's me."

"Melanie? Why are you whispering?"

His voice, as usual, implied he was in the middle of something.

"I don't want the cops to hear. You won't believe what's happened." A flood of tears and then hiccups.

"What is it? Is it something with Chloe? Pull yourself together," he shouted, which stopped the hiccups at least.

"No, it's nothing about Chloe. It's me, not her."

"Wish you'd said that to begin with. Well, what's going on?"

My well-being was clearly not paramount.

"I'm so relieved you're feeling better. I'm not." I said in a snotty tone, hiccups gone. "I'm in the park. Not a big deal really. Just a murder. There's been a murder."

"Melanie, what are you talking about? Who got murdered?" I held the phone in the air. How about asking whether I'm all right?

"If you just calm down a minute, I can tell you." Reassuring him was not what I needed. "Ralph, the caretaker, was murdered and I was the one to find his body."

"You're not kidding me, are you?" He paused. I waited. "Are you all right?"

That was more like it.

"I didn't get hurt if that's what you mean. I'm a nervous wreck. Could they book me on suspicion of murder?"

"No. I don't think so. You don't exactly have the right look." He laughed.

"What look is that? Black leather and a whip?" No answer. "For some reason, I thought it would help if you came down here. It would show we're a responsible couple in the community. Would you do that?"

There was a slight pause as if he considered this. "I can't. You'll be fine. I've got a deadline I have to make by four, with a lunch review at this new Mexican place in Tribeca."

I wasn't a Mexican food lover on a good day.

"Greenwich and Washington," he said. "Why don't you meet me for lunch? You can tell me all about it."

Lunch. Cracked skulls and blood in the rice and beans.

"I just found a dead person. Food is not exactly on my mind like it's always on yours." Bad comeback when looking for sympathy.

"It's what pays the bills so it better be on my mind," he snapped, which was not all true by a long shot.

All of a sudden, a bit of conscience surfaced. "Look, if there's any real trouble call me back. I know they're just going to ask you questions and send you home. If you change your mind about lunch, let me know. It's one of the nouveau Mexican places. They'll have brown rice and goat cheese."

"I'll let you know if I need to make bail," I sniped, and cut off the call.

A picture of Daniel appeared where he keeled over into a pile of beans covered with guacamole and slimy cheese. I jumped up and shook my head as if I could shake out all pictures of death. I'd probably go to hell now, and jail.

Why did this have to happen to me? One of those ice queen mothers like Nicole, she should have found him. She wouldn't have even called the police, just left her kids and walked away, deciding Ralph was drunk and he'd do fine as a babysitter.

I texted my closest friend, Rebecca. *In park. Ralph was murdered. I'm with the cops.*

She replied, *What? Should I come down there?*

Wonderful Rebecca. I told her not now, I would call.

She texted, *Absolutely. I'm here.*

I started to breathe again. I went to the door.

Cops from the crime scene unit walked through the playground, heads down, gathering evidence in plastic bags. Well-trained actors in a Shakespeare tragedy. One cop gave the male detective an empty coffee cup and a paper plate with crumbs. Ralph's breakfast. The detective placed each carefully in a plastic bag, and gave it back to the officer.

"Do you know anything about a baseball bat? Louisa told us that Ralph kept one in a closet."

The blue suit guy with not regulation longish sandy-colored hair, a cowlick flopping down over one eye, was suddenly in front of me. He scowled and sounded impatient, like he wanted to be anywhere rather than here. Something in me snapped.

"A bat? Why would I know about a bat? I don't play ball. My problem was coming to work today to a job I didn't want to be doing. You know what that's like?" I pinned him with an accusing stare.

"Out of the blue, wham, just like that, this strong lovely guy is dead. I mean, I'm not in your business." I stopped and shuddered at the idea. "This has been a first for me. I may not sleep for a year. I don't care about a bat. I just want to get out of here, go home, lie down, and start this stupid day over again." I was ranting.

Janet Brown walked over with an amused smile on her face.

"I think we can interview you now. Let's sit here." She gestured slowly to the picnic table, as she would to a demented inmate. I sat down, suddenly drained, and put my throbbing leg up on the bench.

"Who are you?" I asked the guy in the blue suit. He showed me his badge. Detective Levano, 24th Precinct.

"We'll be quick, right, Detective Levano?" Janet Brown gave him a collegial smile and possible wink. Now I was annoyed again. I might be in shock, but I wasn't senile. "What time did you get here," she asked.

"Nine oh five. I was at 4,790 steps," I said confidently.

Levano snickered in a nasty way. Brown stopped him with a cold look.

"Good thing you tracked your steps," she said with a placating smile.

They thought I was a moron.

"Did you see anyone as you walked here?"

"No, I couldn't even see Ralph from the path. The leaves were too thick and the sun isn't overhead then. There was no one."

Brown continued. "All right. You got down to the playground. You saw no one. What happened next?"

I suddenly remembered the gate. "The gate was unlocked but it wasn't wide open the way Ralph usually left it. I wondered about that. Why it was unlocked but closed. His murderer might have shut it to discourage people from coming in."

Brown nodded.

"I walked in, saw feet sticking out, and ran. That's when I dropped my supplies, tripped and hurt my knee." I turned to Levano. "Ralph kept the bat in the storage building. That's all I know. He never used it."

"We've already checked there. It's gone. Mr. Duvet was hit on the head with a heavy object."

"Do you know for sure it was a baseball bat? Could it have been a rock?"

Levano tried to squash his irritation at my question, but failed. Brown gave him a pointless look to play nice.

"You want a quick lesson in forensic medicine?" he asked. "The indentation in his skull measured exactly to bat specifications-a bat would fit in there nice and snug, like a baby in a sack." He almost growled.

My stomach threatened to rise back into my throat. The morning's events crowded in on me. My fantasy of Ralph turned into a nightmare, blood everywhere, my jerk husband. There was something my neighbor Selma said, what was it? I couldn't remember. I couldn't breathe. I had to get away from here.

Levano took out a cigarette. He tapped it on a pack, put the cigarette back in the pack and laid the pack on the table. He was trying to quit. He'd better not smoke around me.

"Why don't you try ginseng, or cayenne pepper flakes," I said with disdain. "Or acupuncture." Levano stared at me and shook his head. "Smoking's not allowed in the playground," I added.

His face got beet red as if he was about to explode. He took out a cigarette.

"What happened when you ran away? Did you see anyone?" Brown ignored the smoking debate.

"Louisa got here right after I tripped on the concrete edging. The jogger was gone by then. I called out for help but he didn't stop. Louisa and I walked back to the playground together. We knew then it was Ralph. We tried to find a pulse. A few minutes later I called you." After I threw up. I didn't tell him that.

"What did the jogger look like?" Levano asked.

"Just a guy, dark hair, I think, solid type."

"Was the body exactly as it is now when you found him?" Levano looked up at me from under heavy eyelids while he defiantly lit a cigarette. He'd been watching too many Humphrey Bogart movies. I waved away the smoke. He should get a ticket for this.

"Yes, exactly as we found him except for the blanket," I finally answered after my coughing fit ended.

"Right. Next time don't use a blanket, disturbs prints. Makes it harder for our lab guys," Levano said.

I thought Brown rolled her eyes at him.

"Really? Are you trying to be funny?" I took out my phone to be rude and saw I had a text from Rebecca. *Should I come get you?* she asked.

There was also a text from Cornelia Waterbury. *Confirming the girls' playdate today. Looking forward.*

Seriously? I was sitting here being questioned by cops about the murder of a wonderful man I knew, and Cornelia Waterbury, multimillionaire, expected me to show up on Park Avenue in a few hours. She was a business connection for Daniel. Why was this day being spent doing the opposite of what I wanted for my life?

"Can we go back to this murder." Brown looked at Levano and back to me. "How long have you worked here?" she asked.

I told her it had been just since August.

"How long has Ralph worked here?"

Surprisingly, I never asked him.

"Is there any reason you can think of why someone would want Ralph dead?" Detective Brown continued.

Why would anyone want Ralph dead? So many other people could die and the world would be a better place, really. Nothing ever happened to those people.

"No, none at all." I finally said. "In fact, I'm shocked anyone could get to Ralph with a baseball bat. He was very strong, very agile."

Levano eyed me with new interest. "What was your relationship with him like?"

None of your business. My fantasies were mine.

"He was a nice guy and we kidded around, a work relationship." I fought back burning tears. "Ralph helped people out here." Ralph was the perk, the sparkle for me at this ridiculous job. They didn't have to know that.

"It sounds like you were close to him," Brown commented, not unkindly.

"No, I wouldn't say we were close. Just friends here at work."

Levano reached into his jacket pocket and extracted an envelope.

"You have a thing for him?"

Goddamn I was tired of this bad cop, good cop routine. Objection.

"That's pretty insulting. He was a good guy. It's horrible he's dead, and to find him that way."

I shivered to show how upset I was. The shiver turned into violent trembling for some seconds. I grabbed my arms.

He raised his eyebrows. "Okay. Calm down. Ever see any of these men talking to Mr. Duvet down here?" There were eight or ten photographs. Some white guys, some black, Asian. Every race represented but none of them the type you'd want your daughter to date.

"No. Those guys would stand out. I only saw Ralph with the playground crowd."

Levano got up, arched his back. The interview was over. "If you remember seeing Mr. Duvet doing anything that seemed strange. Many phone calls, erratic behavior, an argument on the phone, anything at all, call us immediately." He threw a business card on the table which I took to show I wasn't being booked. So that was it. No putting my valuables in a plastic bag, the clanging of a cell door locked shut.

"Let me through. I'm in charge here." Helene Springer, playground president, arrived, storming into the cordoned-off area, brushing off police. God, she gave me a headache. The prim round collared shirt, starched khaki pants, low-heeled, no-nonsense pumps, and short pageboy pulled back with a velvet headband said she was Miss Purity. But her looks lied. Laurie Talbot, her sidekick, also with a velvet headband, was with her.

They made a beeline for me. She fired comments in that voice of hers that came out of her nose. "They said you discovered his body. What time did you get here? I thought you and Ralph came in at the same time."

I'd had enough. "Are you saying this was my fault? I had a fencing class before work, with witnesses. Where were you this morning?"

"Ladies, cool it." Detective Brown said. "You're the president of the playground co-op?"

Helene nodded.

"In that case, we need your help. Get your local people to talk, someone will have seen something. We are aware, ladies, that this is a community playground."

Levano loudly added, "Don't forget this is a public park and this is a murder case. We're in charge. This guy wasn't just a random hit. I hope you checked him out thoroughly when you hired him."

"What do you mean it wasn't random?"

Not a bad question. My brain was working apparently.

"All his money, wallet, credit cards, jewelry are all still on him. It wasn't robbery. If you're not killed for your money it's usually personal."

Janet Brown shook her head just slightly, so you knew she disapproved. She'd tell him later he should have kept his mouth shut. Just like any married couple. A new wave of nausea hit me. There was silence. "Can I leave?"

Levano waved his hand, dismissing me.

I wanted one last moment with Ralph, but my stomach frankly couldn't take any more blood. The crowd made a path for me, my intimacy with crime gave me status. The ice cream stand was doing well. Murder was good for business. A city as big as New York swallowed and digested much larger disasters than Ralph's demise with not even a telltale burp. Not the case with my digestive system. This would take months to pass through.

What was I supposed to do now? The day stretched in front of me like a black hole. Pick up groceries? Apply for jobs? Everything was different. I wasn't even sure I knew my way home. The ground swayed under me. My legs felt like they would buckle.

Chapter Three

A woman is like a tea bag—only in hot water do you realize how strong she really is.

Nancy Reagan

My phone buzzed. Rebecca was texting. *Where are you? You shouldn't be alone. I'm coming down there.*

I grabbed at Rebecca's message like it was a lifeline. *Meet you in thirty minutes at diner.*

Oxygen flowed back into my lungs. My legs held me up. I breathed in deeply and got a blast of ocean air as the wind brought the smell of the Atlantic up the Hudson. The unexpectedly exhilarating breeze pulled me down the path to the river.

Coming toward me on the path was a scrawny man with a wild beard and shirt four sizes too big. He passed so close I could see the scars on his face and arms, and leaves caught in his beard. I turned around and watched him. When he got to the top of the path, he trudged onto a short span of grass and dead leaves till he arrived at an ornate iron gate. This gate led into the tunnel of the Hudson Train Line, running below the park. I had heard that homeless guys lived in these tunnels. The scrawny man used a large key to open the gate and slipped in, locking the door behind him. This was the first time I'd seen anyone enter.

The river was glorious, the slapping of the water against the concrete walkway was peaceful. Not for me today. I had to follow that man.

Fearing a tick bite, I quietly tiptoed across the overgrown grass and dead leaves and peered through the gate. After my eyes adjusted to the dark, I made out cardboard boxes and plywood construction. Housing. There were two men down below near the tracks. I couldn't hear what they said. A stocky, young looking guy in a T-shirt jumped up and down like he was excited, or high. He pretended to pitch a ball. The scrawny guy with the hand-me-down shirt swung what looked like a bat or a board. He stopped and stared at the gate. I jumped out of view.

What a way to live. No bathroom, freezing in the winter. Rats all the time. The payoff: no responsibilities, no taxes and bills, no trying to keep a family together. Homeless guys. What was it Ralph said about the homeless guys? He said he knew them. He could deal with them. They wouldn't be strong enough, at least not the one I just saw, to kill Ralph. Even so, this was their turf, they'd know who'd been around this morning. Was the scrawny guy swinging the missing bat? A flash of pain from my knee warned me to go lie down somewhere and let the cops check this out.

At Riverside Drive, stay-at-home dad Bruce Salter pushed his three-year-old son Marc in a stroller. Bruce was dressed as usual in a basketball shirt, cut-offs, and a baseball cap on backwards. He did the child care while his wife Betty, a stockbroker, supported them.

"Hey Mel," he called to me. I stopped. "Awful about Ralph. You teach down there, right?"

He took a box of juice out of the mesh stroller bag. He handed it to Marc. Watching a man care for a child made me warm all over. If men did more child care they'd get laid more often. I nodded.

"You were at the playground...oh Jesus, were you the one who found him?" He stared at me like I was a ghost.

"That would be me. Something I never want to do again." A cold wave traveled up my spine.

Bruce was all about being a good person for others. "Can I help you in some way? Are you all right?"

A compassionate man. I should have been a stockbroker to get a guy like this.

"You might be able to help the police. You jog every morning in the park, right? Did you see anyone suspicious this morning?" I asked.

Bruce rubbed his day-old beard. "Yeah, yeah." His head bobbed up and down as he remembered. "Two men, big heavy guys, not joggers, just walking out of the park near the playground. Not gay, not in running gear, not workmen. That's why I remember them. I thought what are two straight guys doing in the park this early if they're not exercising or working or picking each other up?"

"Between seven and eight maybe?" He nodded.

"Could you identify their faces?"

"I don't know. They were pretty far away. You mean I might have jogged by while Ralph was..." He shivered. "This city sucks. I gotta convince Betty to move to the burbs."

Driving around in a minivan all day sounded pretty lethal to me.

"Bruce, if you can, go look at the pictures Detective Levano has at the precinct. You might recognize someone."

"Absolutely, anything, be glad to."

There was a dull pain in my knee. I said goodbye and got into a taxi.

"Miss, you hear about the murder in the park?" The driver had a heavy middle Eastern accent.

"Yes." Cab drivers got information at the speed of light.

A nasal young tenor chanted in Arabic, filling the taxi. The voice was soothing, like a warm bath. "What's he chanting?"

"That is the Koran. He's very good."

"Really relaxing to listen to him."

"I know who did this thing today."

Of course, Muhammed had a theory, and he was going to tell me.

"I take these men dressed like women to the park. They party at four a.m. Drugs make them crazy."

This didn't make sense. Ralph got in at seven a.m. Drug users would be home asleep or passed out by then. In this scenario, there was no motive. Ralph wasn't robbed. I told the driver to talk to the police too.

~ * ~

The lobby of my building was not the type that filled anyone with warm feelings. Dark brown and putrid green walls, unwaxed chipped old

24

marble floors, bulbs in what were once grand sconces added to the perpetual air of gloom. The lobby screamed, "Get out. Let me bring in high paying tenants." The landlord, when enough of us were gone, would make it look like Versailles with the six thousand dollars a month rents he'd get.

Where was Anton, our resident gossip, Pierce Brosnan lookalike, daytime doorman? The front door was wide open. Anyone could walk in.

"Hello, Miss Deming." Anton's voice echoed off the marble and the vaulted ceiling. He walked out from the package room where he had been on his phone. Moments later, in front of our third-floor apartment, I suddenly remembered what my neighbor Selma told me yesterday morning.

"Lock your doors. Gertie Applethorpe's ten-thousand-dollar diamond necklace was stolen out of her freezer last night."

It seemed so unlikely I forgot it. A necklace in a freezer? Gertie's over eighty, lives one flight up, and gets confused. She probably misplaced it. But Selma said the doormen left the front door unattended all the time, like just now with Anton. I confronted my unlocked door. Going inside didn't seem like a good option. The burglar, or a murderer, could be waiting for me, lurking inside a closet, sure I knew his identity. This was probably a crazy thought. I couldn't tell.

"Anything wrong?" Harold Farber, who lived one flight above, was taking the stairs.

Harold was a devoted birdwatcher and old time socialist, developed websites, and clearly did not live with a woman judging by his greasy hair, dried-gravy-encrusted jeans, and union T-shirt from the 1980s, which he wore every time I saw him. But his outfits enticed someone. I heard moaning and bed creaking at least once a week. Maybe his women were other birdwatcher socialist friends. The picture of him going at it with one of these women was almost as upsetting as imagining your parents. Harold stared at me. I realized he had asked me a question.

"I'm fine. Just daydreaming."

He cleared his throat. "You write, I heard. Is that true? Teach little ones?"

"It's all true."

"Have you heard about our online paper, wildwestsider.com?"

"No, not really." I opened the door.

A stained T-shirt birdwatcher was better protection than nothing. The apartment looked undisturbed.

"It's a weekly online paper, all about New York's Upper West Side. People only read on their computers. We're going to cover what the Times doesn't. There's a lot of crime out there that nobody reports. You wouldn't believe the murders, muggings, rapes, burglaries, petty stuff too. The mayor wants it played down so he'll look like a law and order guy, but that's crap."

I had a huge need to laugh. I held my breath and smile maniacally instead. I was nearing hysteria. I wouldn't believe the murders? Something that appeared to be a once in a lifetime experience was happening. Out of the blue, just like Ralph, except this time it could be good, not deadly. Like being struck by lightning twice in one day.

"Harold, can you wait a minute?"

He nodded.

I ran into the kitchen to my herbal medicine cabinet, put twenty-five drops each of California poppy and Passionflower into spring water and gulped it down. I breathed and returned to Harold who waited patiently. A slight calm now held back my mounting hysteria.

Harold started again but this time he sweated with excitement. "Not just crime. Good Samaritan stuff too. Also, politics, reviews, whatever affects Upper West Siders. We've got start-up money, advertisers are coming in. This is a big consumer spending area. I need writers who know the area, who live here, have their finger on the pulse of the place. I have a feeling you'd be perfect. I'm paying." He smiled winningly. "Are you interested?"

He had no idea how perfect I was. It was the best of times. It was the worst of times. A writing job at last. Taking the pulse, or no pulse. Cold and clammy. I shivered but he didn't notice.

"Absolutely. You can count me in," I finally said.

"Great. Start with a piece about that course you give and any local color stories and people of interest in the park. Let's see how you do. Keep it under two pages, five hundred words. And get it to me by the end of the week."

Does blood count as local color? The end of the week. Was today still Monday? Harold gave me his card. We shook hands. He held my hand way too long.

"I know you'll do great," he said.

His smile veered toward a leer. He was still holding my hand. I couldn't tell if he was hitting on me, or he was just awkward. He came toward my face as if he was going to plant a kiss somewhere. The smell was three-day-old garlic mixed with B.O. I jumped away, taking my hand with me.

"Thanks, Harold." I flashed my Mexican wedding band at him to remind him I was married. He backed away, blinking rapidly, waved with a limp wrist, and walked down the stairs. On a normal day, a job offer would have me ecstatic. Instead, I wondered how somehow this good turn suddenly in my life would go belly up and ooze dark slime over everything. I quickly opened the door wide. I tip-toed around, peeked into rooms, and felt stupid making sure I was alone.

It was cool and quiet, the way old places with thick walls can be. Real estate agents called apartments of this vintage a classic six. The place was at least ninety-five years old, which was good because the rooms were big. But being this ancient was bad because the plumbing and wiring were that old too. The windows were the old six-paned type which let in noise year-round and freezing air in winter. There was a decent sized foyer, a New York City luxury. It was large enough for a massive roll top desk that had been in Daniel's family for years.

Four doors led off of the foyer. This gave a lot of options if you wanted to chase a child, or anyone else, around the apartment. Straight ahead was the hallway to the bedrooms. To the right an archway led to the living room. The living room looked out on maple trees and the quiet of 87th Street. To the left was a glass-paned French door leading into the dining room, which faced a dark courtyard.

Immediately inside the front door to the left was the kitchen, big for New York, but impossible to use because of narrow countertops. The glass-fronted ancient cabinets were glutted with cooking gadgets and books Daniel brought home. His parents lived here when he grew up. He took over the rent-controlled lease. Thus, we could afford Manhattan living. I'd now done a sweep of the place. No killers jumped out.

The answering machine on the old landline was only used by my mother, robo calls, and one other person. "Hi dear. The girls have a playdate at our house today at four p.m. Look forward to chatting." Cosmopolitan Club member, Junior League Cornelia Waterbury. There she was again. I'd have to break both legs to get out of this.

I grabbed an ice pack out of the freezer, made for the bedroom, and sank into the lavender and olive plaid armchair in the corner. The sharp point of the Mace canister in my pocket dug into my side. I took it out and threw it into the drawer of the nightstand. I put the ice pack on my knee.

~ * ~

Ten minutes later I limped to a red vinyl-clad booth in one of the West Side's longest surviving diners. It was a miracle these meat and potato places still operated while real estate prices sky-rocketed. Diners always had the most comfortable seats and the worst food. In macrobiotic restaurants you perched on wood torture racks. It ought to be the other way around. Eating five thousand calories at a meal should be done on hot coals. I put my leg up on the cushioned banquette and soaked in the comfort. I heard the next booth's twenty-somethings in conversation.

"My agent won't return my calls. I've left five messages. It's been two weeks since she sent me on an audition."

"It's been two months since I heard from mine. Have you heard this one? What's brown and black and looks good on an agent?" Pause. "A Doberman." Loud appreciative laughter. A group of unemployed actors were having a gripe session. I'd heard the one about the Doberman.

"My God, I'm glad you're okay." Rebecca's warm hug loosened up all the crap from the morning and tears flowed. "Move over." She sat there with her arm around my shoulders while I sobbed. "Someone's gonna think we're breaking up," I whispered through tears.

"Not a chance. Why would you break up with me?"

I giggled. She was right. If we could choose our relatives, which would put therapists out of business, I would have picked Rebecca for my sister even though she was drop-dead gorgeous. She had a perfect body, long straight blonde perfect hair, sharp cheekbones, wore leather jeans as often as the weather permitted, and could have just climbed off the back of an Italian moped. She was married to Paul, an M.D. who did genetics research. One of the three doctors in the country, Rebecca insisted, who didn't make any money. I calmed down enough for Rebecca to slide onto the other seat.

"So, how are you ladies today? Here are menus and let me tell you the specials."

A handsome Greek waiter with dark curly hair hovered over us, ogling Rebecca. Everything, including the Mediterranean lamb loaf and the ham topped with a cherry, was described as au gratin. Cheese and lamb? I looked at my hands that took Ralph's pulse. Death germs could be crawling over my skin. Maybe Ralph had an incurable illness.

"I haven't even washed my hands since I found him." My voice went way too high.

Rebecca put her hand gently on my arm.

"I'm going to the bathroom. Chamomile tea for me."

"Let me hear those specials again," Rebecca said, smiling charmingly at the waiter.

It was part of Rebecca's personality, a kind of reflex response, to flirt with any attractive man, and sometimes more than flirt. In a few minutes I slipped back into the booth.

"So, how's Paul?" I asked to be polite.

"He's either obsessed with a razzle-dazzle computer they put into the lab or he's obsessed with a big-breasted secretary."

"That jerk, he wouldn't, would he?"

"Of course. He's done it before."

Paul had an affair, we thought, with a student a few years back. Rebecca left him for a while. Eventually, they got back together. She'd had at least one affair of her own since then.

"Why don't you hire a detective to find out?"

"Or I could find my own well-endowed secretary, preferably male." Rebecca flipped her hair out of her eyes and pinned me with a

29

stare. "We didn't meet to discuss my marital problems, not that I couldn't complain all day. What the hell happened down there?"

I felt my heart speed up. "I went to that stupid job. That was the problem. I was the only one in the park. I sprayed everywhere with Mace when I saw his feet. I was so terrified. I ran away because I thought someone might still be there. The bushes moved." I put my hand over my eyes. "Louisa came back with me. He just lay there. The blood, I can't describe it. I don't want to." I held my breath.

Rebecca grabbed both my hands and I held on. "Why did this have to happen? He was a bright spot in my boring life. Except for Chloe, and you. He was handsome, sweet. What the hell?" I started to breathe again.

Rebecca raised her eyebrows. "You weren't the only one drooling. I heard prissy Helene Springer was all over him, hanging out after hours with the help."

She laughed through her nose. I laughed too. I had known Rebecca since our kids were a year old and we joined the same play group.

"Helene looks like she could be my mother's schoolteacher," I said sipping my tea.

"Helene was his boss. Gotta be nice to the head lady."

Rebecca buttered a roll. She could put away food and it never showed. Two rolls and I couldn't button my jeans. "I just heard something that might shed some light here," she said.

"Yes? What?"

"Jackie, Jonathan's mother, the one who wears skirts with thigh high slits to buy groceries, called as I was leaving. I told her about the murder. She told me there was talk the playground might be closed. Drugs being sold down there. Maybe Ralph was involved."

"Not Ralph," I murmured. I sounded like one of those mothers whose son has just been arrested. Not my good boy.

"Really, Melanie." Rebecca shook her head and gave me that 'you're too innocent' look. "You didn't know much about him. The way people look on the outside has nothing to do with their lives. Look at my husband. A doctor, decent looking. People think I have it made. Meanwhile his salary is like he's teaching public school, and he may be about to have another affair."

"Why can't one fantasy actually come true?" I protested like an eight-year-old who's just heard those presents under the tree come from Mom and Dad. "What could Ralph have done to get himself killed? He wasn't taking hushed angry phone calls, or meeting up with suspicious characters at work. He was relaxed, fun." I thought, *Ralph could have been into selling drugs. How would I have known?*

"I get the fantasy thing. Reality sucks, right? Daniel is not Prince Charming."

I nodded. "He's growing wider every day. Lunch was more important than this murder." Rebecca snorted loud enough that the out-of-work actors turned around. "Ralph, a lovely man and my fantasy got killed. I'm not tough enough for this. I almost fainted. I actually threw up." I shivered. "What a disaster. My life is a mess. I'm a mess." I heard my self-pity party. Thank God it was with Rebecca.

Rebecca tapped her manicured blue nail on a napkin and shook her head at me. "This is nuts. You're the only woman I know who's taking fencing. Now you're the only woman I know to trip over a murder victim. You're sitting here and not lying in bed with a bottle of scotch which I would be doing. You're one tough woman." Her hazel eyes got serious. "You just think you're a disaster because of your family and your crazy brother." This was what happened when you had a psychologist as a best friend.

"Yeah, they're nuts, but it's time I got over that. I survived. I'm a grown woman with a daughter and a self-centered overweight husband whose main passions are undercooked steaks and divinely decadent double chocolate mousse cake."

Rebecca laughed. "Everybody's got their Achilles heel. Mine at the moment is big-breasted secretaries." Rebecca got an evil grin on her sculpted face. "How nasty can we get? How about some phone hang ups to Helene and that secretary of Paul's?"

"Okay, but add some heavy breathing along with undecipherable muttering. How about an anonymous tip to the cops hinting that Helene was romantically involved with Ralph? She could become a prime suspect." Revenge was a sweet topic.

Rebecca stretched out her black leather-covered legs on the banquette. "We could show up unannounced one night at Paul's lab. Wear masks and bring blindingly bright flash cameras."

I grinned and said, "You're on."

The problem was Rebecca was serious. She changed the locks on their apartment for a week. Paul had to rent a hotel room the last time she found out he was having expensive lunches with a secretary. And I was not really the mask and flashbulb type.

"You'll find another gorgeous guy. Maybe this one will be more than a fantasy. They're out there, just waiting." Rebecca smiled reassuringly.

"If I looked like you, I might have the nerve to do more than dream. I used up my lifetime bravery allotment this morning."

Rebecca shook her head and took a sip of coffee. "You're wrong about that bravery allotment. It's not gone. Look at these women standing up to guys all over the place. They just get better at it." She gave me a look of reproach. "You're way off about yourself. You've got that America's sweetheart look with just the right amount of freckles. You just need some new clothes, like I've also said one hundred times." Her phone buzzed. She nodded while she spoke to someone, then hung up.

"I've gotta make time for this call. Patient is hysterical, needs a phone session. You going to be all right for now?" She looked at me with concern. "Why don't you walk back to my apartment with me?"

The pounding in my chest was way down. "I'm breathing again. I'll live. I'll stay for a while."

She slipped on a soft suede shirt. "You're much stronger than you think. If I ever find a body, you'll be the first one I'll call."

"Great." I stretched my arms over my head and worked out the shoulder kinks. "Well, here's a little-known tip for that moment when you unexpectedly stumble on a man who's been killed. Don't cover the victim with a blanket, as per instructions from Detective Levano." Rebecca looked shocked.

"The detective had the nerve to criticize you this morning? After what you went through?" She bent down. "Imagine being married to a jerk like that. He must give his wife written notes after sex. He's on our list for late night hang-up calls."

I couldn't laugh. "I never want to hear Levano's voice again, even on a phone. I could fill out a complaint form but I'd have to go inside the precinct. Not worth it."

We said goodbye. I watched her walk out the door and down the block. Her blonde hair looked like melted butter in the sun.

Chapter Four

My appetite returned in full force. I called the Greek god over and ordered split pea soup, a tuna sandwich on whole wheat, and sweet potato fries. At least fourteen hundred calories and fifty grams of fat right there.

"Too bad your friend isn't here. She could use some meat on those bones."

My arms suddenly looked flabby, my hips grew an inch. The pale green solid mass of soup arrived, dangerously hot and probably all white flour, all gluten. Was I desperate enough to eat this? I tried to live like the Tsimane tribe. Of course, they lived in the Amazon, not in the middle of Manhattan. Gluten has never passed through their lips, only corn and rice. They have the fewest heart problems in the world.

They do 15,000 steps a day.

I checked my steps. Only 7,952. What a loser. I should move to the Amazon.

I swallowed one spoonful of the gluteny mess, and another. I took out my notebook. I never told Rebecca about www.wildwestsider.com. I also didn't ask Harold how much I'd be paid. Ideas for the column came quickly and suddenly it was there.

Over-achieving parents need playgrounds to be educational. I went to rip it up as I had done with everything, I'd written for years that wasn't a boring corporate presentation. Only something happened. I couldn't shred it.

I was shocked. What had happened to me? I was letting something I wrote and cared about exist. I slowly and carefully took my hands away from the notebook, as if I'd just committed a holy act. I tapped out the column into an email to Harold, and sent it. A mind-blowing change had occurred, like I could fly or move objects with my thoughts. My hands shook. I needed to eat.

One sweet potato fry couldn't hurt. It dripped oil. I rolled it in a napkin and squeezed the oil out. A tablespoon at least. My stomach lurched but I grabbed two more and wolfed them down. From a corner of my eye I saw a hand appear and two rolls disappeared. I jumped up, heart pounding.

"You know if I close my eyes, I can't tell the difference between this junk and an old sock." It was Daniel, standing there chewing away contentedly.

"You scared the crap out of me," I collapsed back into the booth and breathed deeply to calm down.

"Sorry, but you scare easy, always have. You're eating fries? My Mexican restaurant wasn't good enough for you?" he snorted and laughed.

I ate a few more, chewing loudly at him.

"I walked by, saw you from the window." Daniel was in a good mood from the tone of his voice.

He settled his large frame into the seat. Suddenly, it hit me. It was unbelievable, he didn't remember.

"Just as well you didn't meet me though. Food was terrible. I got out of there really quick. I think the cook had cheese whiz slathered all over anything that didn't move. You would have hated it."

His eyes, how they twinkled, his dimples how merry. Since Daniel grew a beard last year and added pounds, he was more and more resembling a Santa, which would be fine if his personality matched his looks.

"Sure, I would have hated it."

I stared at him wondering how long it would be before he remembered that his wife came face to face with a murder victim at her place of work. I'd be damned if I'd get him off the hook and remind him.

I went back to try the soup but I bit into a big lump of flour. I put the spoon down.

"That soup is pretty high in fat," Daniel said and winked at me as he piled butter on a tasteless piece of brown bread. "So, how's your day been?"

I think my mouth dropped open. In a long line of inconsiderate lapses, this was the worst. He had completely forgotten our phone call. I wished Rebecca had stayed to hear this. I coughed heartily on the soup and pushed it away.

"Oh boy, I'm dense. Obviously, your day has not been great. What happened in the park? I assume the cops didn't arrest you." He chuckled.

"They released me on half a million bail. Your mom mortgaged her house." The look of shock on his face was gratifying. "Don't be silly, she'd never do it." I sighed. "I've had an awful day. I'm still a wreck." I held out my hand as evidence and added a few extra shakes.

"Goddamn, I'm really sorry I couldn't make it there. Guess you're upset." His eyes were a little glassy, the way he got when he was sincere. "So, are you going to tell me what happened?"

At this point the tuna sandwich bursting with mayonnaise arrived. I forgot to tell them to leave it off. I wouldn't touch that. A month's worth of fat. I just ordered it to feel better anyway. Also, tuna is way high in mercury.

"Were you going to eat this? Seriously? You must have had a rough day." Daniel reached for the sandwich.

A rough day. That's what he thinks when a co-worker is murdered? I should record this. It's priceless. I told him about Detective Levano being obnoxious, and the bat, that it wasn't a random hit for his money. Daniel was captivated, or as much as he could be while the sandwich disappeared.

"Fantastic, truly incredible." Daniel said in an incredulous tone. "Honey, you're really something. Neurotic blocked writer and housewife who can't stand the sight of a water bug one minute, nerves of steel the next." His large hand massaged mine while the other continued to pop fries into his waiting mouth.

Okay, so I can get riled up about bugs, and disasters that never happened. I have writers' block. Still, he's got big issues, like the food he was chowing down.

"That sandwich has thirty grams of fat with the extra mayonnaise. Six hundred calories at least."

"Fat is what gives food taste. People like food that tastes good. Anyway, you're the one who ordered it." Daniel said.

"Never. Rebecca ordered it." I put on an innocent look. "But why are you eating it? Thirty grams of fat, ten grams of protein. That's the worst ratio. I was going to give it to a homeless person." So I lied a little.

We got the check and walked back to the apartment. After he finished the sandwich.

~ * ~

I made a cup of ginger tea and went straight for the bed. I took out a new notebook and wrote down the order of events from today. There was a dull murmur of a jet circling on its way to La Guardia Airport.

"Melanie, I just can't get over it. You and this dead guy." Daniel burst into the bedroom. "What does a dead guy feel like? Was he cold and clammy?" Daniel acted as if he'd just heard the story. This could be the world's longest double take.

"You mean like a dead fish?" Living with him I should get a prize. "What kind of a question is that? I don't want to think about it. It was awful. Why are you asking?"

"I've never touched a murder victim. I'm trying to get the feel of what this morning was like for you. If I don't ask, how will I know'?" His downcast face looked like a little boy who had just missed the food fight in the cafeteria.

"He was cool and clammy, if that's what you mean." My stomach rumbled a warning. "This is not good for me. I don't want to talk about it. I'm gonna be sick again." I was developing respect for the police. This was their daily bread. Their spouses either asked macabre questions at dinner, or maybe worse, talked about how the lawn needed to be mowed. How did they deal with this?

Daniel sat down next to me on the edge of the bed with its ancient

Ralph Lauren striped quilt. This time he massaged my shoulders. "I know you've had a terrible experience," he murmured. "I want to share it with you."

I doubted that. The massage was great. Still, I knew Daniel and massages. They always led to sex. I didn't mind sex usually, but murder and sex were like crème fraiche and fruit. It spoiled the sex. Necrophiliacs got turned on by dead bodies. Not my thing.

"I appreciate the massage, but I don't want to right now."

"You're angry I didn't rescue you at the park. I was selfish. Let me make it up to you now." He moved from my shoulders, down my arms and right toward my breasts.

I rolled to the other side of the bed and jumped up. Do all men think if a woman sits on a bed, she wants to go at it?

"You must be kidding. Sex now? We're talking about a murder. Remember this morning? You're against the course I'm taking. I find Ralph's body, you don't show up, you forget it even happened to me and now you want to have sex?"

Daniel was quiet as he figured out a defense. The problem with being married to a writer who has deadlines is they always have a comeback.

"You're just feeling too guilty to relax and enjoy my excellent technique," he said with a tone that meant I was the one who had a problem. "Isn't that called survivor's guilt? You're the one in therapy."

"You think finding a murder victim is like stubbing your toe? A few minutes later you forget it ever happened? Really?" I rolled my eyes and fell into the large armchair.

"There's nothing you could have done then, and there's nothing you can do now. Why feel guilty about a guy who swept up the playground?" Daniel was still hoping for a let's get past this and have sex ending here.

"I don't feel guilty. Take it from me, if your boss ever slumps over at lunch, you won't run home and take your clothes off. Anyway, Ralph was more than a caretaker, he was a lovely guy." Suddenly it was quiet in the room. Uh oh. I broke the rule. Never compliment another man. Even if he was dead.

"He could have been in with the mob or dealing drugs. You didn't know him, Melanie," he said scowling.

Rebecca said the same thing to me but without the tense jaw. The jaw would be sexy on Dwayne Johnson, but not Daniel. "So, you liked this guy. You never mentioned him," Daniel said.

"He was a kind man. Why would someone do this to him? The detective said it wasn't random. All his money was on him." My voice squeaked; my throat closed with tears.

Daniel looked at me and finally his face showed a ray of compassion.

"I get that you're in shock. Maybe I was being a little insensitive. Leave the investigation to the police. They'll find out what happened." He straightened up and left the room. I yelled after him.

"A little insensitive?"

Wouldn't it be great to have a guy like Bruce to talk to? He'd give me a back massage and not expect anything. Better still, how about having a guy who wanted to talk suspects and clues? Daniel had been like that when we met. He was turning into Belinda, his self-centered boss.

What had I been doing before Daniel plowed into me? A chronology of today's events. I wrote down everything from the gym on. Along with the theories and information I knew so far. Did those homeless guys have a bat? Who were those two men Bruce saw leave the park? Were women or drugs part of Ralph's downfall? Who was Ralph really?

I showered to get rid of the day, and loosened my knee with hot water. Ten minutes later my body was better, but my mind whirled. I put on a deep green blouse and my second decent pair of black jeans since I'd be on Park Avenue later with Chloe.

Ignatia Amara, homeopathic remedy. Three pellets as often as needed. For loss of any kind. There was a canister in the herb cabinet in the kitchen. I took several and put the Ignatia in my bag.

I had to go back to the park. Did this morning really happen? I had to see for myself that the police were there. I'd go back to the tunnel and find those guys. They'd know something.

"Leaving for Chloe," I called out.

Daniel came to the foyer looking contrite. "Melanie, let me help. I'll pick up Chloe. You can rest."

So, he had a little bit of Mr. Nice Guy in him.

"Thanks, I have plans with her after school." I opened the door. "But you could stay home on Tuesday nights with Chloe while I take the course."

"Not every Tuesday."

"What's your offer?" I said keeping a wounded victim tone.

"Two of the nights."

"Three," I countered. He nodded. "Great. See you later." United Nations negotiators had nothing on me.

~ * ~

The afternoon quiet on the street helped me think. I had no experience with the homeless population. Friends who stayed on my couch when they left their boyfriends were just relocating.

And then, coming toward me from the park, on the opposite side of 90th Street, was the same scrawny figure with a loose floppy shirt I saw earlier who opened the gate to the train tunnel. It was a sign I should keep going. I followed him.

I relied on *Castle* reruns, and *NCIS*. Pretend to read while following. I used a discarded *Daily News* on a bench and peered over the paper. My guy carried big black garbage bags filled with his life's possessions. He turned down West End Avenue. I gave him half a block lead and turned also.

I knew where he was going. They served hot meals at St. Paul's Church at 86th and gave out canned food. It was a popular spot, always had a line. My target did what I expected. He turned left at 86th and joined the meal line. Nobody looked like they just came from a job at Goldman Sachs, but not everyone looked homeless. I could fit in.

I nixed that idea. What if someone I knew came along. I went into the church by a different entrance and asked a young woman with a green and blue mohawk if they needed help giving out lunch.

"Sure. Go down those stairs and follow the noise to the kitchen."

This was a stroke of luck.

"Put on an apron and a hairnet. Wash your hands. Then put on plastic gloves." The head chef, a hefty black woman with a kind face named Gloria, started me ladling mashed potatoes onto plates sitting on trays. There was only one other woman, pencil thin with wild gray hair stuffed into a shower cap, passing out food. She added canned peas and carrots and a slice of meatloaf. Nothing was fresh. Whatever nutrients this food once had were long gone. The city was screwed up. Any kind of protein powder or vitamin could be mixed into mashed potatoes at least.

"Gloria, are vitamins ever given out here?" Her rolled eyes answered the question. "What if I donated a few boxes of multivitamins. And whey protein powder. Would you consider it?" She paused in mid-slice of a meatloaf.

"Are you saying this food's not good enough? Plenty of nourishment in this. More than they get anywhere else. We can't be giving out pills here. Are you from the Mayor's Nutrition Committee or something?"

I'd be kicked out in a minute. "No, no committee. Everyone knows vitamins help prevent illnesses, right?"

"Are you sick with some disease? We can't have you serve here if you are." Gloria stirred and stared at me as if I had spots. "Usually you have to have a letter from a doctor, but we're short staffed today."

She thought I had TB or hepatitis. Did I look sick?

"No, no. Healthy as a horse." I flexed an arm muscle. "All those vitamins."

"Lady, we're just here to get these meals out to the hungry people out there. You wanna help with this or not?"

Right. Get out to where the tunnel guy is sitting. That's why I was here. Not that my idea was bad, frankly, about prevention. "Sure, of course. No problem. I'll take a tray out." The hairnet felt itchy. Did they wash these?

"Start with the furthest table. Give in order. No grabbing. Don't cough or sneeze on anything.

"Got it." I quickly walked outside to the furthest table. The place had filled up. Maybe fifty people. Everyone coughed or sneezed, except me. I was right of course, about vitamins and prevention. I definitely needed a mask. I stopped and took two hundred mg C with zinc, not enough. There was a Purell dispenser, so full I bet it was never used. I considered putting the tray on a table and running out the door. Thank God, I remembered Ralph.

I gave out the meals and got a lot of polite thank yous. No tunnel guy. I turned to go back to the kitchen, and there he was at a table. I slowed down, pretended to do a head count and could hear a little of his conversation. The guy next to him had a cast on one wrist. He wore a blazer with big holes in the elbows. The blazer was talking.

"Hey Shorty, where's Junior?"

So, my guy's name was Shorty. When Shorty answered in a deep voice, he sounded distraught, near tears even.

"I don't know. He said he'd meet me here. He's never late. I'm worried. He's so young."

The love that came from him was like a tidal wave, it almost knocked me over I wanted to fall down on the bench and hug him. This Shorty guy had more love in him than all the Nicoles of this world. Was Junior his friend or his son? At that moment, I saw it in one of his bags. The outline of a long item with a rounded end that could definitely be a bat. Maybe he always carried it for protection, or maybe it was the missing bat, the murder weapon. Shorty had a good heart. I should probably call the police. Still, I couldn't call Levano. Shorty was a nice guy. He'd get in trouble, and for no reason.

"Did you hear about that guy getting whacked in the park?" his friend asked.

Shorty lowered his voice. The only way to hear was to get closer and risk more germs. I cleared the table around them.

"Yeah. Junior and me did. The cops came into the tunnel so we split. Junior went out the exit down near 79th Street. You know the one." The guy with the cast nodded.

"That park guy was pretty decent. Always the good ones, you know how it is." I knew exactly what he meant. Shorty thought Ralph was a decent man. I wasn't calling Levano, bat or no bat. The cops could find out some other time.

"Hi. How are you doing?" I tried to sound casual. "I just heard about that guy in the park too. Did you know him?" They looked at me, surprised that this white woman was listening in. "I worked there so I knew him. Ralph. He was a really great guy. I can't believe someone would do this to him."

The look between Shorty and his friend was definitely a signal between them to shut up. "No. Didn't know him." They returned to their food.

"That's too bad. He was a really nice man. Great with kids. Would you like some vitamin C lozenges with zinc? Good for cold protection. I have a bunch with me."

Shorty's bloodshot eyes narrowed as he looked at me. "Are you a nurse? I need more than vitamin C. I need antibiotics but nobody'll give them to me. I've had a cough for three months." He coughed profusely in my direction.

I jumped back. He might have pneumonia or bronchitis or worse. I covered my face without thinking. He burst into laughter.

"Didn't think you were a nurse. I'll take those vitamins C's. Why not. You want some?" He looked at his friend. I poured out vitamins from the container into his hand. It wouldn't help TB. I had to get out of here.

"Those cops need all the help they can get to find out who did this, in case you remember anything," I said.

Shorty shook his head.

"The police said they were looking for a weapon. I don't know what it was though." I watched his face carefully. There was no flicker of anything when I said the word weapon. I'd swear he had no idea a bat had been used. That's why he openly carried one in his bag.

"Here, take the bottle of C's. Sounds like you need them," I said.

I went back to the kitchen door, ripped off my hairnet and gloves, and used the Purell dispenser. I took a picture of the room, including Shorty and his friend. I announced to Gloria my daughter called and I needed to leave. I also said I'd love to help out another time. She jerked her head away and narrowed her eyes at me as if to say my coming back was a terrible idea. I agreed. On the way out I scrubbed again with Purell and stopped into a drugstore for a small arsenal of cold prevention.

Chapter Five

Vitamin C—the Jimmy Carter of Vitamins.
M. Deming

Take vitamin C, feel better. In liquid form, used on your face, it gets rid of wrinkles. Good inside and out, everyone loves C. Just like Jimmy Carter. I gulped down three thousand milligrams with Airborne in water in the drug store, gulping it like it was jug wine. Now I was in charge of my life.

I stepped off the curb onto Broadway. Something rushed by so fast it skimmed my toes and brushed my arm. Heart-pounding instinct made me step back an inch barely in time. I should have known. As soon as you think you're in control of your life, you're not.

"Slow down, moron," I yelled. I glared at the biker dressed in the total outfit—skintight shorts, skintight top with flags on his yellow jersey, racing like he was alone on the road in the Tour de France.

He turned around and gave me the finger. Perfect. I stumbled back onto the curb and felt a strong arm grab mine. I pulled away sharply.

"Sorry, just trying to help."

What the heck. I turned around to see who had lifted me back on the curb. That's when I got struck by a bolt of electricity emanating from a dirty blonde and silver-haired guy, rugged cheekbones, square jaw and loads of intelligence in his face. A Redford look. Not quite six feet, a lanky body that said he worked out but not to impress. He looked at me with a combination of caring, amusement and flirtation.

"You all right?"

"I'm fine. Crazy bikers. And people wonder why New Yorkers are tense. I could be in a hospital in traction for weeks, because he had to cut two minutes off his personal best."

I had no idea why I was saying all this to a total stranger. He laughed a delighted laugh, which made me instantly feel warm all over. Ridiculous. A pickup on the street like I was twenty.

"That was a quaint word, moron. I would have used something stronger," he said with a sideways look at me. His eyes were blue.

"What word would you use?"

"Two, three, even five-word phrases. You seem to be good with words. Bet you can figure it out."

He was teasing me. I smirked. Just what I needed. A guy with cute repartee who picked up women on the street with the kind of looks that melted hearts. It was time to go.

"So, you won't instruct me in cursing out bikers. You're leaving me in suspense," I said, stepping off the curb carefully this time.

"Till next time. Watch out for morons," he called as I crossed the street.

His charged aura sadly drained away the further I went. I looked back but he had walked on. Rebecca would say he was hitting on me. I wasn't in any shape today to banter with a stranger, especially a guy as magnetic as he was. To be honest, gorgeous guys always made me nervous.

I thought about the biker. Was he aiming for me, or was he just one of the racing fanatics who zoomed around as if they owned the streets? I knew nothing that would make a biker want to hit me. Suddenly I realized the killer might have seen me on the way to the playground this morning and when I found Ralph. Of course. The picture of something moving in the trees when I first saw his boots, came back to me. The jogger on the path. No, that would be ridiculous. No one was after me wearing tight bike shorts on a twelve-hundred-dollar bike.

Two blocks later a cold chill made me think I was either being followed or my blood sugar was off. I looked around. No one was there. No heart throb guy, no killers. I was jumping out of my skin. My sanity was slipping. Or I just needed protein.

Einstein said the universe was friendly. Usually this made me feel better, but today it sounded like bull. If the universe was friendly Ralph would be alive and I wouldn't be conjuring up a stalker.

Where was that place without killers, with love, acceptance and quiet? This was that white light moment where a sane person went to an ashram, or a monastery, or a beach. Maybe changed their life entirely, got divorced. I wished I was the type to tag along with Redford's lookalike and have an afternoon of flirting and laughs. Instead, I was heading back to the scene of the crime.

The light through the trees made a mottled pattern on the red roof of the classroom building. Police cars and vans were everywhere. Network news trucks and dark SUV's lined Riverside Drive. I walked down the path. There was something pink in the bushes, a curlicued ribbon stuck on a branch. I picked it off and dropped it in my bag to use in the class.

"Hey, Melanie." Gabby, a West Side mom, portrait artist to the stars, and parent at Chloe's school, watched the action. "Heard you found him. Must have been awful. Are you okay?"

"Not really. He was a nice guy. Who would do this?"

Gabby looked at me with amusement. "I heard lots of gossip about Ralph. Like he left his wife for a British model type." She stopped and pointed. "That's her by the way."

A skinny, to the point of anorexic-looking, short-haired blonde with heavily outlined eyes and tight silver pants stared and cried next to the cordoned-off area.

"Really. She doesn't look strong enough to crush an ant," I said.

"You never know about people. I think she has a weightlifter boyfriend too. Ralph's wife was pretty outraged. Funny, you work here but never heard the chitchat."

"Nobody tells teachers anything, as if we're pure. Do I look pure?"

Suddenly a red-headed newswoman in a wraparound print dress walked in my direction. She pointed at me. "Miss, can I talk to you for a moment?"

Of course not. Without waiting for my answer, Shelly Miller from New York News, according to her name-tag, stuck a microphone in my face. "Are you Melanie Deming, the teacher who found the victim this morning?" The cameraman was right behind her.

"No cameras." I said. She turned and told him to put it away. What did she have on that tape already?

"Can you tell us what you saw?" The microphone was still at my jaw.

"I can't really talk about it."

"Was he alive when you got to the playground? Was he able to talk?"

"I'd rather not say anything. The police are handling this." Gabby glared at Shelly Miller, grabbed my arm and pulled me away.

"Thanks, Gabby. I've got to go." I race walked in the other direction. Shelly Miller already had me on film and thousands would watch. My heart pounded. Being here in the park wasn't safe either. I'd go to the safest place I knew. Chloe's school.

Chapter Six

New York has more rich people than some cities have people.
Calvin Trillin

"Yoohoo, Ms. Deming!" Serena's Caribbean lilt echoed off the Mercedes SUVs with tinted windows and black limousines. These family limos were double-parked in a long row waiting to pick up their super-wealthy charges on East 88th Street outside the Huntley School. Serena was the nanny for West Sider Sam, a former playmate of Chloe's from preschool, which made us old friends in child years. She was from Trinidad. Large gold hoop earrings dangled out from under her well-cut Afro. Her purple nails and long fingers could have been in a Revlon ad. In a yellow shirtwaist and wide black belt, she was a plus size woman who still exuded sexy elegance. In my dreams I couldn't carry off her look. With three extra pounds, I shrouded myself in black and baggy. I was always glad to see her, especially today.

"Did you hear about Andrea?" Serena asked. "Yesterday Mrs. Powell told her to leave after eight years. Said she was poisoning the kids' minds with religion. No severance. Nothin'."

Juicy gossip was a favorite topic. I wasn't exactly sure why I'd been allowed into the caregiver network. Maybe it was because my clothes said "not rich by a long shot."

Serena continued. "I say people poison their kids' minds with worse than religion." Serena gave a brief knowing nod, and folded her arms across her large bosom. Andrea was a well-respected, Class A, formerly well-paid nanny.

"Sounds like they couldn't afford her anymore. The stock market must be down," was my assessment. Eric Powell was an investment banker.

Serena nodded vigorously. "That's it. I heard Mr. Powell had a fit about how much Mrs. Powell spent on their Hamptons' gardener. Or maybe how much time she spent under the gardener. Ha."

She looked at me seriously. "You know about Ralph. Terrible."

Serena drew closer to my ear. I sneezed from pungent perfume. "Men are stupid, can't keep it in their pants, we all know that. Ralph, especially. He'd had a lot of women from what I heard. But to leave his wife for that skin-and-bones blonde stick thing." She sighed and shook her head.

Ralph left his wife for the white skinny woman who, according to Gabby, also had a boyfriend. Leave it to the babysitter network, quicker and more efficient than the police or FBI.

"Leaving a wife is bad no matter what," I nodded, affirming marital bonds. "But is the blonde stick worse trouble than usual?"

Serena crinkled her eyes and laughed at my stupidity. "No, no. You're missing the picture. Ralph's wife is a baker. Ah." She closed her eyes and blew a kiss. "A professional, makes cakes for the Waldorf, big social weddings. He gave that up?" She fanned herself with both hands, overcome with the idea of this. "If some man offered to bake cakes that good for me, hold on, honey."

I laughed with her but thought, *What is this with people and cake?*

Live for today. Die for the calories. If it tasted good, of course you ate it. Eat everything and die happy.

Not Ralph, according to Serena. Ralph didn't stay enticed by chocolate mousse and crème brulée. Serena's information irritated something in the back of my brain, annoying, like an itch I couldn't reach. I said goodbye and walked to the exit for dismissal.

The Huntley School was located just off Madison Avenue, one of the most expensive shopping streets in the world. An orange cost four times more on Madison Avenue than on the West Side, as if an evil genie cast a spell and those millionaires paid three dollars an orange thinking it was better somehow. An orange was an orange. I'd tasted them on both sides of Central Park. No difference. The very rich had to pay more. It was the only way they could figure out if something was good. Or they would pay more if they paid their bills. I'd been told they used the millionaire payment plan. Pay half of what you owed, if at all. Then throw out legal letters.

Before Chloe went to school here, I never stepped foot on Madison. Now I was here every day. I would rather be almost anywhere.

The line, "You can never be too rich or too thin," was invented for this group. Size triple zero Barbies to their Kens. So, was I jealous? A million would be nice, yet the real cost was way too high for me.

These marriages were life sentence money traps.

I waved at Sandra Crane, dressed in a prim seersucker skirt just above the knee and a polished cotton striped blouse. Prime example. She and her husband had been in church every week since he was seen entering a hotel one afternoon with a younger woman. Sandra wore a large emerald surrounded by diamonds. Her payoff for keeping up the front.

There was Hilary Adams picking up her twins. I had heard she'd been headed for a nasty divorce until her husband had a fatal heart attack while on his private jet with high-priced hookers and cocaine. She smiled and looked relaxed. The brownstone near school, a huge house in Connecticut, and a large inheritance, probably helped. The doctor she was now dating, or maybe had already been dating, helped too. No one was quite sure.

I could never be a wife of a multi-millionaire and not only because I had the wrong measurements. They worked a lot harder than I did and not at a salaried job. I didn't like the job description anyway. The apartment and summer mansions were meticulously decorated and staffed perfectly. Dinner parties comparable to the White House. They had to know anyone who was important and be on the right committees. Look better than the competitor's wife. This was the street where the term trophy wife was invented. Babs Bernstein defined trophy wife.

"Hi, Melanie," said Babs. Long chestnut curls, tall, willowy. Andover and London educated. She devoted all her time to managing the homes and charity work. "We hope you'll come out to Connecticut again. Edward wants to try one of Daniel's recipes with him."

I tried to smile enthusiastically.

"Sure. We'll have to find a date."

That would never happen. The last time we were there her husband told her in front of everyone, in a bone-chilling voice, that her performance overseeing a project was unacceptable. I wanted to smack him.

Rich people clustered. At the same restaurants—Aureole, Tres Georges, Le Bernardin. They shopped at Saks and Bergdorf's for Chanel suits, Prada for shoes, hired consultants for Valentino gowns for galas at the Metropolitan Opera, the Philharmonic, the Met Museum. There was only one street they considered habitable. Park Avenue, with Fifth Avenue a close second. Naturally the private schools clustered near where they lived. At pickup time, up and down Madison and Fifth Avenue, it was a dark-tinted-window SUV traffic jam. With chauffeurs and bodyguards. The children of the rich could be kidnapped.

I saw Sasha Warner. Big star, big sci-fi franchise. Her son went here too. She was not the biggest name. The children didn't necessarily get their parents' looks or talent, interestingly enough. Then there were a few regular middle-class families at Huntley on scholarship or going into debt.

Chloe was here because Daniel's mother went to Huntley fifty years ago and insisted. And she paid. I was a public school kid back in Jersey, so this private school business sounded clubby to me. Daniel and I fought our own public versus private school battle for months until I felt like a party pooper. Private schools do make public schools look like England after the blitz. Chloe loved it. So, I struggled along like a sea turtle who laid her eggs and tried to get back to water, totally out of my element.

"Well hi, how are you?"

The southern drawl was Susie Swertz, Ashley's mother. Susie was a Texas Baptist with long, thick, enviable red hair and perfect creamy skin. Her chauffeur waited at the curb to whisk mother and child to their duplex in the sky. Laura, another size two mother, in silk pants and sling backs that I would only wear to a wedding if I could afford them, joined us. I pushed down the voice telling me to lose ten pounds now. We chatted about school events, music lessons, vacation plans. Colorado and St. Bart's were in spots this year. The Hamptons was the preferred choice for the country home, Connecticut being second.

"They're choosing the roles for 'Oklahoma' today. I just know that Ashley will be crushed if he's not picked." Susie's long eyelashes fluttered. I suppressed a snort. Of course, Ashley would get the lead. He'd had voice lessons since he was three.

"Well, Henry's going to talk to the head of the drama department. The competition is just so unhealthy."

Henry was Laura's husband. Henry loved competition as long as he won. He made his millions by buying low and selling high with insider information. That sounded unhealthy to me. I kept my mouth shut.

The administration had to handle these super-rich, super-spoiled parents who dangled the possibility of donating millions to the school. Glad I didn't have to do it. Thank God the kids arrived.

"Hi sweetie." I grabbed Chloe in a big hug.

I didn't know till this minute that I was worried about her, as if the world had ended when Ralph died.

"Hey, Mom. Don't squeeze my painting. Look at this." She unrolled a watercolor she did in art class.

"Wow. Renoir, right? That's amazing. We'll frame that." I didn't know who Renoir was till I was twenty-one. She could already copy him.

We walked along to Cornelia's. It was like I took Prozac. I couldn't stay down with a bubbling child. I'd never used Prozac, to be accurate. SamE, an amino acid, had the same antidepressant power as Prozac. No prescription needed and buy it anywhere. Just as good.

~ * ~

Park Avenue was chronically serene, like someone had sprayed the block with Xanax. The streets were eerily empty. There were no stores. There were no homeless camped on the sidewalk, no sirens, no busted-up uneven sidewalks. There was no garbage. Where was it?

Garbage sat on the sidewalks twice a week for pickup on the West Side. Rats ran in and out of the piles of soda cans and pizza crusts and half-eaten burgers. Park Avenue looked as if the size triple zeros didn't create garbage, or it was whisked away soundlessly at night after being turned to fairy dust by white-coated attendants.

No one stood on the street talking to their neighbor. It was crushingly boring, or like everyone had died.

Doormen were the only sign of life, white gloved and uniformed.

"We're here to see Cornelia Waterbury," I said.

He called upstairs. We were approved and glided across the polished marble floor, under glittering chandeliers, past butter-soft leather couches and across expensive oriental rugs. Another doorman took us up in the elevator to a private vestibule.

Cornelia Waterbury, with her smooth Martha Stewart-cut blonde hair, greeted us. "We're so glad to see you." Her daughter, Elizabeth, grabbed Chloe's hand. They ran giggling up the wide staircase to a large second floor and an endless hallway with five bedrooms, a playroom and terrace. I'd heard that this at least six thousand square foot apartment was over eight million dollars five years ago when they bought it as a wreck. I was left standing with Cornelia, and the feeling that I was a teenager with my mother, or an immigrant given temporary refuge. We exchanged air kisses. Private schools made for odd friendships.

"They're such good friends," purred Cornelia. "And now we get to visit."

Cornelia's linen cream-colored culottes and silk blouse looked brand new and went perfectly with her tanned skin and large gold bracelets. Her loafers were a gorgeous beige leather with a sculpted metal alligator on the front. I looked really out of place. I had to repeat the story to remind myself how this happened.

We met at a Christmas party for Food Lovers Inc. a few years ago. Cornelia's husband owned a publishing group that bought the magazine. She brought her daughter. I had Chloe with me. The kids hit it off. Kids, like dogs, make friends and the parents follow along behind making friends too. Cornelia liked to keep up on Daniel's restaurant discoveries. Of course, it didn't hurt his standing at the magazine to count her as a friend. Cornelia's future was predictable. When she was seventy, she'd look exactly like she looked now at thirty-eight, only slightly older with the best plastic surgery. She'd still be a size two.

"Melba," she called out, and rang a buzzer connected to the kitchen.

Melba appeared, in a white uniform and apron. She had a sweet round face and was from the Philippines.

"Yes, Mrs. Waterbury." She was properly deferential as expected over here.

"Can you bring those lovely cakes you bought today? Also, the box of herbal teas for Mrs. Deming. I'll have Lapsang steeped for three minutes. Then take out the tea ball as I showed you. Do you remember?"

Is it just me who detected the resentment that Melba had toward Cornelia? I think Melba was a trained chef in her country. I smiled at her sympathetically.

We were in the library. Who has a room in Manhattan that's just for books? Decorators buy books by the yard to make the clients look smart. Handcrafted mahogany bookshelves with eight-inch moldings and cornices lined the walls that were stained and glowed a deep red. Yards of velvet hung from the windows. The whole place screamed life was unfair. Ralph's murder wasn't fair, someone having this much money while others worked three jobs, and on and on. With what they paid the decorator, I could have a babysitter, could write whenever I wanted at a retreat abutting the ocean in Maine.

"So, what's new?" Cornelia's eyes were a pale watery blue oozing sincerity.

For the third time I told the morning's story.

"My goodness, you're a hero."

"Not really. I just hope they find whoever did it. I've gotta work there."

Cornelia was not someone I trusted with my innermost feelings. She shuddered. Her delicate shoulders trembled ever so slightly under her silk blouse. Her small nose wrinkled, as if she held an unsightly diaper. Very quickly her good breeding, the years of charity work, took over. She leaned forward across the table, and faced me squarely.

"I can help you."

Her Cheshire cat smile and wink threw me off. Maybe she was

reading my mind and was offering me money to stay and quit my park job, like Shakespeare and Dante with their wealthy patrons.

"How?"

"Dear, it really couldn't be easier." She settled against the silk cream-striped couch. "All I have to do is call my friend Midge Rogers. She works herself to the bone for the homeless. She's on the Mayor's Task Force. I mean I'll have to buy a table for her fundraiser at the Guggenheim, but..." Cornelia sighed triumphantly, "she'll have to pitch in for the new Children's wing at Sloan Kettering."

These women were tough and terrifying. They knew everyone and weren't afraid to use what they knew to get what they wanted. Cornelia had an MBA from Harvard and had been an investment banker. If she stayed, she'd be making about what her husband made. Six million a year on the books, plus a share of the business, and lots of stock options. Her own daddy's connections with his seat on the stock exchange gave her a trust fund, a running start, and total control of her life and her husband, William. I'd never mess with her.

The tea was delicious. I was having trouble staying awake. Put me in a luxurious quiet setting and serve me food and it was like I was stoned. Nothing was wrong in the world. For a second, I wondered if she drugged me. This was unlikely since Cornelia stared at me waiting. It was my turn to talk. About what? Right, her friend Midge.

"What can Midge do?" I finally said. "Give a fundraiser on my behalf?"

"Ha," chuckled Cornelia. "Silly." She patted my hand. "She's well-connected. She'll find out everything the police know and what they're doing. If there's a homeless person involved, she'll be in the middle of it." Cornelia stood up and stretched, bracing her taut slight shoulders like a Siamese cat ready for action. "I'll call her now." She walked into the kitchen.

I mildly protested. "You really don't have to." But why not let her do her thing? Rich people needed to have a purpose. What harm could it do?

I followed her to the kitchen and sat down in the cozy Mario Buatta chintz-covered window seat. I smirked into my hand. Here I was tucked into these charming pillows in a kitchen that was featured in Town and Country or one of those home decorating magazines while talking about the death of a black man who would never be allowed anywhere near this building. In a few minutes she was off the phone.

"She'll have her secretary make a few calls and she'll get back to me. I hinted a homeless man was involved and she was beyond excited." Cornelia patted my hand in that mothering way. "She'll take care of the poor man and if she can't, well, you don't have to get mixed up in this stuff." She raised her carefully plucked brows. "Leave it to the police and people like Midge who need a thrill they can't get at home, if you know what I mean."

Was Cornelia getting thrills at home? I couldn't imagine it was with her husband whose blood seemed to have been drained out years ago. Did she mean that I needed a thrill?

Cornelia passed me a plate loaded with petits fours, all sugar. I nibbled, but reached for a piece of fruit. There were just so many free radicals I was willing to eat to get information.

"Delicious, aren't they?" I nodded but took a bite of pineapple. "Now how is that clever Daniel of yours? What out-of-the-way bistros has he discovered this week?" We had arrived at the real reason for this play date. She and her friends were starved for food with a passion. Daniel was their entrée. And that was it for Ralph's murder, good deed done and finished with, Park Avenue style.

Chapter Seven

Unquiet meals make ill digestion.

Shakespeare

Piercing sirens on Broadway were too much after silent Park Avenue. I had a brief attack of move to the country, grow vegetables, join a quilting class, go to folk concerts on the village green. Just as fast as the thought appeared, reality set in. All folk songs and trees were the same to me, and I could do serious damage with a quilting needle.

Ralph's handsome mangled face returned.

"Can we get roses?" Chloe's voice pulled me back to buckets of flowers in front of the market on Broadway. She chose pink. A dozen roses on Broadway were one of those inexpensive perks to living here since flowers were delivered to New York from around the world. Unless you lived on Park Avenue like Cornelia. She paid a floral decorator at least five hundred dollars a week for an exotic arrangement of Birds of Paradise with curly bamboo sticks in an exquisitely tasteful antique ceramic vase, like something from a Han Dynasty Palace.

We turned onto our block. A man walked toward us but a sidewalk space away. My God, it was the same blonde guy who pulled me back from the near bike collision. This was weird. I tried to keep my gaze averted, but his intense blue eyes met mine for a second.

We looked at each other, each with a curious expression, as if some otherworldly hand had arranged this. The possibility of bumping into the same person twice in a day in New York is outrageously remote. He stopped. I stopped. He walked over.

"Name's Devon. Think we ran into each other earlier." His eyes were warm.

"Melanie. Yes, what are the odds?" Chloe looked curiously at Devon, and ran off into our building.

"I have to go. See you around I'm sure. Third time's the charm," I said and ran clumsily after Chloe.

I looked back down the street. This stranger named Devon glanced back at me as he turned the corner. If I wasn't with Chloe, I would...Oh, who was I kidding. I wouldn't have done anything. He could be a stalker, for God's sake.

I climbed the four flights to our apartment. 11,762 steps. I'd arrived at five miles somehow during this day of the worst imaginable lows, and some out of the blue high moments, including being hired to write a column.

Daniel was home and annoyingly cheerful.

He scooped Chloe up and whirled her around. I was next. "And you, my brave heroine. How are you?"

"Not as great as you are," I said. Then he actually chucked me under the chin. Four-year-olds might get chucked under the chin by their eighty-five-year-old great uncles. This should be grounds for divorce. Daniel ignored my grimace and blithely talked on.

"Just ran into a freelancer on the street who works for the magazine. Nice guy. Wouldn't want to be him though. Has to hustle for work all the time."

Daniel had forgotten what my life was about, why I was in the park this morning to begin with.

"Remember I hustle for work, too? Like this morning? *Creative writing for Toddlers*." Daniel was unruffled. "Two months ago, I compiled a ten-page list of cleaning supplies from around the world by category and brand for that corporate presentation?"

Daniel laughed nervously. "But now you know what the best floor waxes are. In case you ever got the urge to wax." He looked sadly at our ancient oak floors, and got out of the kitchen fast before I could hit him with one of his Hestan titanium frying pans, which cost four hundred dollars, unless you're a food columnist.

I sat at the kitchen table and dreamed of my own writer's retreat, a large sunny studio overlooking trees and a babbling brook. I hadn't told Daniel about Harold asking me to write a column for his paper. I knew it would go badly. The trumpet of Miles Davis filled the air. My cell phone.

"Allo." I heard a voice with an accent, a muffled TV, canned laughter. This was a wrong number. I went to hang up.

"Hello." The voice lost the accent and was insistent. "This is Nadine Duvet, Ralph Duvet's wife. Is this Melanie Deming?" How had Ralph's wife gotten my unlisted number? I nearly stayed silent and hung up, but a mixture of guilt and curiosity took over.

"It is. Please accept my condolences." Thank God I'd been warned about a wife.

"Is this a bad time?" she asked.

Of course, it was. I didn't want to talk to her. But you don't say that to a woman whose husband had just been murdered.

"I have a few minutes. How did you find me?"

"Helene Springer from the playground was kind. She gave me your number."

Helene was not kind. She was vicious and self-serving. She should have asked me first. The reasons to hate Helene were piling up. Blaming me for not protecting Ralph was bad enough, and those velvet headbands. Now this.

Nadine sighed loudly. "It's strange to hear you say condolences about Ralph. There was always heartache. Still, I can't imagine life without him."

Would I say the same about Daniel if he died? That was a dark place to go with a total stranger. A flash of a headache started.

"I don't want to burden you with my problems."

When people say this, you know that's exactly what they're going to do. Dump it all. This was going to be bad. I took some gingko biloba, also known as maidenhair tree, and magnesium oxide for headaches.

I tried the reliable "I have another call coming in," but Nadine cut me off and started to cry. This woman knew how to manipulate.

"Because you found him, I wanted to know if he said anything, if he suffered. I don't know why, because there were other women. Once you're married, you're connected forever." Her voice softened, obviously changing tactics. "Please tell me if he was breathing, was he able to speak?"

I said nothing. Didn't the cops tell her this already? Did she think he said something about her?

Nadine started again, more irritated, a lot pushier. "Nobody has to know you talked to me." Her voice became a wail. "I want to know for my children's sake. They're crying, asking God to take care of their daddy. I told them he was in heaven. They want to write him letters, want to know if he'll write back to them." She was hysterical, her voice high pitched, sobbing in between words.

Feeling near a breakdown myself, I walked to the herbal medicine chest and took thirty drops of valerian root. The herbal form of valium. Oh well, if I took fifteen drops more I'd sleep through this call.

Nadine took a break to blow her nose.

"I'm sorry but there wasn't..."

She interrupted me. Now she sounded like an indignant schoolmarm.

"You must tell me what you saw and heard. You are a writer. You probably observe every detail."

"I'm not that kind of writer. Screenplays. Unproduced."

What was I saying? Who told her I was a writer? Get off the goddamn phone.

"Oh, I'm sure you're very good," she said slowly, emphasizing very. "Would I have read anything you've written?"

The flattery ploy was obvious, a crazed fan tying Stephen King to a bed.

"Do the police think the blow to the head killed him?" She was unrelenting.

"Why? What else would it have been?" I asked.

"The police don't tell me anything. Who do people think killed him?" She was really a bulldog.

"Maybe a homeless guy or a drug addict," I said.

She laughed, a manic sounding cackle. "Of course not. Didn't anybody look at his forearms?"

In fact, I had often done that very thing. Nadine went on.

"Ralph was a professional boxer and very strong. I see these homeless creatures. They are weak. They could never kill him like that. There are many other people who might have done it, or paid someone to kill him. Like his trainer."

"What about his trainer?" Silence.

"For twenty years his coach has been a bastard named Bennie Resor. He egged him on, kept him fighting for almost nothing. I wanted him to work in the playground. He had a salary at least."

"What does this have to do with his death?"

Boxing normally is more dangerous than being a playground caretaker, but he got killed in this job she pushed him to have. Maybe I should watch my assumptions about what's dangerous. You think if you stay away from sky-diving and rock climbing that should do it. But then you get hit by a brick falling off a building just walking in the street. Nadine had been talking. Stay focused. "Could you repeat that?"

She huffed impatiently. "I said Bennie lied to him. Told him he could win big when he knew Ralph would lose. Bennie and his mafia friends bet on him to lose. That's how Bennie made money. He used Ralph, that's all."

"Nadine, this sounds like old history. Why was he killed now?"

"Bennie was afraid he might win. Ralph had one more fight coming up and he was in better shape than ever. Ralph was sure this time he'd beat the guy. Those mafia people don't like to lose money."

Mafia. Those big guys Bruce saw. "You told the police this, right?"

"Yes. They said they'd check it out. They did not sound interested. Bennie is on Ralph's insurance policy. He'll get part of the money. It's disgusting." I heard her spit. "Then there's that drug addict girlfriend of his. She was always after him for money. One of her dealer friends could have killed him."

There was no money missing from Ralph's body.

"You need to talk to the police, not me."

"I did. They don't believe me. They act like I did it." Nadine's voice got shrill. "Why would I hurt Ralph? I loved him. He's the father of my children." Now she was into high-pitched wailing. She needed a

61

psychiatrist and a sedative.

"Is there someone there who can help with the kids tonight?" I tried to sound soothing.

"I'm perfectly fine to take care of my children all the time, thank you."

Good. Nasty was better than crazed sobbing.

"Goodbye, Nadine." I hung up and collapsed into a kitchen chair.

That call was like being stuck in an elevator with a claustrophobia group on a field trip. I was panicked, and it wasn't me who was afraid of elevators. I didn't lose my husband, she did. This time I took California Poppy. Twenty drops. I should be in a coma by now.

The landline rang and Daniel picked it up in his office. He shouted to me a few moments later that Cornelia was on the phone.

"Hi, dear."

"Cornelia. I can't believe you're calling so soon. Did you find out something?"

"Darling, what did you expect? Midge is very well connected." She paused dramatically.

"Cornelia, you're killing me. What is it?"

"Your worries are over. They've arrested a homeless man and are questioning him probably as we speak. Midge, of course, is up in arms and on her way over with a pro bono young stud from Skadden Arps." She sighed.

"Are you sure?"

"You're questioning my reliability?" She sounded miffed.

"That's not what I mean. I just got some information that makes a homeless man seem like an unlikely suspect."

"Well, Midge agrees. You could be friends. According to Midge, they harassed him till he became incoherent and Midge went to rescue him. Any more than this is not in my domain."

My back ached. I needed to lie down. One more question. "Did Midge say what evidence the police have on the guy?"

I heard Cornelia tap her pearly beige nails against her inlaid telephone table. "What did she say? Yes, it was a bat. Baseball bat. She said they're trying to blame him for it just because he had a baseball bat."

"I think Midge is right."

The guy I spoke to at the soup kitchen had too much love in him to be a killer. And he was too weak with that cough. I sighed heavily.

"They've got the murderer. You know what I think the real problem is here?" snapped Cornelia.

Did she know I'd almost overdosed on herbs in twenty minutes? "You don't know how to accept a favor and let people take care of you."

Cornelia majored in psychology at Vassar, where she slept with the department chair which turned into the love affair of her life. Doing it with a professor gave her such intuitive powers that she felt she must bestow her insights on her friends. Her insights were occasionally right, but her timing was always off. I don't let people take care of me, but that's not my current problem.

"Maybe you're right. I'll take you to lunch. I know a great macrobiotic restaurant on the East side."

"Spare me the details." She hung up.

The room spun around. Ralph's storytelling voice, his lifeless body, the blood, his wife's hysteria, too many herbs swirled in my brain. I lay on the living room floor, put my feet up as I'd been instructed, shed a few tears and listened to a meditation app. I breathed into my lower spine, and released through the top of my head.

Daniel found me on the floor. "Should we go out or send out?" This was the question most often heard in NYC apartments everywhere at dinnertime, but rarely here. Food critics never casually ate restaurant food. Daniel's voice was kind and he smiled sweetly. This was his peace offering.

"Whatever," I mumbled.

"I'll order from that new Chinese place. You look like you're exhausted." Whoa. Compassion. Take this before it disappeared.

"Perfect."

"What were all the phone calls?"

My stomach knotted sensing trouble.

"It was Rebecca. Problems with Paul as usual. And Cornelia about

63

a play date."

Daniel left to call the restaurant. My stomach unclenched. How easy it was to lie. I felt lighter than air, as if I was running down a path on a mountain hillside.

Note: Eating healthy with Chinese food means brown rice, plain steamed vegetables and tofu or chicken. Use your own tahini or low sodium tamari.

Chapter Eight

No place has delicatessen like New York.
Judy Blume

And nitrates.
Melanie D.

"Did you remember Belinda's having a cocktail party this afternoon for Brian's new cookbook or are you too busy interviewing suspects?"

Daniel's voice wafted into the kitchen where I counted drops of herbs and made a protein smoothie with frozen kale and berries. It was three days after the murder. Chloe was at school.

"I'm getting a medal for heroism from the Mayor, but I figured you couldn't make it."

"Very funny." He opened the front door. I stared at him and couldn't resist the obvious question.

"Which is worse do you think, forgetting a party or a murder? Like on a scale of one to ten."

Of course, I didn't remember the party. I didn't want to go because no one, including me, cared whether I was there or not.

Daniel's tired look said he was giving up the skirmish. His briefcase bulged with books, his hair curled wildly. Belinda Williams was his editor at Food Lovers Inc. Brian was another staff writer.

"I don't have time to pick up the cheese Belinda needs," Daniel muttered loud enough for me to hear. I said nothing. "Can you do it?" He looked soulfully at me.

I swear he asked me to marry him with the same tone. *Be kind*, I reminded myself. He could walk out the door and get hit by a bus. I always feel kinder when I think someone could get hit by a bus.

"You want me, the enemy of cow's milk, to buy cheese?"

He ignored this and produced a two-page list, about as long as the Declaration of Independence.

"Zabar's will have everything. Charge it and the magazine will pay us back." His eyes lit up. "Zabar's is the best place to get your mind off violence. It's uplifting, the people, the smells, the cheeses, the roasts, the Chicken Kiev."

Daniel looked irritatingly rapturous as he cooed about the famous gourmet store on Manhattan's Upper West Side.

It wasn't his rapture that annoyed me. He continued to have amnesia about who I was. He still hoped one day he'd wake up and I'd be frying bacon and sausages and piles of pancakes in lard.

"Zabar's makes me think a lot about violence actually," I said with a smirk. "Violent deaths like heart attack, strokes, colon cancer."

Daniel looked like he'd been doused with ice water. My God, she wasn't Julia Child after all. What a shock.

"Just don't say anything to get my name linked with yours."

"I'll announce I'm your wife when I walk in. I'll get a lot better service." He turned white with terror. Humor used to be something we shared. I momentarily felt guilty.

"That was a joke."

Color returned to his face. Daniel left.

~ * ~

I jogged to Zabar's. and entered the swinging wood and white double doors like Mother Teresa might have felt walking into a Roman orgy. Overwhelmed by a room filled with everything evil like fermenting cheeses and barrels of pickles, I walked straight into a hanging sausage that smacked me in the head. It was like a haunted house. Fat and salt were gods here. Squabs stuffed with truffle pâté. Salmon cooked every way in cream sauce, sixteen brands of caviar, pounds of chocolate, pastries, breads, bagels, and twenty-five different kinds of cream cheese. There were many rooms, all packed with buyers.

This all came about as a result of World War II. An immigrant family decided no one would ever starve to death again. So, they opened an upscale palatial food bazaar on Broadway, feeding wealthy people who didn't look as if they'd ever starved a day in their lives.

The huge cheese department had a line of dairy fans at the counter. I took a number. The wait was long. I pawed through bins of already packaged stuff to get out quickly. Cheddar from Ireland, Fontina from Denmark, brie and camembert older than I was from France. It all tasted the same anyway. Just throw in anything and pay. That gourmet crowd would never notice once the labels were off. My hands were numb from the icy cold of the refrigeration making me think of morgues.

I marched up to the counter where the lone cheese cutter was overwhelmed and nowhere near my number. My impatience with spending still another hour doing what I didn't want to do finally erupted.

"Shouldn't these cheeses have to list the nutritional value and fat content?"

A small black-haired guy with a two-day growth looked up from cutting a large chunk from a tire-sized wheel of brie. "They don't have to."

"Why don't they have to?" I yelled too loudly.

"Lady, we're waiting here. See the manager." A big-chested woman in a paisley shirt with a full shopping cart stared daggers at me for delaying her one thousand calories of brie.

"She has a point. I always wondered the same thing." A sleek ponytailed blonde in black and white leggings and tank top took my side.

"Google the fat content," said a tiny thin woman with big eyeglasses wearing a Sierra Club shirt.

I took out my phone and put in "fat content brie." I had a text from Daniel. *How's it going with the cheese?* I ignored him.

"Brie can have almost thirteen grams of fat, five grams protein, one hundred and fifty calories per ounce." I announced. "Feta cheese, by the way, is saltier than seawater."

"Who are you to tell us what to eat? You're no doctor." The

paisley shirt pointed at me.

A lecture came up like bile in my throat. Was I trying to help or was I just fed up with being here?

"Eat what you want, but cows' milk products are bad for you after the age of five because you stop producing lactase."

A crowd had gathered. They'd start throwing yogurts at me any minute.

"This is a load of crap. Go munch on some grass. Hey, I need my cheese." The paisley top gestured to the guy who stopped cutting.

"In Japan they live longer than we do and they don't eat dairy products," I yelled.

If I scared them all away, I'd get Daniel's list a lot quicker and could get out of here.

"Yeah. In Japan they just die from nuclear disasters." A big guy with muscles everywhere, including his calves, had ten wedges of cheeses and five gallons of organic milk.

He stared at me. "Wait a minute. You're the one who found that guy in the park. You probably starved him to death. Now you're spreading more trouble."

Shelly Miller from NY News and her camera guy had made my face instantly recognizable.

"You don't know what you're talking about. He was a good friend." My voice shook, my insides were quaking.

"What are you doing here, lady? You're blocking the counter." The in-charge cheese man behind the counter had arrived and leaned into my face. He had deep lines from his nose to his mouth and anger in his eyes. He looked at the smaller one. "Call security."

For a person who'd never even gotten a parking ticket, I was having too many close calls with law enforcement. A beefy guy in a uniform stormed over. This was not good.

"I'm going." I turned and walked to the exit. Cheese or getting arrested? No contest.

The Sierra Club member, the ponytail and a young round-faced guy with a Jay Z T-shirt followed along.

I whispered to my followers, "Goat cheese is good for you though.

It has a different protein structure."

I felt a tap on the shoulder. The sweet-faced guy stared past me as if he'd seen his favorite burger. I jerked my head around and was confronted by wide doe eyes and shaggy short blonde hair. It was Carey from the park, Ralph's girlfriend. Her see-through body as out of place in Zabar's as my attitude.

"You're Melanie, right?" she whispered

"That's right. Who are you?" Gabby had pointed her out but she didn't know that.

"I'm Carey Longert, Ralph's fiancée."

"I didn't know he was engaged. I thought he was still married."

"No, that's a lie." Carey's eyes instantly became dark and angry. "We were going to get married. As soon as the divorce came through."

Sure, sure, and someday I'd be a millionaire.

This couldn't be a coincidence being at Zabar's with her at the same time. She followed me in. I was pinned up against a refrigerated section.

"Who would want him dead? What do you think?" I asked, moving away from the sub-zero temperature, stepping over baskets filled with cutting boards and brightly colored slicers for sale.

Carey fumbled with her op-art jeweled brass belt atop orange skin tight bell bottoms. What could she be buying here where nothing had a fat content lower than ten grams? She bent her head closer to mine. "Actually," she mumbled, "there's something important I wanted to tell you."

I pictured the headline: 'Suspect confesses amidst blue cheese. Case stinks.'

Carey's mouth quivered. She bit her lip. "Ralph got a letter about six months ago. It upset him a lot." She rubbed her eyes and stared past me.

"What kind of letter, what did it say?"

Was Carey a stalker, or was she the not-too-bright child she appeared to be? My already bad mood was getting worse.

"I guess you'd call it a threatening letter. The person called him horrible names. They said he deserved an early death."

My heart raced. "Do you know who sent it?"

Carey's eyes darted around the store and she chewed on a finger. "Not really. Maybe somebody connected to boxing? I mean, couldn't it even be his wife?"

"Do the police have the letter?" I asked, hoping her answer would be the right one.

A cheerful voice boomed out from speakers. "We have a nice sale going on in delicatessen, lowest prices ever for whitefish and lox. Would the lady who left her champagne truffle pâté please come to the meat department." The loudspeaker kept droning on about squab, duck pâté, and truffle ice cream.

Carey continued. "Uh, I've got it in my apartment. I mean, I forgot about it until yesterday. Ralph just said people are crazy. He never took it seriously."

"That was a mistake, don't you think? Carey, why is the letter still in your apartment?"

Why didn't Ralph pay attention? He might still be alive. Why didn't he tell the police? Maybe I should go see the letter. Someone needs to. What would the cops think if I walked in with it? My throat closed up just imagining Levano. I spoke up and my voice was too loud.

"You've got to give it to the police immediately." The tall redhead next to us had been sniffing packages and wrinkled her nose in my direction.

"It's not that easy. I can't," said Carey in a whiney tone. "That's why I need your help."

Ralph seemed to surround himself with annoying women. "All right, Carey. And why can't you give it to the police yourself?"

"Because they'll think I wrote it myself to get them off my case. I mean it makes me look bad that I didn't give it to them. That's right, isn't it?" She looked at me woefully.

It wasn't a point in her favor, but there's a murderer out there.

"Holding back is worse, it's compounding the problem every day you don't give it to them. Lying is always a mistake. Once they see the note, they'll forget about you."

I had no idea if this was true but why was she making such a big deal about it? So she held the letter an extra week. Unless there was another problem.

"Do you have a visa?" I asked.

She stuck her hands in her pockets, stared at the ground and mumbled something unintelligible.

"Speak up, I can't hear you." This woman could get anyone furious.

The doe eyes looked up. "My visa's fine. I can't go to the police because I lied about where I was when Ralph was murdered. When they find that out, they aren't going to trust anything about me. They'll think I killed him. Which is so stupid. The only man in the world who ever cared about me, loved me. I'd never hurt him."

Oh, come on. Every guy who looks at you is in love, okay, lust with you. Love, tears, hurt, all this was spinning in my brain. But I had to keep on track. What was it she buried in there? That she lied about where she was that morning? I hoped I didn't hear that.

"Look, Carey, this is too complicated for me. I'm just an innocent bystander in this mess."

I backed away from her and crashed into a guy's shopping cart who stared daggers at me. I looked around and the security guy had disappeared. "I've got shopping to do." I waved the list at her.

"I'll help you. I'm quick at shopping." She perked up and smiled endearingly, like a sweet child. I gave her part of Daniel's list.

I went to the counter as they called my number. The crowd was gone.

"You're back," the younger guy said. He looked around nervously for help.

"I just have to get this for my husband. I promise not to say a word." I handed him the list. He quickly filled the order.

"Your husband has good taste. You must have one weird marriage." He smirked as he handed me piles of cheese.

"Aren't they all?"

Carey was clearly born to shop. She was done.

I paid and raced out of the store. My panic subsided. We crossed Broadway and sat down on a bench in the center divider while traffic whizzed by on either side. This had been New York's attempt at a grand street one hundred years ago on the West Side with gardens in the wide middle divider. Unlike Park Avenue, the plants were overgrown and newspapers wrapped around the trees.

Carey had a shy smile atop pale pink cheeks in an ivory complexion. The devil disguised as a Botticelli angel in skin-tight pants on Broadway.

"You'll come to my apartment now to get the letter? You can take it to the police." Someone in her life had once told her just look adorable and keep asking for what you want.

"That's not happening, Carey. You're the one who withheld evidence and lied about where you were the morning of Ralph's murder. I'd be crazy to get involved with you. You broke it, you fix it."

I need to see this letter, I argued with myself. *If I look at the letter now, do I have to go to the police? I could just take a quick picture. You don't have time. Leave now.*

I picked up my shopping bags and threw back my shoulders. Carrying three hundred dollars' worth of food in these famous orange and white bags raised anyone's status.

"You should go to the police. It's your problem," I said.

An emaciated bearded man sat down on the other bench with his assorted bags. He settled himself gingerly, arranged his possessions near him, and closed his eyes for a nap.

Carey slowly crumpled on the bench, knees tucked up to her chin, her face rested on her knees. I touched her thin arm.

"One more time. Tell me where you were that morning."

Her smile was gone. She wiped her eyes with the back of her hand.

"I can't tell you. It's a big mess, but it has nothing to do with Ralph." Carey sounded distraught, so why did I feel like I was part of a staged scene?

"You've got to tell somebody."

"I have people to talk to. I don't need you," she yelled. I jumped as if a car had backfired.

The homeless guy opened his bloodshot eyes and looked at us.

Maybe he'd been to enough group therapy sessions that he recognized the lingo. He looked familiar. My God, it was Shorty. Do all exhausted homeless guys look alike to me? It was Shorty. He wasn't under arrest. He'd recognize me from the soup kitchen, and I'd bet he overheard this conversation. If he told the cops what he just heard, Carey was in trouble and I was too.

I raced across the street. I knew Zabar's felt like death to me.

Chapter Nine

I really regret eating healthy today...said no one, ever.
M. Deming

The bags of cheese got heavier with each passing block. Being surrounded by high fat food lovers made me feel insane. I started fights with total strangers in a place I didn't want to be. What was wrong with me?

Carey followed me to Zabar's. What in the world had I done that suddenly I'm being followed by strangers? I'm not interesting. I've always led a boring safe life. Why did Carey choose me? Now I was withholding evidence too.

I threw the bags on the kitchen counter, angry at everyone. Shorty overheard Carey when she said she lied. He might have heard about the letter she was hiding. Would he go to the police? What awful secret could she be keeping that she had to lie about her alibi? I was involved now for no reason.

I quickly jotted down notes with everything Carey said, and chomped on celery to restore my sanity. There were messages from Rebecca and Cornelia who both wanted to know about my emotional state, each telling me to "stay out of this mess."

I started another column about homeless guys living in the parks, but didn't mention the murder. Finally, I began the Herculean task of finding anything to wear to the cocktail party. There were only two ancient options. I went with a kind of short skirt and a leopard print top with a jacket that seemed sophisticated when I bought it years ago. I had an uneasy feeling it was all completely out of style, but I had to leave.

The A train took me to Spring Street, a few blocks west of the heart of Soho. The day was warm but the air had a crispness to it, like vanilla ice cream over hot apple pie or unsweetened rice dream over gluten-free apple crisp. The cool air gave an edge of excitement to life on the street. People walked faster. Conversations sounded more urgent. Life started fresh every year in the fall.

SoHo was one of the chic places to be seen in Manhattan. It used to be a home to starving artists who took over abandoned lofts and made the place a hip spot. The artists were gone, pushed out by real estate developers who descended like army ants. Except they smelled money, not blood.

There were high-priced restaurants, designer clothing stores where a T-shirt could be two hundred dollars, cars bumper to bumper on the narrow streets, and crowds on the sidewalks.

The Zabar's bags were not doing a thing for my outfit. I pushed past pencil-thin young girls who made any slip of a dress look elegant, and guys in tight suits or muscle shirts with tattoo covered arms. This scene aged me by ten years.

Belinda Williams, Editor in Chief, lived one flight up over the Hampshire Gallery. As I pressed on the buzzer, I pictured Daniel running down the stairs to relieve me of the cheese. No such luck. I had an annoyingly optimistic friend who insisted she got good things to happen, like finding a parking spot, by using positive imagery. Whenever I tried it, I ended up right where I started, carrying shopping bags up the stairs. Bad karma.

At the top of the incredibly long and steep flight of stairs was a huge open metal door. I heard a party going on. I was greeted by a sculpture that was composed of a wire hand holding a spoon and a plate. The apparition had a basketball for a head and tennis balls for boobs. The plate held business cards, which I didn't have.

Belinda's husband was an art dealer. The large open plan loft and the space upstairs was their home, their office, their salon where they entertained people while convincing them to buy, to advertise, to see it their way. Everything was a tax write-off. Nobody just lived in a duplex like this. They were just like my cousin who lived and worked on his goat farm in Vermont.

I hovered at the door, looking for Daniel. A six-foot-high poster of Brian's book jacket was plastered on one wall with a 'before' picture of a heavy woman wearing a babushka. Next to the before photo was an 'after' picture of a thin woman wearing a babushka. We were bonding with the Romanians over cabbage soup, the hot way to lose weight. Brian was not a close friend of mine but he'd been an ally to Daniel, which was why I was here.

A few people in the crowd glanced my way. One of them, dirty-blond hair with a slight hint of silver, great abs judging from his flat stomach, tweed jacket, priest collar shirt, made his way toward me. The charged air I felt was startling and familiar. It was Devon, the twice-in-one-day guy who had grabbed me away from the biker.

"So here you are again. I'd say you were following me, but it looks like you're catering this party," he said with that amused smile. His blue twinkling eyes gave me an approving look. His rugged midwestern aura and his voice exuded sexual pheromones more than any man I'd encountered in a long time.

"I thought you were following me. Maybe our life lines are colliding?" I looked at my palm. He laughed. Flirting with him suddenly flowed naturally. It had been a long time since I'd wanted to interest a man. "Belinda likes to have too much. And no, I'm not catering. Just cheese." I held up the by now pathetic looking bags. The contents had warmed and I could smell the nauseating mixtures.

"So, you're Upper West side." He smiled and I had an instant picture of basking in that glow over a long candlelit dinner. What the heck was going on? I felt flushed and unsettled around him and a sense of danger.

"Not hard to figure out with Zabar's bags. I guess you're not a psychic. Do you work with Belinda?"

"Psychic is one of the few jobs I've never had. Freelance journalist, novelist, once in a while do a travel piece for Belinda. Let me reintroduce myself. Devon McIntire."

He held out his hand which clasped mine warmly for a confident long moment. I began to sweat under my shell and was tongue-tied.

"Melanie Deming," I finally blurted out.

"Are you related to Daniel Deming?" he asked cautiously.

"Only by marriage," I quipped. I watched hesitation quickly come and go as he glanced away and back. He returned to looking at me, possibly more intrigued than before.

"Melanie, you're here, finally. Where's the cheese?" Daniel's booming voice and large presence overwhelmed my tête-à-tête. Daniel pecked me on the cheek and grabbed the bags.

"I see you've met Devon. Great guy. Remember I told you I met a writer downstairs last week? That was Devon. Come over and say hello to Belinda." With his free hand Daniel took my arm and pulled me through the party. Was this jealousy? Devon was the freelancer who had to hustle to make money.

How often had I ever felt blasted by heat three times like this from a man? Never. I allowed myself a seductive wave at Devon. I wanted to get back to talk to him. Had meeting me affected him the way it affected me? He probably threw out sexual vibes to every woman he met.

With Daniel at the helm, I sailed through a sea of black. Black shiny nylon sheaths, black leather and suede blazers, black turtlenecks, black lace, black silk suits. This crowd would never have to stand in front of their closets worrying about what to wear to a funeral.

"Melanie. You're an angel. Daniel told me. Do you have a drink yet?" And there stood Belinda. Neon fuchsia silk pantsuit, black hair so short you could see her scalp. An endless mouth and earrings that appeared to be two acrobats in the missionary position.

"Do you know Melanie, Daniel's charming wife?" she addressed the three people gathered around her. One was an older—for this crowd that meant over forty-five—woman with a grey pageboy in a grey silk suit. A tall young guy in regulation black pants, crew neck sweater and black rimmed glasses. A Black woman in a voluminous brown and black caftan. I smiled. We all nodded. Belinda said the names so fast I'd forgotten the first one before the next introduction. The smile faded off Belinda's face by the last name. She glared at someone. I shifted my gaze and saw her husband and a gorgeous blonde wearing a black furry micro mini skirt in a serious conversation. John held her by the elbow and openly leered.

"Oh John, can I see you a minute?"

Belinda raced off, fuchsia flying, to remind him of his marital status. I turned to Daniel, who stood like a sergeant waiting for orders, with the bags.

"Where can I get a drink?" I asked.

Daniel blinked like he had awoken from a trance, a state he was often in around Belinda. Probably brought about by total terror.

"Over there. I've got to give this to the waiters." He peeked into a bag and looked up, his face stricken with shock. "You got Danish fontina instead of Australian?"

"Wow. That's terrible?" I guessed Carey's expertise was limited, but who would give a damn.

"By the way," Daniel whispered, willing to forget the cheese disaster, "the grey pageboy is an agent. Maybe you should talk to her. Get some ideas about what's selling."

Well, this was new for Daniel. Thinking about me writing something. His mouth got tense. "But no mention of the murder to anyone, agreed?"

Why in the world would I want to tell strangers about a wonderful man like Ralph? Why did Daniel even have to remind me? He left with the smelly cheese, I looked for the bar, not that sparkling water with cranberry juice would help my mood. I made my way through the chattering crowd.

"Can you imagine? They sent a five-page piece back with ten pages of notes? Then they expect her to redo it for no money."

"Those editors should be tarred and feathered." A tall white-haired man with deep worry lines lit his pipe. Really, he could smoke here?

"Paul's in Paris for the fall shows to do a piece about which models eat at what restaurants. You know the angle."

"That's a joke. Paul doesn't care about food. Unless he can have a young designer for dessert." Two young women laughed.

"Models don't eat, do they?" I commented as I walked past. They just stared at me, or at my clearly out-of-style jacket.

It was downright enlightening to walk through this group. The bar, with a crowd around it, was a masterpiece of cherry wood and black slate that said these premises were meant for serious drinking and partying. Necessities for the magazine world.

I sipped my cranberry cocktail and tried to think of a clever way to start a conversation with the literary agent. Daniel had disappeared as usual, leaving me on my own. I had time to assess the footwear of the female population. I realized that my shoes, Ann Taylor pumps, were hideous and wrong. Chunky and high or four-inch stilettos were the only possibility in this downtown crowd, or any clog type thing could pass. My shoes announced to the room that I was an out-of-work mother who hadn't had a creative thought in years. Barefoot would be cooler. Or I could run downstairs and buy anything that cost hundreds of dollars.

"You the identified driver?" Devon and his come-hither eyes had returned.

"Nope. Too many calories in alcohol. I like to save myself for food." Devon was making a move here despite Daniel. He clearly remembered our moments on the street. Maybe he got turned on by married women. Was he here with someone? No one was running up to grab him away. I felt flushed and like a teenager at her first dance.

"Devon, how are you? Haven't seen you since Frankfurt last year." It was the agent with the grey pageboy. I stood there smiling stupidly while Devon went through repeat introductions and said her name. Susan something.

Susan turned to me. "How many children do you have?"

The shoes. I knew it. They were a dead giveaway.

"Just one daughter. She's nine, a great age."

Wrong answer. Better to say I had had my tubes tied. The agent's mouth turned up in a polite smirk. She and Devon proceeded to do a publishing chat. Who'd been fired, rehired at which house, which companies merged or were bought, how much everyone got. What was selling: apparently any book by a celebrity who had a spiritual awakening after being addicted to drugs and alcohol. An abusive childhood or a jail sentence thrown in wouldn't hurt. Any world-coming-to-an-end fiction thriller with a main character hell bent for destruction and heroism, but first held captive inside a UFO. Or could it be celebrities who were held captive by UFOs? Devon had forgotten I was so alluring.

I stood there becoming the incredible shrinking woman soon to be stomped on by a stiletto heel. The feeling grew like a balloon that this was my last chance before I remained forever frozen as an unsuccessful writer in the wrong shoes tagging after a chunky husband who got acclaim. The thought became stronger and horribly urgent. With a final desperate push, I was off the diving board head first into bottomless water.

"I write too," I announced to no one in particular.

"Really?" Devon turned his eyes back to me with that same warmth, but now with slightly more respect and a hint of competitiveness. Or was that my imagination?

"What have you written?" asked the agent in her professional tone. After all you never knew where the next *Bridges of Madison County* might be.

"Just some screenplays still sitting on the shelf." Their faces immediately glazed over. Boring. I was still shrinking.

"But," I said loudly, "I have this great idea for a mystery."

The agent perked up. Devon was attentive. I had my audience now. I proceeded to tell the story of the murder of an African-American boxer, now a caretaker. They liked the playground setting and really got into the homeless guy with the bat, the white girlfriend with a secret, the ex-wife who baked for the Waldorf, the boxing coach who stood to inherit but was in trouble with the mob, the teacher who discovered the body. The amateur sleuth who was followed by suspects, and finally an attempt on her life. This was fiction.

"Melanie," a voice that I didn't want to hear at this moment interrupted me.

I swiveled my head around enough to confirm it was indeed Daniel, but I kept looking at Susan. She seemed upset I had stopped telling my story. Which was a good sign.

"Sorry," Daniel apologized. "I have to steal her away to meet someone." He smiled through clenched teeth that only a wife would notice.

"What's the rush Daniel? Let her finish," urged Devon protectively. "We have to know how it ends."

I wanted to tell the literary agent about my column in the *WildWestsider*, but I hadn't told Daniel yet. "Actually," I admitted, "I've got several endings."

"Well," said the agent, "if you ever get it done, send it over." I nodded and moved away, relieved to have scored a partial victory over oblivion. Daniel still had a tight grasp on my hand.

"Hey, what's the problem?" I snarled.

"What are you doing telling them about this playground business?" he growled back. "They'll think I'm married to a nut job and I might have to agree with them." He let go of my hand and cradled his forehead as if to say I was a headache.

"You've got it all wrong again." I quickly looked around. "And by the way, you're making a scene." Judging from the stares, a few people already noticed Daniel's dramatics. I smiled my best Katie Couric smile and put my arm through Daniel's lovingly. "I was trying to sell an idea for a mystery if you must know. And the agent was actually interested."

Daniel's angry brow and pursed lips showed he was not impressed. I could write a screenplay for TV and win an Emmy and he'd still be worried about how he would look. Ralph would approve and Devon stood up for me. Probably this was how Grisham got started, trying to impress young law associates at a cocktail party. Now that I'd taken the plunge, the idea was born. The story was going to have its own life.

"Don't talk about it anymore."

Daniel's face was red with anger or fear. Hard to tell. He looked around and noticed a few people watching him. He broke into a smile for them.

"What's wrong with talking about Ralph's murder like a story idea? Have you had a lot to drink?" I assessed him. "What's wrong with my pitching an idea to an editor?"

"Because your 'idea' is a true story and I don't want to be in it. It makes me look bad."

"Whoa. This is not about you at all." His criticisms in one form or another had been coming at me for nine years. I suddenly realized what was underneath all this.

"Daniel," I said quietly. "I'm not your mother. I won't embarrass you."

"What are you talking about?" he muttered. His mother always embarrassed him in front of guests. I was right. When do men believe their wives' insights? Never.

The too bright fuchsia was flaming her way through the crowd. The point of Belinda's deep maroon nails waved in Daniel's direction like distress signals. He shrugged and left me to help her. I took his arm.

"Let's go have dinner somewhere. I'll tell you about my idea for the book," I suggested, remembering when years ago we had been a team backing each other up against the rough world.

"I can't leave and I already know your idea. I'll see you at home." He turned his large back on me and walked away.

"Maybe you won't," I muttered.

What the hell. I didn't come just to messenger his damn cheese. I wasn't buying into his negative vibe. I wanted to scream at him, but there were too many agents and connections here.

Screw him. Living well is the best revenge. Writing well is the best revenge. Where was that agent? Where was Devon? I couldn't see either of them. Laughing giants in five-inch heels surrounded me like a wall.

I spotted the basketball head and made my way toward it, past a shirt-sleeved guy in a vest and a woman in a black leather skirt with a thigh-high slit who seemed to be doing a bit from *Slaughter on Tenth Avenue*. Everyone here was doing what I had done with the agent. They were trying to sell something or get something from this party. Damn, I almost had a deal until Daniel took over. Then I'd have to actually sit down and write. Was I capable of writing a screenplay anymore, or a thriller? Short columns for the *WildWestsider* didn't count.

"Which magazine are you with?" A woman with tortoise-shell round glasses and chunky heels stopped me.

"*Women's Health,*" I answered, which seemed right for me and my shoes.

"Really? Are you doing a piece on Brian's book?"

"Absolutely," I replied confidently. "Eating healthy in Moscow.

You'd be surprised how many low-fat ways you can cook with vodka. Actually, not cooking it at all works too." She laughed. I laughed. Maybe I should pitch this to a magazine.

Finally, there was the entrance. I started down the stairs. Daniel and I left parties separately many times, but the void between us this time felt bigger.

"I hope you're not leaving." Devon stood in the doorway as if he had been waiting for me, a sexy angel delivered from some heavenly messenger service. He didn't want me to leave. What did I do to deserve this? Could this be my Fifty Shades opportunity? I considered inviting him along. For a moment I was twenty again and the only thing I had to worry about in screwing with a stranger was whether or not I had a toothbrush, a condom, and thong underwear. Damn, nothing was really safe anymore, not sex, not playgrounds. Also, I had a nine-year-old at home. Not to mention that husband.

"Looks like it," I said with forced perkiness.

"Do you have a card?" Devon asked. I looked at him dumbly. Wasn't it obvious I wasn't the kind of woman who had a business card? I pretended to rummage through my bag.

"I think that story idea you told is worth pursuing. It could work for a screenplay. I've been thinking about writing something for TV, if you want to work together on it. There's also a group I'm in. We read each other's work in progress. Maybe you'd want to join."

He calmly watched me with an assured look that somehow acknowledged I was an appealing woman and a writer, although I wasn't sure in what order.

"If you're interested, call me. Here's my card anyway," he said.

I took it, trying not to grab his hand which I wanted to feel again.

His agenda was writing, not lust. Times had definitely changed since I was last out meeting guys at cocktail parties. Devon was sweet and generous, so why did I feel like one of Dr. Seuss' creatures with two heads, one wanting to be successful, the other to be sexy? All I could think about was throwing out these shoes.

"That sounds great. A group might be perfect."

Daniel and Devon. Who would I rather write with, or be undressed with? Whoa. Stay with the topic.

"Nothing of that mystery's on paper yet, except notes, but if I get something together to read, I'll definitely call you."

A thought jumped out. *What the heck, give him your number.* "How about I call you now and you'll have my number?" I called him.

I could feel his eyes watching me as I clomped not gracefully down the stairs in my school teacher shoes.

On the subway I was filled with that glowy feeling you get when you've met a new guy. Like when I was eighteen. Unless my thermostat was completely wrong, this wasn't only about work. Was my karma changing?

Since I had stumbled across Ralph's mangled body, time was closing in. Gravity wasn't holding me back with its usual grip. I was filled with nervous energy, careening down a swerving, unstoppable and dangerous bobsled course

Chapter Ten

Ten at least Harmful Effects of Sugar
The Science of Eating.com and Melanie

"You trip on a murder victim at work and you don't tell me?"

The following Saturday morning, Selma, my senior citizen neighbor, stood in our kitchen doorway in cranberry and silver velour workout gear. Her hair today was a vivid purple, cut in a short punk rock style. Every few weeks she tried a new color. Two weeks ago, it was green. She said life was too short not to experiment. I don't think she just meant hair. Hands on her hips, back straighter than anyone forty years younger, her posture said I'd insulted her somehow.

"It just happened. I haven't seen you. It's a police investigation."

"I could at least bring you chicken soup."

Chicken soup was her cure for any problem, death or a bad hair day.

The elevator opened and out walked Janet Brown. A detective in my hallway on a Saturday morning without calling me first couldn't be a good thing. I was trapped standing in the hall with nowhere to hide. No buzz from the doorman. Brown wore a royal blue pants suit that was exactly the color of the suit from the playground. Interchangeable slacks. Shoes were casual silver Steve Maddens. I didn't see a gun anywhere.

"Hello. Janet Brown, detective with NYPD. We interviewed you at the playground." She shook hands. She smiled at Selma. Did she think I'd forgotten her less than a week after the murder?

"I'm Selma Greenburg. I live right next door." Selma pointed to her apartment door and gave her a defiant look. "What's happening to this city? Crime is rising. My friend goes to work and she finds a body. Do you know who did it yet?"

I saw Brown's back stiffen. She expected Selma to be a sweet older lady.

"We're working hard on this. We'll solve it. I think crime is down, not up." She turned to me. "I need to talk to you privately. I have more questions about the victim."

My stomach was in so much pain I almost doubled over.

Selma's eyebrows shot up.

"Melanie's been through a lot. Does she really need to answer more questions? I'll stay with you." She took my arm.

"I need to speak with Ms. Deming alone," Brown said firmly, her expression grim.

Selma narrowed her eyes at Brown but returned to her apartment.

I worried how long I had on a Saturday morning before Daniel and Chloe barged into the kitchen. I'd have to lie about Janet Brown, say she was a fellow writer.

"We can sit in the kitchen but we may get interrupted." I cleared my throat. "I haven't talked to my daughter yet about Ralph. She knew him." I got teary thinking about Chloe.

"How old is she?" Brown asked.

"Nine going on twelve."

"My kid's eight, a great age." Brown looked at me. "Tell her he had an accident. If you're okay, she'll be okay."

"I'm not okay, believe me. This was my first, and I hope last, murder." The detective's face remained impassive. "I'll say you're here about a writing job we may work on together. I can tell her later."

Janet Brown shook her head in disbelief." You're talking to a detective with the NYPD. We don't lie about who we are."

"What about undercover work? You change your identity." I sounded desperate, like a suspect being dragged away in handcuffs calling back to the weeping children, "I'll be home soon."

"I'm here to ask about Ralph. This won't take long." Brown's rigid mouth said she didn't care about my emotional issues.

Maybe I should have a lawyer present. Her almost-black hair

reflected the kitchen light. My hair never had a shine like that. Why would a woman who had such great hair become a cop? And her nails were dark red, more District Attorney than NYPD.

"Where did you say Ralph bought his breakfast?" she asked.

"I didn't say. No one asked me. I saw Dunkin Donuts bags mostly. Usually donuts. He'd ask me every day if I wanted one. Except he knew I didn't eat donuts. Why?" What was this about?

"Some people eat the same thing every day - a bagel, an egg on a roll, a blueberry muffin from the same place. Would you say that was Dunkin Donuts?"

I tried not to laugh but a snicker crept out. Food again.

"I didn't check the garbage every day but I'd say Dunkin was it." If this was a male cop asking, I'd figure there's some sexist bias behind the question. Women knew what men liked to eat.

"A few times I saw him with a fried egg on a roll. I can't tell you if that included bacon or not. At least that was better than donuts. There was some protein in the egg and bacon, though bacon is bad because of nitrates. Donuts have absolutely no nutritional value. They're all sugar. Do you know what sugar does to people?"

Brown sighed and drummed her fingers on the table.

"Sugar leads to a fatty liver which means bile is not being eliminated. Sugar causes inflammation. The use of sugar has been directly linked to obesity..."

"Enough. I get the point but it's irrelevant. Ralph's sugar level was not what killed him, so stay on track and just answer my questions. I don't have much time." Detective Brown tapped her foot.

Not much time before she arrested me?

"It doesn't hurt to be informed. I mean I'm not saying you have anything wrong with you, but you ought to know about the dangers. *National Geographic* said we're all addicted to sugar."

"No insult taken. Look I don't want to set you off again, but just tell me if you ever saw him eat cupcakes? Please stick to the question."

What does she mean set me off? She thinks I'm unbalanced.

"No, never. He usually ate donuts. Not the cream filled ones so not as huge a sugar rush and a big crash." My words spewed out of my mouth as if they were scalding water.

"I mean it could be relevant, right? This was a strong guy. Why wasn't there a struggle? How much energy he had left could depend on how long after ingesting the donuts he was attacked. Maybe he was on the sugar crash side and about to fall asleep. Did he have diabetes?"

I was walking in the woods without a compass, going in circles. Brown was leading me somewhere unknown. This could be a trap. My heart pounded as if I'd just finished a hundred-yard dash. If I took herbs now, she'd think I was taking drugs. Try tea.

"Would you like some tea? I have all kinds of Yogi teas." A soothing tea could help. I filled a teapot and turned it on. "I have chamomile, very calming. With honey. Also ginger tea, good for the stomach. Cinnamon Berry, a probiotic tea. You want to look at the rest?" I opened the cabinet. Detective Brown stared at the thirty boxes of teas as if they were suspects.

"We probably have Lipton or an English Breakfast with caffeine."

"Not now, thanks. I'm a coffee drinker. Mind if I look at your herbs?" she asked.

"Sure." I opened the herbal medicine chest. I babbled on. "Sorry, I don't know how to make coffee, too much acid."

Why was she looking through my herbs? I finished pouring hot water over the tea bag. I prayed chamomile and ginger would stop my mind from picturing a jail cell. My stomach acted like I had dysentery.

"Why are you so interested in what Ralph ate?" Suddenly, I remembered the smell of vomit around his body.

Brown picked up a canister of pellets, a homeopathic remedy. She read the label. She put it down and looked at me.

"We just found out that Ralph was poisoned, before he was hit over the head. The autopsy told us which poison was used. We know where it came from. A box of cupcakes was found laced with the stuff. Cyanide and traces of arsenic. Cyanide works in minutes."

"We need to know who made the cupcakes. If the cupcakes were purchased at a store or if they were homemade by the murderer. Were they purchased at a place that Ralph frequented? Did he know the murderer who brought it to him as a gift? The box was no help. It was a plain white bakery box. Did anyone ever bring Ralph baked goods?"

"Poisoned cupcakes?" I repeated. Poison *and* a bashed skull? "Someone really wanted Ralph dead." I shivered.

"Right. Do you have any thoughts about baked goods and Ralph?"

Nadine, of course. I wasn't going to name her. The police had to already know she was a pastry chef.

"I never saw him with a bakery box. I only knew him for a few weeks. Wouldn't his wife be the right person to ask?"

A small swift cockroach emerged from under the toaster oven and disappeared again before I could squash it. Cockroaches have a million places to hide.

"Did you find the cupcakes at the playground? I didn't notice any bakery box when I got there." I clutched my own hand.

Brown hesitated, then made a decision. "No. They were found further down in the park in the rotunda near the boat basin. Next to a body. We have a second victim. "

"What?" I jumped up and knocked the chair over, making enough noise that Daniel would come in. "What do you mean? Who died?"

"Are you sick? Do you need a few minutes?" she asked.

"Poison is terrifying." I shuddered. "Now there's someone else?" My hands shook. I couldn't pick up my mug with ginger tea.

"It was a young homeless guy. He had the box with him. Just ate one frosted cupcake. The Rotunda at 79th street. Bums go there to sleep it off because it's protected from weather. We had two guys patrolling, and a drunk ran out yelling that someone had died." Brown seemed to enjoy telling the story.

"That's where Shakespeare is performed. In that Rotunda. I know the place."

"Well, this wasn't any Hamlet." Janet Brown smirked.

"It's a really peaceful place but it's twenty blocks from the playground. That's a long distance for a cupcake to travel. How did it get there?"

"Bums go through garbage pails. Whoever gave this treat to Ralph must have thrown it away to hide the evidence. The homeless guy took it out of the trash and kept moving. Nomads." She said the word with disgust.

"The murderer watched Ralph die and threw away the evidence." That same person may have watched me from the woods.

She nodded. "Two guys drank booze at the Rotunda. The younger one offers the older bum a cupcake. He's not interested. The older one passed out. When he woke up, he shook the kid, trying to wake him. The kid was covered in vomit, completely grey. His skin was cyanide pink. This new victim was Caucasian, by the way."

Ralph was darker skinned.

"The victim mumbled two words," Brown said. "The older guy thought the word was Short. 'Short don't.' is what he heard. He thought the kid was talking about him because he's real short. The kid died minutes later. This older bum came running. By the time our guys got to the victim, the kid was staring at nothing."

Shorty, the man from the soup kitchen who talked about his friend Junior. The kid he loved and was worried about. The kid was dead now.

My insides were up in my throat. "I'll be back."

I ran inside and threw up again like the day of the murder. I'd never be able to write anything with a death scene if I threw up all the time. Cyanide, arsenic? I rinsed with mouthwash and tried to breathe.

"You look a little green. I'll leave in a minute." Brown looked at me with pity.

"When I found Ralph, I smelled something. I told you that when we first talked."

"Your nose wasn't wrong. You smelled the cyanide and vomit. Nice combination. He threw up in the bathroom, stumbled out, and got struck by a fatal blow. Someone really wanted him dead because the poison was doing the job just fine. We would have caught it before the autopsy because the victim's skin color turns very pink with cyanide. Since he was dark skinned and there was so much blood from the head, the change of color wasn't obvious. He died from asphyxiation. The cyanide molecules ate up the oxygen in the bloodstream. The blood turns cherry red." Janet Brown finally stopped her horror story.

Everything red suddenly leaped into view. The apples and nectarines in a bowl shone ominously. Call 212 POISONS, the red letters from the sign stuck on the refrigerator years ago glared at me. The room spun around.

"Cyanide is so premeditated," I managed to say.

"That's what it is. The most. Unusual in the realm of homicide. Of course, it could be an accident, or a random killer who worked in a bakery and got his or her kicks by lacing a few creations. The odds are slim that cyanide got in there through either of those methods. Cyanide could be in the form of rat poison at a bakery. A trace of arsenic could have been an ingredient that got changed in a factory. It wasn't what killed him but it was there. There's a lot of unanswered questions. This is a double homicide."

A child could have eaten those cupcakes. This Junior guy sounded very young. So terrible.

"Shorty's friend," I muttered without thinking.

"Where did you hear about Shorty?" Brown's lips were tight, her eyes suspicious.

I was trapped. "I've got this friend who knows a woman at the Coalition for the Homeless. She heard from her friend at the coalition that a guy had been picked up with the bat. She told me since she knew I found Ralph."

"Small world. Well, since you're this well-connected, you may hear more. Let me know what you hear. A case cracks through piling up of tips. If the public understood they might talk to us instead of each other." She stood up.

"I'll be glad to." I risked another question. "The homeless man is not the killer?"

"A homeless bum has no place to sleep, much less find a kitchen to bake poisoned cupcakes. The kid who died was his pal. There's no motive that we can find." She walked over to my herb cabinet. "This is called Arsenicum Album 30 c." She's holding the tube. "Why do you have this?"

"I don't remember. I haven't used it in years. The label says what it's for." I read aloud, "Symptoms of food poisoning, or stomach distress." The word poisoning was there. I looked at Brown. "It's to cure food poisoning, not cause it."

91

She actually thought I could kill Ralph with that? Arsenicum is derived from, but is not, arsenic. It's diluted many thousands of times. My hands were sweating. What lawyer did I know?

"I'd like to show you something." I opened the cabinet under the sink. "I have a multi-pure system on my faucet to screen out lead and arsenic. A lot of public water systems have arsenic levels over the allowed level."

Brown looked at the tank.

"You're saying the cupcakes were made in a kitchen with higher doses of arsenic in the water. That's something we can check."

"Yes, and definitely not in this kitchen." How insulting.

Daniel walked in. His eyes darted from Brown to me. "I thought Selma was here. I'm Daniel Deming, Melanie's husband."

"Good to meet you. Detective Janet Brown, investigating the murder in the park. Just asking your wife some questions." She shook his hand.

"She can't be a suspect. Can't even squash a bug." Daniel laughed.

"Hey Mom, can I go to Samantha's?" Chloe rushed in. Her eyes widened when she saw Janet Brown. "Are you a cop?"

"Actually, I'm a detective. You must be Chloe." Janet Brown smiled for the first time that day. Daniel's mouth got tense.

"I'll walk you over to Samantha's. Let's go." Daniel took Chloe's hand. He glared at me as if I had brought evil into the house and around his daughter.

"Wait, Dad. A real-life detective. Like on *NCIS*. This is cool. Do you have a gun?"

Daniel looked horrified. We never watched cop shows.

"Yes. When I'm at work I have to carry one. It's part of the job." Chloe was gleeful and stayed put even though Daniel pulled on her hand.

"You came to talk to my mom because she worked with Ralph, right?"

"You're very smart. Yes, I wanted to ask her questions about him. She's been very helpful."

Detective Brown bent down to Chloe. "Everything is fine though, and I think your playdate is waiting."

"Okay. Us kids knew Ralph, too. Maybe we could help apprehend the criminals who whacked him."

Daniel's eyes and mine widened.

"You knew all about this?" I was shocked but proud of her spunk.

"Sure. All the kids talked about it at school."

It had started, the parenting phase where I'd never know what's going on in Chloe's world outside of the family. Wishful thinking to call it a phase. This was a change that would last a lifetime.

"I'm ready to go to Samantha's now." Chloe gave Daniel a look that said she called the shots here. "See you later." She gave me a hug and walked out.

Chloe calmly left as if we had detectives in the kitchen every day. Daniel looked back at me and shook his head with disapproval. Chloe was definitely the more mature of the two.

"You don't have to worry about her. She's a good kid. I need to take a picture of this." Brown laid the arsenicum canister on the table.

"Didn't you just tell my daughter I was so helpful? Am I a suspect? You can buy it a block away at a health food store. I just explained about tap water having arsenic." Really, she was annoying. "My stomach's upset right now. I'll take six pellets." I popped them in my mouth. "It's harmless."

Brown stepped back unconvinced. "Okay. I get your point." She took a picture of the canister anyway and left. I only started to breathe after the door closed. I never mentioned Carey and the threatening letter. I was now withholding evidence.

Chapter Eleven

Thirteen million Americans drink water with arsenic above federal standards.

Palms up to the heavens, slow in and out. Three deep breaths are a meditation. Ralph was killed twice. First a cupcake with cyanide and arsenic. Second, a deadly bat swung with hatred. Poisoned cupcakes sounded like a woman. A bat sounded like a man. Could there be two different killers? Does Janet Brown think I'd bake a poison cupcake? I never baked anything unless it was a mix.

A run to clear my brain. I pulled on leggings, an old Nike shirt, and lace up sneakers. The downstairs buzzer rang.

"Rebecca's on her way," Anton announced.

"Rebecca's an old friend, Anton, but you're buzzing me. Why didn't you didn't call me about the other woman who was here?"

"She said not to." He coughed profusely.

"And you went along with that?"

"She showed her badge."

Janet Brown wanted to surprise me, catch me off guard. A bolt of fear went through my chest.

Outside the kitchen door Rebecca's blonde hair bobbed up the stairs.

Seeing her drove away the terror that Brown left behind. My shoulders, which had reached my ears, suddenly dropped. My hands unclenched. "What brings you here?"

"I'm the goodwill wagon and I'm checking up on you." She sank into a kitchen chair. "Wanted to make sure you were alive and out of jail."

Sure, but that wasn't the whole story. Her pale cheeks looked flushed and her usually sparkling eyes were grave.

"What's wrong?"

Tears welled up in her eyes and slid down her cheeks.

"That bastard husband of mine. I got a call from the wife of a doctor who works in his lab. She saw Paul and the big-chested secretary at a restaurant near the hospital. They weren't just politely eating. She just wanted to let me know. God, it was embarrassing, mortifying. As if I didn't know already."

She wiped her eyes with a napkin on the table. "So, plan A and B are in action."

"He's a bastard and he doesn't deserve you. I'll tell him that if you want. I hate to ask, what are plans A and B?"

Rebecca's grim expression turned into a broad wicked smile. "Remember that guy at the Analytic Institute who wanted to have lunch last year?"

"Right."

"I called him. He oozed warmth and was dying to see me. We're having lunch next week. That's plan A."

"What's plan B?"

"Plan B is vengeance. My spies have informed me the bimbo lives in the Bronx. She's married, of course. Her husband is going to get a phone call. You know, do unto others as they do unto you."

"As you would have them do unto you. I think that's the way it goes. Not exactly the way it was meant."

Rebecca was fully in the swing by now.

"Phone calls late at night, heavy breathing, whispered unrecognizable words." She paused, looking at me with determination. "That's where you come in. It would be better not to use my phone."

"Oh no. Not mine either." I put up both hands. "Not a good idea. Too many cops in my life right now. My phone could be tapped."

Rebecca pondered this for a moment. "You think? No, not possible. They'd have to get a warrant and you're not really on their list, right?" She leaned toward me, her hands on her knees. "I want to call the bimbo's husband now. You get him on the phone. I can't do this alone;

you're moral support. I'll talk."

There was clearly nothing moral about this. But it didn't matter, Rebecca was my best friend, and I would give her a kidney. I wouldn't refuse.

"I'm blocking my number. Otherwise he'll call me back." I activated private number on my phone. She took a piece of paper out of the back pocket of her leather jeans and unfolded it. I dialed the number. I heard a man's voice say "Yeah?" like a growl.

"Hello. Does your wife work at New York Hospital?" Another growl apparently meant yes. "There's someone here who has information for you that you need to hear."

If you're exposed to enough violence and police, after a while nothing seems wrong or strange. Or the cupcakes were making me sleepy. I listened while Rebecca spoke using a high-pitched voice.

"You'd better keep an eye on that wife of yours. Especially around a certain doctor in the lab," she said.

"Who the hell are you?" he said.

The shocked and angry voice jolted me awake. This was more than a high school trick. It could have serious implications. He could beat up his wife, or Rebecca's husband. He could kill someone. I grabbed the phone and pressed "end call."

"What's going on? It was just getting good." Rebecca sounded a little annoyed, but more cheerful.

"Nothing. He knows, he's not happy. This makes me queasy. Let's talk about something else."

Rebecca folded a napkin on the table, looking self-conscious, which was unusual for her.

"Fine. Fine. You've been under a lot of stress. Probably wasn't right to ask you to do this. I just can't stand that jerk husband of mine getting away with it again."

"I can't either because you are a fabulous woman and friend. Take him to court or to another therapist or a sex addiction program. Maybe he's a sex addict like all these guys." I gave her a hug. Her face brightened.

"You know, you may be onto something. Sex addiction. I'll

threaten him with meetings. Your turn. What's been happening?"

I told her about the cocktail party, my book idea based on Ralph, the agent, and meeting Devon. I told her how attractive he was, but not the electricity I felt near him. She was satisfyingly jealous. I told her about the poisoned cupcakes and that I might be a suspect. Rebecca swore she'd keep it to herself.

"That detective took a picture of arsenicum album. It doesn't even work for stomach problems."

"Jesus, they aren't kidding around." Rebecca stopped twirling her stray lock of hair and pinned me with a concerned look. "The writing sounds great, but really, stay away from this murder investigation. Whoever did this is crazy. It's exciting, but..." she put her hand on my arm. "Can't you just become this more assertive sexy woman, which you are anyway, by talking with your shrink, like everybody else does? Become a black belt, hit a board?"

"Rebecca, you're telling me to deal with my issues by whacking a board after that phone call?" I laughed and went on.

"Finding Ralph, the writing job happening on the same day, these women who loved Ralph, meeting Devon and the agent, maybe it's all fated. It's my karma."

Rebecca assumed the lotus position and put her elbow on her knee, her head in her cupped hand, and thought about this.

"Karma I don't know. Sex I do know. Focus on Devon. He sounds like a lot more fun."

"He is. Devon is about business, you realize. Money and scripts."

"Yeah, like Reddi Whip's only for chocolate pudding."

My cell phone rang. I didn't recognize the number so I listened to the message on speaker.

"Hi, this is Devon McIntire, from the party the other night. I have more ideas about..." Rebecca interrupted.

"You'd better talk to him. If you don't I will and I'll say I'm you." Rebecca went to grab my phone.

I raised it out of her reach. I was fifteen suddenly and girlfriends teased each other about guys all the time. I made a face and took the call.

"I was on my way out the door. How are you?" Rebecca gave me a satisfied smile.

"I'm great," Devon said. "Even better now that I'm talking to you."

No one had come on to me that way for at least twelve years, or really ever. I was suddenly weak all over. Rebecca moved closer trying to listen in. I switched the phone to the other ear.

"Well, glad to make your day," I said as if men flirted with me every day.

My heart was beating too fast. I didn't remember how to do this, and I knew I shouldn't. I didn't want Chloe to have divorced parents and spend years in therapy to get over it. Who said I was getting divorced? It was just a phone call.

"What can I do for you?" I asked. Rebecca burst into too-loud guffaws and I threw a roll of paper towels at her. I mouthed, "Go to hell."

"That's a great question. I'm writing a list right now which starts with a glass of wine." I held the phone away from my ear. A man was saying this to me and it wasn't a wrong number. I walked away from Rebecca. Devon's midwestern voice made me sweat even when he tried to stick to business.

"*One* of the reasons I'm calling is to talk more about that story idea you have. I meant it, about working with you on this. Maybe for TV. How about getting together for coffee and talking it through?"

Coffee and what else? I put my hand over the receiver and whispered, "He wants to meet me for coffee."

Rebecca nodded her head and mouthed, "Say yes." I was starved to talk to another writer about what happened to Ralph. It couldn't hurt, to have coffee.

"Do you know anything about boxing?" I asked.

"A fair amount. I do know people to call. How about the day after tomorrow at two at the cafe at Barnes and Noble? Get some research done, get to know each other. If you can use a collaborator, I'm looking to collaborate."

"I guess. I don't know." I was suddenly tongue-tied.

Rebecca prodded me in the arm nodding yes, yes, yes.

"Fine. I'll meet you at two. See you then." I quickly hung up and dropped into a chair.

Just a phone call with Devon was exhausting. I'd never make it through coffee. I just won't go.

"Aaah, right." Rebecca jumped up and grabbed my hand, shaking it like a farmer with a full cow.

I looked at her sternly. "It's just for coffee, and to work on the script idea about the murder. Aren't you the same friend who just told me to stay out of this?"

She wrinkled her elegant pointy nose. "The murder, silly, not the man. So, what are you going to wear? Not that I hope?" She pointed to my leggings and faded shirt.

"I wasn't planning on it. Come on, what difference does it make? It's just business."

She looked at me as if I was a child playing dumb, which I was. My body was not acting like this was business.

"I don't think so, from how red your face is. Anyway, why take a chance and make a bad first impression? Let's look in your closet." She pulled me down the hall to my cramped closet in the bedroom.

"Believe me, Rebecca, there's been nothing sexy there for years." I hung back.

She stood in front of my embarrassing row of hangers. "There's got to be something."

I looked listlessly at boring black, grey and navy tops. Rebecca grabbed a short sleeveless shift with large flowers that I forgot I owned. "How about this Hamptons look? Upscale, chic."

"Rebecca, I'll be ridiculous in that at Barnes and Noble."

"This is perfect." Now she held up a long low-cut black dress I'd worn to a wedding ten years ago.

"With this hat." I grabbed a floppy straw virtuous maiden hat with flowers that had been unused for years as well. Rebecca strode over to my dresser, a disaster area piled with ancient perfume, tangles of jewelry, and years of birthday cards and buttons.

"This is essential," she said. She'd managed to find the only pair of red lace thong underwear I owned from the days when I was single. I'd never worn them back then either.

"I'll definitely wear those."

I grabbed them from her and stuffed them back into the drawer. It was two twenty. "This is really fun but I've got to leave for Chloe."

"Sure." Rebecca was only half listening as she browsed through my shirts, holding up a silk black sleeveless top with gold buttons and the patterned leopard number I'd worn to the party.

"He's already seen that. You can stay if you want and shop, but I'm out of here." I felt more butterflies now than before.

"You have to buy some new clothes. This thing," she made a sweep with her hand, "looks like you committed fashion suicide years ago. Go to Victoria's Secret at least."

Rebecca stopped when she saw the panicked look on my face. She took my hand.

"Melanie, you're gorgeous whatever you wear. You've got to promise to call me after you see him. I want a detailed description of every minute." She left and I ran to the park.

Twice around the reservoir. Three miles, six thousand six hundred steps, brought the day's total to 12,147 steps. Suddenly I remembered I'd found a pink ribbon in the bushes the day Ralph was murdered. The kind that bakeries use.

Chapter Twelve

You are What You Eat so don't be fast, easy, cheap or fake.
C.A.C.F.P.

The tenth day after the murder the playground reopened, which meant I was back to teaching. To stay calm, I ran to a fencing class. I was surprised to see that Blanca still had her job at the gym. Maybe she was the only receptionist who didn't leave for Broadway auditions every day. She stopped me on my way out.

"Did you really find that man in the park?" she asked.

I nodded.

"Was he still alive? Did you have to try CPR?" I shook my head.

What a strange question, though there had been many of those in the last ten days. "Did he have any last dying words?" Blanca asked breathlessly like she was watching a soap opera.

I ran out the door shaking my head.

At the classroom, it was more of the same.

"I heard Ralph had AIDS. He slept around. One of his women got it from him and killed him." Linda Best told me this in a low tone after dropping Curt off at class.

"Ralph was perfectly healthy," I insisted.

Linda's triumphant expression turned sour. She crossed her arms.

Maureen, Sarah's mother, put her hands in a T calling time out. "Wrong. It was either a drug deal, or he was a pedophile and a victim took revenge. I have it from a good source."

At least these crazy theories made Helene look bad at screening employees.

"Who's your source?" I nearly shouted. "Don't you think we should wait for the police before we spread rumors about the man?"

Maureen and Linda walked out together whispering and looking wickedly at me.

I wanted the truth as much as they did but not rumors without evidence. The only truth so far was no killer had been charged. I had nightmares about faceless masked people chasing me in the park. The cops left us one guy in a patrol scooter up the hill on Riverside Drive.

Nicole brought her son since she'd never miss out on childcare even though she'd made it clear I was incompetent. She wore leggings with large amounts of fishnet and a way too short black Lululemon workout jacket. She avoided me as if I was strapped to a bomb, which was happiness for me.

A few caregivers hung around ready to lay down their lives for their charges. Some kids clung to their sitters. Glances were passed in my direction. There were whispered conversations like those heard at a wake, where no one dared to ask the bereaved the gory details of the last moments, though everyone wanted to know.

"Melanie, it must have been bad for you finding him," Patrice, a nanny, sounded consoling but really wanted information.

I bobbed my head up and down and took more Ignatia Amara.

Helene, much despised playground president, breezed in at the end of class like a speck of sand blown in your eye, uninvited and unwanted. As the children left, she shook hands with each adult, always the politician. Her sidekick was off today. I looked down from my height of five feet five inches, at Helene, barely five feet two, and her plaid headband.

Helene's blonde hair was in a pageboy style that was big in the 1950s. She had on Anne Klein patent flats, a plaid skirt and a white blouse. This outfit was almost exactly the uniform for private school girls at an East Side school. The uniform was topped by a forty-year-old's face and boobs. Maybe it was a Halloween costume.

"I'm surprised to see you," I said clenching my teeth to not laugh.

"Why are you surprised? It's the first day back and I'm making sure everything goes smoothly. How are your numbers for today?"

Helene had another agenda here. We were a subsidized school in a playground. Numbers didn't really matter and she knew this.

"Almost all, maybe two were out. That's normal in the class."

"Good. We don't want them giving up on the playground because of this unfortunate accident."

Now Ralph was an unfortunate accident. This was her p.c. statement. Of course, there was more. She pretended to read the poems by the kids hung on the walls. I waited, staring like a cat at a hole in a wall. Finally, she got to it.

"What do you know about Ralph's personal life?" She smiled benignly but her body exuded deadly serious. I could see it in her hands that were rigid and curved into fists by her sides.

I almost laughed again. She wanted to know who Ralph hooked up with.

"Not much. I heard he was married. You know more than I do. I heard he had children."

"Really? You never heard he had a girlfriend? A white younger woman?"

Bingo. That's why she was here. Someone saw me with Carey at Zabar's and now she wanted whatever I knew.

"I did hear he had a girlfriend. But it's none of my business." Or hers.

"Really." Her angry eyes were trying to burn a hole into my brain. "Someone mentioned you spoke with her last week."

"A lot of people spoke to me after the murder. I don't recall a girlfriend." Even if someone had videotaped me with Carey, no mike could have picked up what we said. There was too much noise.

I could see Helene thinking about whether to push further on this.

"If you do get information about his girlfriend, I'd appreciate it if you'd let me know. It might help solve this. I happen to know his girlfriend was quite jealous."

My gut told me Carey's jealousy was not the problem. How involved had Helene been with Ralph?

"I hope you've told the police you think his girlfriend killed him. They'd be interested in that," I said pointedly. Helene continued looking around the room.

"Looking for something?" My muscles tensed. A fuse was lit. Trouble ahead. My shrink would probably say watch out. Choose silence, the safe route.

But I didn't want to play safe. I had a writing job now. Harold paid me more to write a column than teach here, and there was no Helene or Nicole to deal with.

"I meant to remind you that I don't want my personal phone number given out to other people unless you check with me first."

Helene's head snapped up, as if I'd slapped her. This was satisfying.

"As a matter of fact, I think all my personal information is protected. The forms said that when I filled them out. It's illegal to give an employee's information to anyone without getting a release from them unless it's to an official like the police. That includes my phone number."

I had no idea if this was true but it got the right result. By now Helene's eyes were wide and a little frightened to be outed without her sidekick, Laurie Talbot. She edged toward the door of the classroom, but she couldn't let me win.

"I have no idea what you're talking about. The strain must be getting to you. Maybe you need to take some time off."

This was psychological warfare. I could play this game.

"That's called projection, Helene. What you're doing. You're the one under stress, not me. Spreading rumors about Ralph's murderer being his girlfriend. Giving out my phone number to his wife. It's not your usual style." I grabbed a can of organic room deodorizer that was made with sage and lavender.

"There's too much toxicity in this room. We need to get rid of it." I sprayed everywhere. By the time I got near Helene she was out the door.

Louisa, watching from a corner, looked at me sternly.

"What are you doing? She's the boss. She'll fire you." I forgot Louisa was here.

"If she fires me, I'll survive." Damn, Louisa must be worried about her own job.

"She won't get rid of you. She likes you." I put my hand on her shoulder. "Sorry if I made you tense. She's such a bitch. Spreading rumors about his girlfriend when she's just jealous of her and she had nothing to back it up. I couldn't help myself."

"Did she really give out your number?"

"Absolutely. Ralph's wife told me that's how she got it."

My arms suddenly felt like a rag doll, all that great adrenaline drained away. I dropped into a tiny chair. More DHEA would be good right now.

I turned brightly to Louisa. "You should take my job. You'll get paid more. You'd be great. I'll give you the plans."

"Come on, Melanie. I wouldn't do that to you." She scratched at a stripe of purple crayon on the desk.

The idea of getting away gave me a surge of energy. "Think it over. We'd both be better off." Louisa shook her head, but she had a hint of a smile.

We locked up and walked together to the top of the hill. I drifted several blocks down Broadway, loving the special peace that comes in a big city, being alone surrounded by crowds.

A guy sold produce out of a basic wooden pushcart that looked like it was still 1910. I took peaches and a pineapple, good anti-inflammatory, highly dense fruit. I handed him ten dollars, and waited for change. He handed me back the money.

"For you lady, it's no charge." He nodded knowingly. I blinked.

"Why? That's nice of you, but I'd like to pay."

"We saw how you found that man in the park. No charge today." He insisted on giving me back the money.

I took the bag reluctantly. "Saw where? On TV?"

"Yes, yes, on TV. Also, wife reads online. WildWestsider thing. Said you teach there." He turned to another customer.

Suddenly, I felt naked, like the whole city was watching. Even though no one else gave me a second glance. Harold did put a picture next to my column online. Maybe that was a bad idea. I never thought anyone would read it.

Daniel was home. I went straight to the bedroom and grabbed a notebook to get down every word Helene said, and a detailed description of her plaid skirt and pink lipstick. I heard Daniel talk to someone at the front door. I started work on another column for Harold.

"Hey hon, you got to try this." Daniel stood in the hall off the bedroom with a plate filled with gobs of something gooey.

"You know someone who's this good at baking and you didn't tell me?" he mumbled with his mouth full.

What was he talking about? I'd entered the movie ten minutes in and had to catch up to the plot. I ran after him to the kitchen. Daniel's mouth was filled with vanilla cake and chocolate goo, an open box was on the counter, a white bakery box, the pink curly ribbon lying next to it. My mouth opened in a soundless cry. My tongue suddenly as dry as the desert. And that old nightmare where you want to scream but you can't was suddenly totally real.

I managed to half shout, half sob. "No."

I grabbed the plate from him with one hand, grabbed a paper towel with the other, and swiped cake out of his open mouth. I picked up the box and threw it across the counter, past the framed prints, the wooden clock, the hanging pots on the wall, and into the stainless-steel double sink.

"Oh my god, oh my god," I repeated, shaking and hysterical. I turned to face an astonished Daniel. "Don't swallow, spit out what's left in your mouth." I handed him a paper towel. "And rinse every bit off. Maybe soap."

I picked up the bottle of dishwashing soap and put some on the paper towel. He was wide eyed, mouth drooping. With great aim I used the wet towel and swiped goo off his tongue. He grabbed my hand and said, "Stop. You're out of your mind. You're off the deep end."

He swallowed what was left defiantly. It had to taste like soap.

"This sugar thing is now over the top," he said furiously.

"Even if it saves your life?" I yelled.

I pulled away from him and started to dial the number for the poison control center. I finally had a use for the number.

"What are you talking about?" he hissed at me. Hissing meant he was still alive which was a good sign, although my desire to save his hide rapidly dwindled.

"Poison is what I'm talking about," I hissed back. "That cake may be poisoned."

Daniel gave me a look you reserve for the truly pathetic former mental patients discharged prematurely to the street turned vagrant.

"Look, Melanie. You've had a rough few weeks. You should go to bed. I'll pick Chloe up, grab some dinner with her. I'll clean up in here."

"That's a great idea," I said spitting out the words, "except you may be in a hospital, and I'm completely sane."

How much should I tell him? The possibility that he'd been poisoned was growing slimmer as the minutes ticked by, but I didn't know how long this took. I should call an ambulance anyway. They'd have to pump his stomach. I think you can't eat or swallow after that for days. Tracheotomy? He's not gonna like not eating. That's not the point. He could die. Poison control didn't answer. I called 911.

"I have an emergency here. A possible poisoning victim. Can you send an ambulance?"

"What the hell are you doing?" He grabbed the phone from me. I had to tell him.

"Who sent that cake?" I asked. I ran over to the box that landed upside down. Good shot, considering. With paper towels, I gingerly lifted the box looking for a card. The top layers of vanilla and chocolate cake with vanilla butter cream icing had slid off the bottom layer.

"You looking for this?" Daniel asked producing a white card from his pocket. "It's from someone named Nadine. She says thanks." He looked up and handed me the card. "Who's that?"

"Oh, just a suspect in Ralph's murder investigation, his ex-wife. She works for the King of Cakes chain as a baker, and the Waldorf."

I saw the elderly couple across the courtyard puttering around the kitchen. He wore boxers and a T-shirt, she was in baggy shorts and a long white blouse. They seemed so peaceful.

"What's the problem?" Daniel asked, his eyes narrowed.

I looked at him, and felt what? A tiny amount of glee. No damn, a huge amount of it. I'd go straight to hell for this. A rich cake filled with poison? It's what I'd been telling him. Sugar kills. Of course, this particular instance wasn't quite about sugar but still...

"The problem?" I sniped. "The detective told me Ralph was poisoned from eating cupcakes given to him in a bakery box, like the one we got. With a pink ribbon."

I remembered again the pink ribbon I picked up at the scene. Suddenly, Daniel blanched and leaned against the wall clutching his stomach.

"Jesus, you're sick, oh no. Ambulance." I picked the phone up off the floor just as it rang at the same time. It was 911. They actually called back. Did they do this because they cared, or because otherwise people would sue? Was this really the issue? Daniel could be dying. What was wrong with me? I couldn't keep one thought going at a time even in a near death moment.

"Hello. Yes, it's my husband. Send an ambulance. He ate poisoned cake. I didn't poison it."

"No, no," he grabbed the phone again. "I think I'm just making myself sick. I think. He assessed his condition. "What was the poison she wants to know?"

"If it's the same as killed Ralph it would be cyanide mainly, that's what it was," I yelped. "And it works fast. I think you should get checked out. There's a Doc in the Box place a block away. Can you make it? Although you'd be throwing up and pinker by now." I looked at him closely. He was all red from anger, but not pink.

"Thanks for the medical lesson," sniped Daniel. No one that obnoxious could be dying. I breathed easier.

"What?" He was still on the 911 call. "Maybe ten minutes ago. Oh. Okay, that's good to know. You don't have to send anyone." He listened again. "If you have to go ahead." He hung up. "They have to write up a report that the call came in. They just wanted us to know that."

He stood up straight and his arrogance returned. "They said if I'm not having symptoms by now, it's not cyanide. I should go to a doctor to make sure. They have to say that. I want you to stop talking to people about this murder," Daniel ordered. "Stay out of this."

Cake was everywhere. On the floor, in the sink, gobs on the counter, on the window sill. Like our marriage, once in a neat bakery box with a pink ribbon, it was now splattered everywhere in plain sight. It hit me with a jolt that I felt happy.

"What century are you living in? Forbid me? Well I forbid you to eat a cake that's sent to me. Poisoned or not."

Bubbles of laughter burst forth. I was giddy from relief. I couldn't stop laughing. Daniel's eyebrows furrowed and I thought for a minute he'd let himself laugh too. But no, haughty control won out.

"Somebody should tell the police that we may have evidence here in our sink."

His back was rigid, he moved stiffly trying to keep his best martyr face. My laughter died down. I put my arms around his waist to give him a hug.

"That's okay. I'll call them and put this mess back together. Don't worry about it. As long as you're alive."

Chloe and I would be miserable if he died, self-centered guy that he was and all.

Daniel looked with great affection at the remains of the cake, a friend being laid to rest.

"Great cake. Moist, sweet, hint of butter and vanilla. Nutmeg? Fabulous real butter cream, unusual for a bakery. What did you say the name of the place was? I'll have to go interview her. There might be a story here." His eyes glazed over.

"Daniel, get real," I said with a sigh. "She could be the number one suspect in a murder investigation. You want to eat more samples of her pastry?" Daniel's brown eyes with the crinkly edges looked at me with a hurt expression.

"That could just make this an even better story." He pointed his finger. "That butter cream is groundbreaking, but you'll never know because your fastidious self doesn't touch cream or sugar." He shook his head and stormed out.

I started giggling again, laughing so hard I couldn't breathe, and then the hiccups started. He was such a show, what a relief. I put on rubber gloves and picked up the cake. I shoved the mess into a plastic bag, labeled it do not touch property of the police. I placed it gingerly in the back of the freezer. I dialed the number I had written on a pad.

"Hello." The accent was Nadine.

"It's Melanie Deming." My heart beat way too fast. "I wanted to thank you for the cake. My husband said it was excellent."

Her voice was stiff. "Of course, it is. I'm the best." And she's modest. Nadine asked, "Did you try any?"

"No. I don't eat sugar, but I was really surprised you baked for me and knew where I lived. Was that also from Helene?"

"Yes. I wasn't supposed to know?"

"Actually, not unless there's a reason to need my address." I paused, not sure how much to push her. "Why did you send me the cake? I don't even know you."

"You are not able to accept gifts," she said in a clipped voice. "I can see that. It's simple. You were nice the other night. You've been through a lot. Finding Ralph."

I wasn't nice at all. "Well, thanks for the gift. I thought you sent it because I'm married to a food critic."

"How dare you say that!" She spit out the words.

Guess I hit a nerve.

Suddenly, I heard banging and a buzzer through the phone.

"That's the police. They said they'd be here today. I have to go." She sounded breathy, on the verge of panic.

There were many voices in her apartment. She hadn't disconnected. I heard Nadine shout at them. One sounded like Janet Brown. I heard the word search. There was movement near the phone. Drawers were opened. I heard a child say something. Brown said, "Take one of those paintings. Photograph the others."

Nadine yelled, "Get your hands off my paintings. You're taking water? Leave my kitchen..." Then Nadine came closer to the phone, "I'm calling my lawyer." With that the connection went dead.

My heart pounded. They must have had a warrant to search her apartment. Water would be for the arsenic level. If that was so, why take a painting? I grabbed some paper and wrote down what I heard. She must be a serious suspect now.

I wanted this cake out of here. I called Levano's number. A Sergeant Carruthers answered.

"This is Melanie Deming who found the playground victim."

"Yes, I've heard your name. I work with Levano."

"I thought you'd want to know that Nadine, Ralph Duvet's wife, just sent over cake in a white bakery box with a pink ribbon."

"Why'd she send you cake? I wouldn't touch it."

"She said I'd been through a lot and I was nice. Does that sound plausible?"

"No idea. We should look it over. I'll send an officer to get it."

"Good. I don't want my husband eating anymore."

"He already ate some?" Carruthers sounded shocked.

"Yes, but he's okay. Now I wonder if Nadine sent it because my husband's a food critic."

"I would have no idea about that. Will you be home or is there a doorman?"

"Is leaving evidence with the doorman allowed? It's in the box but it fell so it's a mess."

"Did you drop it?"

"I threw it in the sink I was so freaked out."

Carruthers laughed. "Since your husband did us a favor and tested it, you can leave it with the doorman." He was a lot friendlier than Levano. I tried for more information.

"Have there been any arrests about the murder?"

"Not yet but we're getting closer. We'll pick up that cake." He hung up abruptly.

He wanted the cake. They must be building evidence to arrest Nadine. They'd already searched her apartment, took a painting and tested her water. Ralph's death could be connected to importing art illegally.

Tomorrow I'd meet with Devon. Plenty to talk about in plot complications. I kept walking while I mixed drops from ten bottles of herbs. I drank them mixed with spring water to restore internal balance and detoxify. I loved herbs. I knew what they did. There was nothing to figure out.

Chapter Thirteen

Spinach increases blood flow below the belt.
Eat This, Not That.com

Daniel left this morning with a terse goodbye, still annoyed I hadn't let him eat the cake. For the first time in our marriage he didn't know anything about my life, about today's meeting with Devon. A ripple of hysteria ran through me. Up and down the stairs endless times, extra lunges at fencing. I raced through teaching and almost missed seeing Bruce Salter as I left the park.

"Hey, Melanie." He called out, stopping me. Bruce had a self - satisfied grin. "Wait till you hear this." He paused dramatically. "I looked through those pictures with the detectives. I'm pretty sure one of them was a guy I saw leave the park. They got all excited. Levano said I was a big help." He beamed.

"That's great. Did you hear a name? Was anyone arrested?"

"I don't know about that." He looked distraught since he lived to please. "I think they brought the guy in for questioning." Bruce brightened, like a retriever waiting for a pat on the head.

"That's really great. Good job." I almost scratched him under his chin.

At home, my usually delicious spinach, tofu and seaweed wrap was impossible to swallow. My heartbeat and sweat everywhere meant panic. What was I going to wear to meet Devon? The remains of Daniel's twelve hundred calorie French toast with whipped maple butter from breakfast stared accusingly at me from the sink.

I tried on Rebecca's choice of tight skirt and black sleeveless top. There was no way I could lose five pounds in the next five minutes. My brain kept repeating "Don't go. Nothing looks right." I tried on a blouse. Too boring. I pawed through drawers of clothes. Nothing. Rebecca said I'd look great in anything. I don't. I felt like I was sixteen again.

A slightly wrinkled black silk shell, lower cut but still way above showing cleavage, suddenly appeared in the mess. With a soft charcoal blazer, it said working female. Someday I'd buy new clothes.

I grabbed the notebook with the details of the case so far and the *WildWestsider* article and threw everything in my bag. Now I couldn't open the door. The walls of the apartment swam around me. From being hot, I went cold. Massive fear encased me in a web. I fell into the blue dotted couch in the living room. Where did I think I was going? I only lived life through fantasies and Rebecca's affairs. I never actually did anything.

Fantasy worked. Don't go meet a man this attractive, even just for work. Books didn't get written while women lived their fantasies. *Fifty Shades? Gone with the Wind? To Kill a Mockingbird?* The women sat home and wrote. They didn't have coffee dates with hot men.

Meeting Devon was wrong. One step and an evil genie would stop me from writing for the *Westsider* and break up my marriage, destroying an often unfulfilling, but otherwise safe life. I called my shrink.

"It's Melanie. Do you have a minute?"

"Just about. What's up?"

"I'm meeting that cute guy who's a writer, to talk about a screenplay about Ralph's murder. I think I shouldn't go because Daniel will leave. Chloe will hate me and I'll never write again." My heart pounded away rapidly.

"You're having a panic attack," Pam said quickly. "Writing with someone is not grounds for divorce. Unless you plan to jump into bed? Just keep your boundaries."

"There aren't any beds in Barnes and Noble."

"You know what I mean. Gotta go."

Writing was not grounds for divorce. Maintain strong boundaries, like Israel and Egypt. Be tough. I locked the door behind me.

~ * ~

The huge B&N on Broadway was a dinosaur that should have been extinct by now but hung in there. No one knew how they paid their massive rent in New York City when ebooks, like termites, devoured hardcovers, page by paper page.

The cafe on the mezzanine level opened to the first floor. Devon lounged at a table in the back, his face buried in Hemingway. I took a deep breath and repeated business, business, like a mantra.

I stood at his table and coughed. He looked up with a smile that spread over his boyish face framed by that thick blonde turning silver hair. A blue turtleneck over flat abs and just the right faded jeans made me start to sweat again. Leave before he sees you. *No*, I argued. *He's just a guy.* Why was I sweating? The sweat was spinach and tofu causing an increase in my blood flow and estrogen. Sure.

"You're here. That's terrific. I wasn't sure you'd show," he said.

My mouth dropped open. I might be drooling. I turned away to check. No drool. His breezy smile faded a moment. "You all right?"

"Yes. Fine. Am I late?"

"No. I'm early. Why don't you sit down?" This was apparently his living room. "I'll get you some coffee. Something to eat? They have great hazelnut scones."

"You live here?"

"Practically. It's my office. So, what would you like?" He stood there with a smile that to me read let's get naked now. I went through a short list of what I'd like, all having nothing to do with food, and one of which had me running down the stairs and out the door.

"Peppermint tea and lemon," I said. "But I'll get it."

If he bought tea, was this a date? Not a date, work. My mind was exhausted already, keeping this straight.

"Oh, you're an herbalist. No caffeine or sugar, I bet," Devon commented.

"Right. Or milk. Among lots of other things."

"Herbal it is. I'll get it." He ran off, probably in relief. Nobody got turned on by healthy.

"Still can't believe you're here." He gave me the tea.

Why did he look at me like I was a prize of some kind? I was done for. I couldn't hold a boundary with Devon with the 42nd Infantry as backup.

"So, you want information on boxing?" he asked sitting down. "I know the owner of a gym in Brooklyn really well. You should meet me there and I'll introduce you. You can talk to him yourself." Devon's hands were rough looking enough to be masculine, tanned, and not shaking a bit like mine were.

I stared vacantly at him. Devon didn't know that the plot of the murder I told at the party was true. He assumed it was fiction, and all I needed was local color about boxing when what I really needed were facts about Ralph. I had to tell him the truth to get his help. I was puzzled he hadn't read about the murder or seen me on TV since even the fruit stand guy knew.

"A few scenes happen in a gym. I haven't decided if the murder is connected to the victim being a professional boxer."

"Well, let's see what you've got so far. Any notes?"

Business it was. Safe territory.

Devon took out a pad and pencils, pushed his sleeves up. "I've been thinking about that Food Lovers' party. Talking to you was the only good thing to come out of it."

"Really? That can't be true. There were a lot of interesting people there." A red-hot flush crept up my neck. Keep it about work.

"You're a lot more interesting than you think," he said leaning toward me.

I jerked the chair backwards, almost fell over and had a coughing fit.

"Should I try the Heimlich maneuver?" he asked with an amused smile.

"Spare me, I need my ribs," I managed to squeak. "I'm still breathing. Maybe we should talk about the story?" Back to the project.

"Some of the scenes you described sounded ready-made for a TV screenplay." He took the top off his pen.

My heart leapt. Ready-made. The warmth spread from my neck everywhere. Damn, look how easily I could be seduced with just a mention of a movie or TV. I reminded myself I was in Barnes and Noble, not a backlot office at Paramount. I took out my notes on Ralph's murder. For a while we got serious and worked on creating scenes in order. Devon was quick with ideas, focused and said what he thought.

"You've got a lot of detail about the characters here. Funny scene with the food-obsessed husband eating the cake. Is this based on Daniel?"

I ignored his question. "Have you ever been married?"

I could hear Rebecca saying, *No, don't ask.*

He raised his eyebrows. "Really? Okay. Yes, was married. Not anymore." His eyes dropped their humor, replaced by a coldness.

He had a story I was not going to hear. At least not now. In a few seconds Devon's blue eyes looked deeply into mine.

"Food is definitely not my top priority."

Did he mean sex was his priority? Drops of sweat formed around my neck. This was a wrestling match. I had to strike back.

"Food is actually a top priority for me," I said with disdain. "The right food I mean. Like there's no reason to use white flour or any wheat in that scone you're eating, or sugar." I pointed at it like it was a dead fish." He stopped seducing me with his eyes and looked at his plate.

"So, journalism's your top priority," I said, taking over the conversation. "Lucky for me. Any books where I can find boxing statistics?"

Devon was still with me, but the seduction was gone.

"Online's the fastest way, but there'll be something upstairs to start. Not sure what you're looking for." He eyed me skeptically.

We took the escalator up to the second floor. I kept my head down to avoid seeing anyone I knew. In the sports section there were five books about Mike Tyson, three about Muhammad Ali, Raging Bull, and then finally a boxing almanac. I sat on the floor, and flipped through the pages looking desperately at the index for Ralph's name, from the years 1992 through today. I forgot about Devon and where I was as I searched for any clues about Ralph. Evander Holyfield, Oscar de La Hoya, these were rising stars. Ralph had never been any kind of champion. Devon sat down next to me on the floor.

"Are you planning to tell me why you're so interested in the man who was killed in the playground the other week? You're not just looking for general stats." He looked at me with the patient expression of a seasoned investigator.

Shame flooded my body. What the hell? How long ago had he figured this out? He'd been playing a game with me.

"If you knew the story idea, I told at the party was about a real murder, why didn't you say something?" I came back at him.

"Why didn't you?" Devon retorted. "You thought I might grab the story for myself? That's what you figured?"

"Totally wrong. Wow, you have no idea who I am. For that matter, I have no idea who you really are."

This was a disaster. There was bad chemistry already. Time to go, but I kept talking.

"Sounds like we're not a great match." I said, and noticed Devon's eyes changed to a darker blue. I went on. "I'm curious, how did you know about the murder?"

The dark moment passed. "I have contacts in the police department and I read the paper and watch the news. Just like anyone. So now, Melanie, tell me why you're interested in this murder?" Devon leaned back against the books, close to my shoulder radiating heat.

"I'm not sure I want to tell you," I said. It sounded as if Devon hadn't seen me on the news.

"Why not tell me? I showed you mine, you show me yours?" He laughed.

I felt turned off and turned on at the same time.

"Mine's more complicated than yours," I said smirking.

"Women always say that." Devon smiled. Suddenly he sat up and faced me. A light seemed to have turned on in his brain. "Oh my God, it was you. You're the teacher. You're the one who found him. That's why you're so interested." He sat up straight and beamed at solving the puzzle. Big deal.

"I'm so interested? What do you think I'm doing, researching *Little Women?* Have you ever found a murder victim? Do you know what it's like to find someone you know who's been killed violently? It's a lot more than being interested."

"I get it. You've got skin in the game. Must have been a nightmare." Devon's face softened. His blue eyes gently caressed my face. I decided to trust him for the moment.

"The idea came to me at the party when I wanted to get the agent's attention. I worked with Ralph. I found his body. I called the police. The murder happened just before I met you. Then I realized there really was a story. The agent was interested and so were you. Or maybe it's easy to get your attention," I smirked.

Devon stretched his arm up along the bookshelves brushing my shoulders. "Yeah, us freelancers will follow anything in a skirt," he chuckled, joking about himself.

I liked him again.

"It's not that different from what writers do all the time, lift ideas from newspapers and any media," he said. Abruptly Devon sat up straight and stared.

"With you there's a really important difference. You didn't lift the story. You are the story."

"Good for you. You're finally catching up."

He ignored my snarky tone. "Of course, the cops haven't arrested anyone and you're waiting to see what happens."

That did it. I got up off the floor and looked down at him.

"I'm not waiting to see who they arrest, as you put it. I'm actively working on getting information whatever way I can. I've met the wife and girlfriend. Been grilled by cops. That's why I needed boxing background on Ralph. Though I don't know if that's what got him killed."

Devon threw the book on a pile in between shelves. "You'll never find anything on Ralph in these books. He was a small player. Probably never made more than two hundred dollars a fight."

"He was important to me and to a lot of kids, even if he wasn't front page news." I stopped. "You didn't think this story had enough potential to do it yourself?"

"It didn't really grab me. I have other projects. Now I can see you're a hot commodity."

"What in the world does that mean?" My voice squeaked like I was eight.

"It means you have the first-person account. Everyone loves a true story by the person who lived it. What might sell this is that you found him in the park, and that you knew him. His life, and yours, could be a thriller by the time we're done." This was the first good idea to come out of his cute mouth. It didn't sound like a line.

"You're just using me. Why should I hook up with you?" Oh God, bad choice of words. Devon laughed and I did too.

"It's your story," Devon finally said. "But I have the connections and I think more experience than you have?" His face was way too confident. "I'll use you and you use me. We have a deal?" He put out his hand. I wasn't doing even a handshake with this man.

"Before I agree, I need to know your end of the deal. You'll get information for me from your police and boxing sources?" I sounded more experienced than I felt. I was out of practice in business partnerships, flirting and keeping boundaries.

"That's why I'm here. Whatever you need." Devon took out his phone and looked through his contact list.

"My friend's a walking encyclopedia on New York boxing lore," Devon continued. "If there's anything worth knowing about Ralph, he'll tell us." He played with a book on the shelf, suddenly uncomfortable. "You can actually trust me. I'm known as being pretty ethical by journalists."

I made a split-second decision.

"I have more names to give you. You're right. I'm a hot commodity and we could write a decent screenplay and sell it." I heard myself say "we."

"Can't see how we'd miss. My contact is at the gym in the evenings. Let's talk to him together. Meet somewhere first for dinner."

Red flags appeared. "No dinner. Just ask your friend for any information connected to Ralph as far back as twenty years ago when he was at his peak. He abruptly stopped competing. He went back to the ring sometime in the past few years."

I was talking too fast and too loudly, but I didn't care. What a relief to have someone else to talk to. My shoulders which had been tight ever since the murder, relaxed. Devon was interested as a writer. He could help me unravel this. Maybe he got off on flirting, but at this moment he didn't scare me.

I took out my notebook and made a list of all the suspects I had. I remembered the guy Bruce identified.

"A parent, named Bruce Salter, sat down with the detectives at the 24th precinct and went through pictures. He identified one of them as being a guy walking out of the park that morning. Can you find out if the police brought the guy in? Get a name?"

"I'll call now." He got a sergeant named John on the phone. "No problem. He'll check into it."

"The police are building a case against Nadine. They suspect she baked the cupcakes."

Devon watched two kids run through the aisles. "So, the poisoned cupcakes are true?"

"Yes. No more half-truths." I took a deep breath. "The autopsy showed cyanide as being the real cause, with some arsenic thrown in. The detective examined my herbs at home. Janet Brown took pictures of arsenicum, as if it could poison anyone. They thought I kept cyanide in that closet too."

"You being a suspect makes for an even better story." Devon smiled happily.

"That's just great."

I paced up and down the aisle of books and fell into a large leather chair. Maybe I could live here. Books and quiet. Devon sat on the arm of the chair. He put a hand on my shoulder for a moment.

"The cops do occasionally solve murders. It's not all up to you." I heard his words, but all I could think about was his hand. I slid out from his warm touch and moved to the other side of the large chair.

"Ralph deserves justice. The police haven't made any arrests and it feels more urgent the more complicated it gets. My therapist said a screenplay is my way of getting closure."

Devon sighed. "Well, hold on then for a wild ride. You've been bitten. The story's gonna control you even when you don't want it to.

Like any passion and obsession." His eyes were back to seducing me. It felt like he was seeing through my shirt. "I warn you, though, there's a letdown when it's over." He smiled as if he was remembering a story. "The ride's great while it lasts."

This man was either outrageously sensitive, or this was his standard pickup line.

"You're a lot more intense and driven than I imagined," Devon said. "We'll definitely work well together."

I burst out laughing.

"My ego's not big enough to take this in. I've got to go." I pried myself out of the chair. Devon followed me downstairs.

On the street, vendors lined up in front of Barnes and Noble, taking advantage of the crowds to sell Harry Potter scarves, puppets, used books. Light clouds dotted the sky.

Of course, part of me yearned for adventure and change, to be reckless, have a passionate affair with the handsome stranger, leave everything behind while day and night we solved the crime and wrote a hit screenplay. The problem was, I couldn't.

"Thanks, Devon, for the tea and your help. Let me know if you find anything." He put his hand on my arm.

"We'll have to stay in touch regularly. We need a detailed list of scenes. We can split up the writing. You'll see. You never know where these things lead."

Did he mean lead like to a Netflix deal, or to us all over each other in some secluded hotel room? I had trouble breathing. Devon was half real guy, half fantasy guy.

Broadway was spinning. Keeping a work boundary was exhausting. I looked into Devon's intense blue eyes.

"You're a perfect writing partner, nothing else. I'm married. Have a child."

"I don't think I said anything about getting married." But at this moment he looked at me like no man had in a while, no man like him anyway. I swung my bag over my shoulder, concentrating on not falling down.

"No, you never did. But you've come on like it's more than just writing." Time for some reality here. "You and my husband know each other. It would be a soap opera. So, let's just be about the work and we'll do great. "

"Absolutely," Devon said looking amused. I ran across the street and didn't stop till I was a few blocks away. I sat on a brownstone stoop, taking deep breaths till the street felt solid again. I walked to the East Side.

Chloe chattered about school while my mind was on Devon's eyes and his touch on my shoulder. We picked up turkey for burgers. Low fat organic turkey is a perfect food. Way high in protein and low in everything else. Daniel put at least half a pound of melted cheese on his.

Chapter Fourteen

Eat to Live, Don't Live to Eat
From Socrates

The next morning, I heard Daniel leave for work. "Have a good day," I called out.

"It'll be good as long as no police come to the apartment," he snapped.

"I'm having an open house for the twenty-fourth precinct cops later. Around five."

"Not funny," Daniel said and slammed the door.

He was making it easy to dream about Devon, who had bedroom eyes and understood my need to write about the murder.

A few minutes later the doorbell rang. It was upstairs neighbor Harold Farber, so excited he bounced from one foot to the other.

"Melanie, this is fabulous. It couldn't be more perfect."

"Really?" I tried to look modest. "You liked my column that much?"

His bouncing stopped. "Sure, your piece was fine. I'll use it. That's not what I'm talking about." He brushed my column aside.

Then he leaned toward me with eyes narrowed and one arm on each side of the door frame, so close I sniffed his armpits. I gagged, and took a step back. If my column was not perfection then what was he excited about? I bet it was a bird. A red hawk who lived on a billionaire's Fifth Avenue windowsill got tired of being rich this week. The hawk flew west. I was really wrong for that story.

"I can't stand the suspense," I finally said, trapped by his armpits. "What are you talking about?"

"You discovered the caretaker in the park. You've been holding out on me." He squinted and wagged a finger almost in my nose. Yuk.

"You've got to write a firsthand report. You found the body. You knew the victim personally. You worked with him right where he was killed. Use whatever angle you want. *City Loses a Good Man,* you lost a good friend, rampant crime. Of course, it'll be highly emotional. But you know the facts better than anyone else. It'll be great. Who knows, this could be taken by larger papers. It could go viral, or run online everywhere. It would be great for you, and for me, and for the *Westsider.*"

I stared at him. Two lines he said flashed in neon. "Taken by larger papers, and run online everywhere."

Since meeting with Devon, writing about Ralph's murder was the plan. Like an answered prayer, Harold was here giving me a path to follow, and maybe an audience. Yes, I'd do this. But it was going to cost Harold because I needed money. I played hard to get, like an agent would.

"I'm not sure about this, Harold. It's still very upsetting for me."

"Not a problem," he interrupted. "Didn't you ever hear of sublimation? Write your way out of shock. Use your feelings."

I knew what sublimation was. I was just surprised he did. Maybe he was in therapy, though you'd figure his therapist would be all over those stained shirts in the first session. I stayed silent, which turned out to be a good bargaining technique.

Harold broke into a full smile overflowing with energy and goodwill.

"There's money in it. We're still working out the finances, but it's looking good. There's more money in websites than in newsprint."

Great. He brought up money. "Harold, do you have a ballpark?"

Harold finally agreed to four hundred dollars up front for two columns about the murder, with more possible. I was thrilled. The best part was I owned the columns. We shook hands. He clutched my hand, not letting go, and stared at me too intensely. I threw out a mood destroying bomb.

"Speaking of crimes, Gertie's diamond necklace was never found since it was stolen two weeks ago out of her freezer. Does the super have any idea who could have taken it? Did you hear anything the night she was robbed?" Harold lived on her floor.

He quickly pulled his hand away looking annoyed.

"No. I was out. The cops asked me a few questions. She misplaced it and forgot where it was. She's old you know and a little…" He touched his head. "Nice woman, though."

"But the apartment door open? Seems like someone came in."

Harold edged toward the stairs. "You've got a reporter's pushiness, Melanie. You find out anything, let me know." With that, he was gone.

Bringing up the robbery worked. Harold was a rent-controlled tenant who paid much less than market rate. He was always terrified he'd be kicked out, though laws protected him. He acted like a mouse around the super, who reported to the landlord. If Harold caught a handyman with the diamonds around his neck, he'd never say.

First, I lied and announced at the party I was working on a thriller about Ralph when I wasn't. Next, I agreed to write a screenplay with Devon. Now I had a deal to write actual articles about the murder. The shift in my reality shook me like an earthquake. Daniel still knew nothing.

Do something. Make sure you're registered for the course. Find the starting date.

I went online. Screenwriting. Started in two weeks. My courage faded. I needed a jolt of adrenaline, which meant Rebecca. She was home.

"I'm so glad you're there."

"Me too. Nobody's here. It's blissful," she said dreamily.

"Great. I need a quick fix of courage from you. I think my marriage will fall apart."

"You already did it with Devon, and Daniel found out? You've gotta be more careful."

"Of course not. You know me."

"What happened when you had coffee? Come on, tell."

"He took the project seriously. We're working together on a screenplay, I guess. He has contacts for information. The problem is he looked at me like it was more than work."

I didn't want to admit, even to Rebecca, how turned on I was. "He has nice hands." I sounded like I was twelve. "It just might work."

"You just shook hands? Even Sex Ed teachers tell you hand-shaking is okay. Whatever, this is so exciting. It's about time you had a guy appreciate you."

I could hear her grinning. "I have a regular job now writing for an online paper, the *Wildwestsider*, with my Socialist birdwatcher neighbor. You remember him?"

"Right. Disgusting. Who could forget?"

"He's published two of my columns already. Now Harold wants me to write about the murder. I'm hiding all of this from Daniel and he's still barely talking to me. I signed up for the screenplay course. Now I have to call the sitter. Am I digging my own grave in this marriage?" I paced around the foyer.

"Maybe a tunnel out of it." Rebecca jumped in. "I'll dial the sitter for you. Give me her number. I've been wishing you'd do any of this for five years."

"No. I can call her. I just needed to hear you tell me I'm right."

"Beyond right. You've made my day. You're working with a hot guy who's into you. I mean I'd go to a hotel, but do it your way. You have a new job. Anything is possible now. Maybe life on Mars. Or I get a poem into a journal. That secretary in Paul's lab falls off a cliff."

"Glad I'm such an inspiration, but I could get an ulcer. I'm hiding so much from Daniel." I gulped more California poppy.

"Well, of course. Daniel's on a need-to-know basis. You're already in the deep end of the pool so now is not the time to panic. You know how to swim. Just take the next stroke."

"I know how to swim," I repeated.

I clicked confirm for the course and downloaded the syllabus. I grabbed a few supplies for class and ran down the stairs. I was late. I ran to the park.

Just two blocks from the entrance, I heard heavy breathing coming up fast behind me. The breathing got louder and louder. Suddenly, it was too close and terrifying. A large hand deliberately reached out and shoved me, as if I was a garbage pail to be thrown aside. I dropped into a lunge in the opposite direction from this lunatic and stayed up. I saw an arm reach out again but he missed me as he kept running.

"You maniac," I yelled.

He never stopped. He was either a random psychotic or it was a deliberate attack. A hoodie hid his head. Somebody wanted to scare me.

He got what he wanted. Gasping and shaking I ran full out to the entrance. Instead of the concrete path, I ran down the steep grass and rocky hill at dangerous panic speed. Running as if somebody was after me, running to get to other people and safety. My feet got tangled up and I fell, rolling over and over on the grass. I grabbed a rock to slow myself down and stopped on a bunch of thorny bushes, scratched and hurting. Yuk. Dog poop could be on me. I leaped up.

"Melanie, are you all right?" Louisa charged up the hill, blonde curls and everything else bounced. She brushed twigs off my sweater and hair. "You flew down here like you were being chased."

"It's the quickest way to get down," I joked, catching my breath. A scratch on my right hand stung. "Some crazy runner just tried to shove me out of the way on my way here." That might be true, or it was meant for me.

"I don't like this, Melanie," she finally sputtered. "I can meet you on the street. We'll walk down together."

"Then we'd both get hit and trip each other."

I laughed to reassure her but felt the sting of the scratches, and fear. Louisa knew. She put her arm around me. At least I was over 5,000 steps.

We climbed through the hole in the fence which placed us directly behind the storage building, right at the spot where we found Ralph. I'd avoided this corner. Tears rushed to my eyes. I took five pellets of Ignatia Amara. This was more than sadness and more than writing a column and a screenplay. I was scared. Daniel was right. I should stop now. In the bathroom I washed off the scratches with disinfectant and took massive amounts of arnica.

The kids came in. We started the class. No sight of Helene. At the end of class, Louisa checked off the kids as they were picked up, a new procedure. Nicole, in red tight capris and boots with four-inch heels, came to pick up Cody. We had a brief contest as to who could stare with more contempt.

"You are Melanie?" I jumped at the voice from behind me.

Turning around I saw a small, compact woman, maybe forty, in jeans and a flowing flowered shirt. Like she was teleported in. A matching bandana was tied around her hair, worn in an Afro. Her complexion was light brown with freckles across the bridge of a cute nose above a small mouth in dark red lipstick. She looked wholesome, not hysterical or bereaved. I knew from her voice who she was. She was clearly not in jail.

"I am Nadine Duvet." She stuck out her hand.

I shook her hand, worried a handshake meant I'd agreed to something. Queen Nicole watched, taking mental notes to be conveyed to President Helene.

"Be right back." I trotted over to Louisa. "Can you stay around in the playground? This is Ralph's wife and I might need a witness."

"Of course, I'll stay. You don't have to talk to her." There were worry lines between her eyebrows. I nodded but slowly returned to Nadine.

My column and the screenplay needed this woman.

"You are wondering what I am doing here, correct?" French accents were usually charming. Hers was not.

"I'm surprised." I hoped she wouldn't get hysterical again. I didn't have enough herbs.

"Can we sit down?" Nadine asked impatiently.

She glanced at the twenty tiny chairs and tables.

"Sure. Help yourself." Like a circus act, we simultaneously maneuvered ourselves into the seats. Louisa expertly walked Nicole out the door.

"Why are you here?"

Nadine's shoulders slumped. Her mouth trembled as she talked. "You must know by now poison killed Ralph." I nodded. "It's horrible, disgusting for someone to kill him that way." Her hands twisted in her lap. Her face contorted in anger. She slammed her fist on the table. I moved my seat back.

"Someone is setting me up, as you call it. Destroying my

reputation as a chef, getting me in jail. The stupid police. They were ready to arrest me, but my lawyer said that they had nothing."

Her face showed disgust. "Anyone can bake cupcakes. You don't have to be a graduate of Le Cordon Bleu to do it. You can just get a mix, anywhere, for Christ's sake." Nadine spit out the words.

I only used mixes. How plebeian of me.

"Maybe you can tell the cops to analyze the ingredients. If it's Pillsbury, you're off the hook." I said.

"You are joking. They couldn't give a damn whether I'm one of the best pastry and dessert chefs in the city. Le Bernardin called, they want me. I am honored of course, but the Waldorf accommodates me."

She leaned forward and gestured way close to my face. "The police are Neanderthals. To think I would have poisoned a dessert is to think that Michelangelo would throw tar on the Sistine Chapel. Desserts are my life."

Nice dramatic touch with Michelangelo, and I was impressed by Le Bernardin. No wonder Daniel wanted an interview. Just because she said she'd never poison a tiramisu didn't mean she didn't poison Ralph.

"Nadine, I get you're upset. What I want to know is why are you here?"

"You must help me. Explain to the stupid detective that you know me. I'm honest, hardworking. Never in a million years the type to do that. Tell them Ralph told you. You're a teacher, they'll believe you."

She moved forward, so close I could feel anger coming off of her.

I jumped up. "I just met you. Never heard of you before. I don't have a hot line to the police. Get your lawyer to negotiate."

She gestured wildly. "They don't listen to my lawyer. I have an alibi. I was at work all night. Afterward, I was out power walking with a friend before I took the children to school."

"So, you have a witness for your alibi. What's the problem?"

Nadine's eyes darted around the room. "People with visa issues are not home for questioning by the police."

Another alibi problem. Nadine stretched her arms and rotated her shoulders. As she stretched, her shirt rose up. There was a shiny brown object, maybe five inches long, sticking out of her pants' waistband.

Could it be a gun? Her shirt was back in place.

Nadine looked grim. "I have an idea who killed Ralph, but I have no proof yet. I am at work on this. I'll tell you everything I know, but I still need a day or two to get proof. You need to stall them."

I didn't believe her. How could I get Nadine out of here if she had a gun? I paced around the room.

"Please leave. Tell the police what you know about other suspects." My pacing brought me to the wall of windows which had metal gated covers. No way out. That brown shiny object bothered me. I eyeballed the distance to the front door. Nadine stormed up to me. I jumped back.

"Other suspects like Carey, Ralph's slut girlfriend."

"That's me." A British accent announced Carey, at the doorway in form-fitting black leather jacket and bell-bottoms. Her timing was perfect, or awful. She walked in as if she was on a runway. The room was instantly too crowded and dangerous.

"Now listen, you two. I don't want any trouble." I yelped.

Oh God, did I just say that? How embarrassing. What if an agent heard me talk like that? I'd never get any writing jobs. I was John Huston in his worst western.

"I'm not fighting anyone," Nadine said in a haughty tone. "I have a right to know why Carey is here."

"I don't have to tell you anything," Carey sniped as she edged her knife-thin silhouette into the room. Carey made a wide circle to get to me and whispered in my ear. She fussed with a startling-looking belt buckle shaped like an arrow that pointed toward her crotch.

"It's that letter. You've got to come look at it and walk me over to the detectives." Carey wheeled around.

"What letter?" demanded Nadine.

"The one you sent threatening Ralph's life. That's what letter." Carey crossed her arms, feet planted firmly next to my feet like we were line dancing. I darted away.

"You're psycho," yelled Nadine. "I didn't have to send Ralph a letter if I was mad at him. I saw him every day. You knew that. Just like you knew he was coming back to me despite your tricks." Nadine's mouth was in an angry grimace, her fingers jabbed a rapid staccato at Carey. So much for how she didn't love Ralph anymore.

"Ladies, calm down," I said uselessly. "Aren't we all in this to find Ralph's killer?" Breathing was getting difficult, my chest felt like it was caving in. I was having a heart attack.

"All she cares about is the insurance. Ralph was just her meal ticket." Carey's high-pitched angry voice was wild, her eyes with heavy mascara like black slits in her ivory face, a leopard about to pounce on her kill.

"Ha," Nadine's laugh sliced through the room. She took two steps toward Carey. "You almost conned him into that marble high-rise trap until I saved him to be with his kids and his own people."

They advanced on each other like wolves in battle. Nadine grabbed what she could of Carey's blonde pixie. Carey let out a scream and grabbed Nadine's Afro. I saw Nadine's hand spread flat, mashed against Carey's face, Carey's hand in a tight squeeze had Nadine's other arm in an impressive lock. At this point the room spun around, a sharp pain laced my forehead, and I collapsed on the floor. Louisa ran in. She pulled Carey off of Nadine and wedged in between them.

I held my head in my hands that vibrated, and laid on the floor. These two were hell bent on mutilating each other. The danger in the room was terrifyingly familiar, like when I was ten. Only I wasn't ten. Come on, grow up. I sat up too fast and the room spun around.

"What's the matter with you?" Nadine stood over me.

This crazed woman was annoyed I stole her big scene. I burst into laughter.

"There's something the matter with me?" My voice sounded hysterical. The teacher was having a breakdown. They all looked uncomfortable.

"It's just an anxiety attack," offered Carey. She rubbed her scalp and glared at Nadine.

"Good news, doc. Not a heart attack. I'm relieved you're here to diagnose. One thing I can diagnose," I said. "I'm the only one who couldn't commit a murder."

Carey and Nadine backed away from me. I took slow deep

breaths, the dizziness lessened. Wayfaring tree is an herb that increases oxygen intake. I needed some.

Louisa snapped at them. "What the hell are you doing? Ralph was a special man. He's gone. Fighting now is a waste of time."

"I deserve a look at that letter. It may fit in with my theory about who did this to Ralph." Nadine's voice was haughty. She put her hands up and showed us her empty pockets. "I don't have a gun, nothing on me at all."

"What's tucked in the back of your jeans?"

In one swift movement she reached behind her and held up a black object. I ducked behind a low table. Something clattered on the floor. Nadine's cackling laugh filled the room. She held a cell phone. Very funny. There was also a brown handled knife lying on the ground a few feet away. "What's this then?" I picked up the closed switchblade.

"If you worked the hours I do, you'd carry a knife. I don't need it anyway. I have plenty more."

"I wouldn't know how to use it." I dropped it in my bag. "What about you Carey, any weapons?" I asked. Louisa signaled she wanted to call the police. I shook my head.

"Please, don't insult me," Carey said. Her skin tight outfit had no bulges.

"We get the letter and go to the police." I said loudly.

"She just attacked me." Carey's chin was way up in the air. "Don't come near my house." She was right.

"Nadine, I'll send you a picture of the letter before Carey gives it to the police. I'm not going anywhere with you both."

"That was my plan. Let's get this over with." Carey was near the door. I wasn't leaving yet.

"Write your address here for me." I handed her a pad. She wrote down her address, shielding it from Nadine, and handed it to me.

"I need to meditate. Either stay or go. I'll meet you."

"I meditate all the time. You should use Meditation Moments. Here," Carey, pushing her phone in my face.

"Insight Timer is the best," insisted Nadine.

Good God, they were fighting about their apps.

"Your apps aren't working. Either sit down and shut up, or leave."

Great words to achieve serenity and bliss. Louisa and I sat on the carpeted naptime area. I closed my eyes, breathed in Deepak Chopra's soothing words about erasing anger and achieving balance. Calming sounds of water and chants filled the room. A chime signaled the end of the session.

Carey was still here, busily examining her nails. Her pants were too tight, I guess, for any deep cleansing breaths. Nadine was gone.

Chapter Fifteen

You are a perishable item, live accordingly.
Unknown

I locked the room. The clean air outside was like a cold compress. Louisa grabbed my hands.

"Melanie, don't go. They were ready to kill each other. Go to the police. Tell them about the runner this morning. Tell them about the letter. When you're done, just go home and lock your door." Her brown eyes showed fear.

I squeezed her hands. "The address is 315 West 82nd. Her name is Carey Longert. Nothing will happen. I'll call you to check in." I didn't recognize my voice sounding confident, even brave.

Louisa hugged me tightly and left.

Through the trees, up on the street, was a blue and white police scooter. If I told the cop, the expedition was over. I wouldn't get the story about the letter for my column. I texted Devon.

On the way with Ralph's girlfriend to see letter threatening Ralph
He replied in seconds. *I'll meet you there. Text the address,*
Best alone. Talk later. I sent the address to him for security.
You forgetting we're partners? he replied.

~ * ~

Charming one-hundred-year-old brownstones with pointed tile roofs and overflowing petunias and geraniums in window boxes lined West 82nd Street. These houses had a parlor floor up several steps. Three steps going down led to an apartment below sidewalk level which had its own entrance. Carey stopped in front of number 315 and looked down at the basement apartment.

"Oh God no!" she shrieked. "Oh no!" I followed her frantic eyes down the steps to the entrance and the small concrete courtyard. The apartment door was wide open, and from the street we saw the mess. A chair lay on its side half out the door. Papers flew like a light snowfall. A baseball glove and a blue plastic box with trucks and action figures were strewn amongst the wreckage of tables. Feathers floated lazily in the air. This was the scene of a robbery. Carey ran down the steps. I yelled after her.

"Where do you think you're going? The burglar could still be there. Call the cops."

Carey yelled, "They're gone! No police!" She went in.

How could she know the burglars were gone? I stood on the sidewalk.

I wished Devon was here. I did have a problem accepting help. Cornelia was right. Too late now, I needed this story. I took pictures outside, and walked into the apartment.

When you live in New York just out of college without much money, you're going to live in crappy buildings. You're gonna get robbed. When you live in Harlem on a top floor, you get robbed more than once, so I was something of a burglary expert. Carey's place inside didn't look as bad as the worst. No filthy graffiti scribbled on the walls, or ketchup and shaving cream and sticky syrup poured on the floor. No one had peed on a wall or a couch, but I hadn't reached her bedroom yet.

Feathers from ripped cushions floated inside this small front room, like petals off a tree. A brick fireplace painted white had photographs of sleek models hung starkly on it, all untouched. One was of Carey in a sequined evening dress.

The kitchen looked like an earthquake shook the place. Cabinets emptied, canned goods, boxes and bottles thrown on the floor. The refrigerator door was flung open, which made it easy to snoop. Refrigerator snooping was one of my secret pleasures, giving me insights about people you couldn't get any other way.

Carey had Weight Watcher TV dinners, many six packs of diet sodas, chai tea drinks, a quart of orange juice, and more low-fat yogurt than I'd ever seen in one kitchen. Lots of Califa cold coffee latte drinks. Not a leaf of lettuce or even carrots. Carey never cooked and was into low fat everything, the one feature we had in common. She starved herself to stay that thin. What did her son eat? I saw pizza boxes in a corner and crushed McDonald's bags.

"It's gone," Carey yelled from the back room. Down a short hallway, past the bathroom, Carey stood in the bedroom surrounded by piles of clothes. Every drawer had been emptied. A double mattress stood on its side, the top nearly reached the ceiling.

"Gone?" I parroted. "Do you mean the letter?"

Carey was silent.

"Are you sure? Maybe it's mixed up with your stuff." I lifted a pile of socks with my foot and let it drop.

"It's gone. I know." Carey's voice quivered.

She sank down to the floor and threw her arms gracefully onto the box spring, like a dying swan. Her head flopped down next, and she cried in big wrenching gulps. I sat down next to her. Her supposed fiancé had been murdered. Her apartment robbed. Even so, my gut said there was something else.

"They're trying to scare me," Carey whispered so low I could barely hear.

"Who are *they*?" We sounded like a scene from an acting class.

"The blackmailers. The ones with the pictures." She whispered this as if I knew what she was talking about.

"What pictures? I'm here about a letter."

Carey stared at the floor. This had nothing to do with Ralph.

"Are these nude pictures?"

She nodded.

I wasn't surprised. I did an article for a fashion magazine about models and the porn business. Young models ended up in X-rated movies believing it would lead to a cover on Vogue. Women were rising up in protest now.

"It was ten years ago, when I was eighteen," Carey said haltingly.

"Now they want five thousand dollars or they'll send the pictures around to the showroom where I work and to my parents." She looked at me, her skin smeared with tears and mascara. "The ones I got back are gone." Her head drooped listlessly to one side.

Why hold on to pictures or even give money? Everything was stored on someone's computer forever anyway.

"Carey, you need a lawyer, not money. Join the #MeToo women. Go after whoever threatened you. They're the ones who are in trouble, not you." I wondered if her story was true.

"No one came here for your pictures. That was just a side bonus for them. Focus on the damn letter. Where did you leave it?"

"I'm not sure."

"How could you not be sure you didn't hide it somewhere? Where were the pictures?"

"In my underwear drawer."

"So where was the letter?"

A strange thought crossed my mind: the letter had never been here.

Carey finally sputtered, "In the bathroom. I think I hid it in the bathroom. In the medicine chest. I think I left it there. I thought no one would look there."

I went into the bathroom. There was no letter in the cabinet. There was Xanax for Carey. Ritalin with her son Everett's name. There was Fen-phen. So, diet pills were the secret to that model thinness. They could make you hyper, irrational and disoriented. Not surprisingly, no letter.

I pawed through the garbage feeling stupid, my hand wrapped in a paper towel to avoid germs. Suddenly a growling man's voice yelled, "Police. Come out now."

Goddamn. I held my breath. The voice was Detective Levano's.

"Yes. We're here. Don't shoot." I shuffled out of the bathroom. Carey tiptoed out of the bedroom at the same time.

Detectives Brown and Levano looked as surprised as is possible considering detectives' facial expressions are frozen at graduation from the Academy. Levano had his gun drawn. I covered my eyes. This was my second time around a deadly weapon. It wasn't getting easier.

"Is there anyone else here?" I shook my head, my eyes still covered.

"You never saw a gun before? Scary, huh? Open your eyes." He waved the gun in the air. I dropped to the floor. Levano locked the gun back in the holster. "I don't know why the hell you're here but you're not cut out for whatever it is you think you're doing." He gave me a look of disgust, as if I was a water bug.

Brown crossed her arms, reminding me of my high school principal. She spoke coolly to Carey. "What's going on? Have you been robbed or are you decluttering?"

She gestured that we should sit down. The detectives grilled Carey. She cried and told them about the letter. Nothing about the nude pictures. Levano turned to me. For the first time I really looked at him and the effect was jarring. His mop of sandy hair was too youthful. It didn't go with the deep lines on his weathered face. His lopsided closed mouth smirked.

"Why are you here?"

"Carey came to see me at the playground around ten fifteen and asked me to look at the letter. She refused to take it to you otherwise. We agreed that after I saw it, she would go to the precinct. When we got here it looked like this, a burglary."

Levano turned back to Carey. "Why didn't you give us this letter when we first interviewed you?" His rage was barely under control. He cracked his knuckles, a sound that had the same skin crawling effect on me as fingernails on a blackboard.

"Scared. I don't know," mumbled Carey.

"Scared?" Levano shouted, his anger burst forth like a fighter hearing the bell. "You've got this ass backwards. You're scared if you cooperate? You have a lot more to be scared about now. You withheld information from the police in a murder investigation. That's a crime." He stood up and looked at Carey cringing in a chair. "Maybe we'll book you on tampering with evidence. She'd have a great time in jail, right, detective?"

Brown nodded and looked amused.

"What's going on, Carey?"

A strikingly handsome black-haired thirtyish guy in shorts and a tight T with enormous biceps and a small waist stood in the doorway. He could have played Superman. He glared at Levano, a bad idea since he didn't have a cape and wasn't about to repel bullets. Carey was transformed. She jumped up and ran to him.

"Who are these people Carey? I won't let anything happen to you." He gazed at her and took her hand. He was definitely ripe for a superhero role.

"Well, well. Is this your other boyfriend, Carey?" Levano stood up.

Though he was older and shorter, he seemed amused by the idea of doing damage to this guy.

Janet Brown faced the superhero in position with Levano. "We are detectives with NYPD, investigating a robbery here and also the murder of Ralph Duvet. We can talk here or go to the precinct."

"This is Richard. He's my friend and he lives upstairs." Carey clung to Richard's arm.

Richard's beautiful face lost its bravado. "I live on the third floor in the back and I sleep late. I didn't hear anything."

"You must be one sound sleeper. You've heard from your dear friend Carey about the murder of her fiancé?" Levano grinned at the word fiancé.

Richard pulled away slightly from Carey's clinging arms. "Carey had broken off the engagement. Ralph continued to show up. Her son, Everett, liked the guy, and he did work around here."

I stifled laughter. Carey was a con artist. She lied to Richard, to me, to the police. What was the truth about the letter?

Levano exchanged a look with Janet Brown who gestured toward the front door. Outside there were deep grey rain clouds. Detective Brown pinned me up against the concrete wall with her dark unswerving gaze, standing so close I could see a hair growing out of a mole on her chin.

"What the hell do you think you're doing hanging out with this woman? She's under investigation for murder. Her alibi's a lie. Her boyfriend's suspicious, too. You followed her back to her apartment like a trained poodle." She squinted at me. "What's your real interest in this case? You barely knew Ralph Duvet."

I suddenly realized the cops being here was not a coincidence. Shorty told them what he heard sitting on the bench on Broadway. Shorty told them he saw me with Carey, about the letter, about Carey's alibi problem.

"I'm reporting for an online West Side paper. There's a story here about Ralph."

Brown smirked scratched the back of her neck and looked up. "Really. You're on a goddamned research project. As if I believe you're reporting for anything. Who else have you talked to?"

"No one." It was none of her business.

"Withholding information is obstructing justice. If you know something you're not saying, we'll find out. Stay out of this or we'll arrest you."

"Look up www.wildwestsider.com," I said. "You'll find my column. You're not the only one who has to make a living. I'm a reporter."

Brown abruptly turned and went back into the apartment.

I ran up the steps to the street and didn't stop running till my cell phone rang. It was Pamela, my therapist. I had forgotten another session. There were fifteen minutes left.

"What's going on? You missed again."

"I was tracking down a story and frankly forgot. I have a job writing a column for an online website and I'm covering the murder and the investigation."

"You sound out of breath."

"I was at a robbery scene. The detectives showed up. One of them drew a gun."

"A gun?"

"The cop had his gun drawn. It was frightening." I started to shake. The terror of the moment finally hit me. Right then I heard a text come in and saw the sender walk toward me.

Where are you? Should I meet you? texted Devon. He was here. My shaking stopped.

"Melanie, this is too dangerous," Pam said. "I understand the opportunity to write. It's what you've wanted. Did you sign up to report from the Gaza Strip? Guns are too much. You're addicted to the excitement. Let this go. It's dangerous."

"Pam, it's been nine very dry writing years. At least I'm working, even if it's just columns for a paper. I've got to go." I hung up on my therapist and smiled at Devon who stood in front of me,

"You don't take no for an answer," I said.

"Not when it matters. It looks like I missed the action. Are you okay? Did you see this letter?"

He sounded worried. Did he really care about whether I was safe, or was he here for the story? Around Devon I bounced between wanting to be a serious journalist, or a damsel in distress. I'd just hung up on my therapist for him. He'd better be the good guy he seemed to be.

"Carey's apartment is down there. She was robbed." I pointed to the end of the block. "The letter was gone, along with some nude pictures. She says she's being blackmailed but she's not what you'd call a credible informant.

"Then Levano and Brown walked in. Her Superman-lookalike boyfriend, Richard, swooped in to rescue her. By the way, he's definitely strong enough to have killed Ralph. Carey told Richard she was no longer engaged. She told everyone else she was."

I took a breath. "Shorty tipped off the cops. They've probably been watching her." Fear suddenly gripped me.

"Is this what it's like, Devon? Cops with guns drawn? Levano waved his gun around like it was a toy."

Devon shook his head. "Rarely. If it was a robbery, he might draw a gun. Waving it around sounds like he was trying to scare you. He was being a smart ass."

I shivered. "My gut says Carey knew the letter wasn't in her apartment. So, why drag me there? She's a con artist. She lies to everyone."

"Now you know. We stay detached, we write the story. Everything that happened goes into a scene. It's not up to us to solve this thing. You had the nerve to put yourself in the middle of the story, which is great reporting, though not always safe."

Devon's words were the support I'd wanted. I felt an urge to hug him but stopped myself.

"Someone shoved me aside this morning on my way to work. I don't know if it was a random crazy or I was being warned. The therapist I've known for years just told me to get out of the investigating business. She says I'm addicted to excitement and it's dangerous and bad for me."

"What do you think? Do *you* think it's bad for you?" Devon asked quietly.

We stood close together on the corner.

"It's bad for my marriage. It's good for me." I felt a pain in my forehead. "I'm writing again. I have a job writing for an online paper. Chloe's happy as long as I'm happy. Daniel doesn't want crime around Chloe. If he knew what I was doing, it would be war or worse. Why do I have to make a choice?"

Devon took me by my shoulders and looked intently into my eyes. "You don't have to choose. You're doing what you were meant to do. You're following your heart, your instincts. You have what it takes to fulfill your dreams. Trust that." His faith in me and the excitement of being close to him sparked heat all over my body where it shouldn't have been. I took a step back.

"You're a great coach. I'll keep going. As long as I don't get whacked, as Chloe put it."

The moment passed. We kept walking.

Devon probably told a lot of women to follow their bliss. A man with his smile, body and charm had a lot of opportunities. I was sure he didn't feel as turned on by me as I felt around him. For him, this was about selling a screenplay and I was a hot commodity. If I backed out, he had no screenplay told by the woman who found the body.

We were near my apartment and talked about scenes for the script. Suddenly Devon stopped.

"I'm going to that boxing gym in Brooklyn tonight. Come with me? I know a French bistro nearby."

"French restaurants at night are not my thing. A bright salad bar maybe. Another time?"

"When? You decide the time and place. We need to get these new scenes in order and lay it all out. See how it works." His laughing eyes said he meant more than the screenplay.

Devon's phone rang. He turned away to take it but I could hear his voice.

"I'll send what I can. You know I always do." He listened to whoever was on the phone. "Of course, I miss you too. I've been busy."

I waved good-bye and ran across the street. The person on the other end was someone he knew well. There was a long history and it wasn't all over. Ex-wife? Girlfriend? And I was a lovesick puppy mooning over an affair that could destroy my marriage. "Grow up," I mumbled to myself.

Chapter Sixteen

I may not be perfect, but I'm sure as hell gonna get close.
Hasfit.com

At home the apartment was quiet, but I couldn't sit still. I blamed it on Gertie's diamond robbery upstairs and checked inside all the closets, like when I was ten and home alone. All these years later I still didn't have a clue what I'd do if a burglar jumped out.

Sublimate, Harold said. The voice of a birder with stained Grateful Dead shirts was loud and clear. Write the column. Devon's voice told me to follow my instincts. Write what had happened up to now. I wrote about that morning, the man I knew as Ralph, finding him, the shock, the horror, not too much gory detail but enough. The swarm of police and the effect on the playground, on the community, on me. His wife, his children. That boxing was his passion. A few subtle jabs at Helene. I gave it the headline "Rocky of Riverside." It began,

Down in the wilds of Riverside Park, a man originally from the deep South and a professional boxer, was a hero to the children who played and learned there. And to their families. He guarded their forested city oasis. Ralph Duvet did not deserve what happened to him while he worked.

At the end I hinted that his murder may be connected to the death of a homeless man, but no details since that was still not public. I gave the names and numbers of the police to call. This column was just the first. There'd be more to come as the case unfolded.

I faxed it to Harold, feeling as if I was on a roller coaster at Coney Island with the same chills and stomach-churning thrills. Ralph's death led me to my own column, to Devon and to a path back to myself. Life was happening fast while I was busy looking in other directions. Where would I end up next?

~ * ~

I put on exercise gear, ran down the steps, and headed east to Central Park. The air was clean. I gulped it like a swimmer taking a breath. The dirt track that encircled the Central Park reservoir with its elegant wrought iron fence was fairly empty today. Seagulls squawked. Ducks, swans, and egrets dotted the lake.

I increased my speed and watched the view of the city like a panorama shot as I rounded the reservoir. There was the slinky toy design of the Guggenheim Museum, the Citicorp building with its giant TV screen top. At the southern end, the long green roof of the Plaza Hotel. Clouds crowned the picture in threatening shades of grey.

I sailed around and back to the West Side for one full circle, and saw a small woman I didn't want to see join the runners up ahead. I turned around and ran in the opposite direction. Other runners gave me dirty looks.

"Melanie, I need to talk to you," Nadine called out. She had seen me and caught up. Nadine was in no shape to keep going at this pace. Too much pastry.

"I'm busy," I called increasing the distance between us.

"I know who sent Ralph that letter."

"There was no letter. It was gone. Go away." I jogged faster.

Gasping for a breath, Nadine yelled, "Ralph got beat up six months ago."

Ralph got beat up? Damn. I needed to know this. I circled back.

"You know if you stopped eating pastries and cake you'd be in better shape."

"Who the..." Nadine stopped mid curse which was immensely satisfying for some reason.

"Just keep walking and talk."

Nadine scurried along trying to keep up with a fast walk. The

Metropolitan Museum's glass wall that housed the Temple of Dendur from Egypt faced the track. It was a miracle this wall of glass had never been vandalized at night. People in glass houses shouldn't throw stones. I was really far from perfect. And the rules of engagement were different for investigators. Whether I liked or trusted Nadine wasn't the deal. I needed her information. *Shut up and listen*, I told myself.

Nadine gasped for breath between words. "Six months ago, Ralph came back from the gym beat up. His nose was bloody, he had cuts all over his face." She gulped and gasped for more air.

"He never got that way, not with all the padding they used when they practiced their stupid boxing. He said a young guy came at him about some old grudge. I tried to find out more but he wouldn't tell me. I went to the Kingsley gym after the park because I knew that snake Bennie, Ralph's trainer, wouldn't be there. The girl who was the receptionist was chatty. We got around to Ralph and then to this fight six months ago. She remembered it very well. She gave me the name of the guy who beat him up. She said she didn't know anything about a grudge."

"What's the name?"

"Andreas Martines. He lives in the Bronx."

"This name belongs with the police. Let's go there." Why did I bother to say this when I knew what her answer would be? I had to decide whether I was here as a journalist getting a story, or as the innocent bystander who had a responsibility to the cops. I knew the answer. I just sent in my column.

"There's nothing to tell yet. I can't. They'll ruin it all. They could not get a five-year-old to tell them the truth."

"Or you."

"Come with me to take pictures of Martines. Use your iPhone. Mine is not working. The bus to the Bronx from Riverside Drive goes right where he lives." Nadine grabbed my arm.

I jerked my arm away. I was done being used. "I came out for a run. If you have nothing else to tell me and refuse to go to the police, I'm gone." I sped away from her, running fast, for me, a nine-and-a-half-minute mile.

~ * ~

Back in the apartment, I headed straight for my herbal pharmacy. I mixed all my herbs, and swallowed half of an L-Theanine capsule, good for relaxing. Menacing people in a nightmare kept coming at me but it was broad daylight and only one o'clock. These women were master manipulators and I was frantic, furious, jumpy. I laid flat on the rug in the living room, breathed slowly. Andreas Martines had invaded my brain.

I tried the internet. There were twenty guys in the Bronx with the same name. That wasn't going to help.

I should call Levano or Brown, but the detectives just told me to stay the hell away from this case and these suspects. This was my story now to cover and write about. I texted Devon the name Andreas Martines and asked him to check on him with his contacts.

Devon texted, *Why did you leave? Sorry about the phone call but I had to take it. I can explain.*

He didn't owe me an explanation. He wrote, *We're getting closer. Be careful.*

There was a fight between Ralph and Martines. They probably fought about a woman. Ralph was far from perfect. He was a seducer. Yet in my fantasies, Ralph had been perfect, and probably had been the same for a lot of other women. He must have enjoyed that. Louisa and Gabby both said Ralph was a real Don Juan. Both thought his death was connected to messing with the wrong woman. I was the one who said no. It looked like I was wrong.

Chapter Seventeen

I suggest ginseng, shown to help men...and women boost desire.
Dr. Kat Van

The next morning breaking clouds revealed a startling blue sky. Chloe left for school. Daniel was sprawled in a kitchen chair reading a cookbook and eating three poached eggs on toasted French buttery bread covered by a canned Hollandaise sauce he'd been sent. His eyes left his eggs for a moment.

"You're looking especially delicious this morning." He reached out, grabbed me around the waist and pressed his cheek against my breast. Thoughts of Devon must have swirled an erotic aroma around me.

"Good enough to eat, that's me," I said lightly, feeling like Daniel might swallow me along with his eggs. Just another tasty dish.

Daniel's arm stiffened, his hand slid away from my ass and he sat back down to breakfast. "So that's your cute way of saying that all I do is think about food. Is that right?"

"It was a joke, Daniel, that's what it was. Anyway, you used the word delicious. I think that word is used to describe food?"

He looked up from his paper. "I doubt you meant it as a joke, but I'm horny."

What a romantic come-on. I had to take one for the team here. We hadn't done it in a while. Besides, I felt guilty working with Devon in secret. Daniel stood up and returned to my ass and breast. Almost instantly, the kissing started. I ignored the taste of eggs and Hollandaise. His hand moved to the front of my jeans and he managed to unzip them.

"Are we doing this in the kitchen?" All I saw was a hard floor and chairs that wouldn't hold both of us.

"Meet you in the bedroom," he said.

I trooped along behind. We had sex pretty well established. There was the usual ten minutes of foreplay. Daniel was more caring in this department than in the rest of our life. Orgasms and a guy who could support himself. He still came through in those areas.

I laid back, enjoying Daniel's pretty good technique and forgot what a jerk he had been. Why deprive myself? I had to admit I imagined being with Devon while "researching" in the stacks of a deserted library.

It's not cheating, in my moral code, to think about other guys or kinky locations like airport bathrooms. I think about whatever I want. He could be thinking about *foie gras* or Sofia Vergara's cleavage. I didn't want to know. Rebecca and I talked about this. She had fantasies about her yoga instructor, professors at her institute on an analyst's couch, or her dentist.

How turned on can you get after twelve years by the guy who slurped his eggs, flossed his teeth, and snored next to you? And then said, "Let's have sex, I'm horny." People who insisted they're just as excited today by their partner as they were twelve years ago lie, or maybe it wasn't that great to begin with. They could be dressing up in bunny costumes to have sex. You'd never know.

As a weight loss tip, climaxing during sex burns more calories, according to the How Many Calories Burned website. Two hundred and two calories for me. One hundred and one for him. I won.

"Well that was a nice surprise," I said while we lay there.

"Your turn to ask next time." Daniel kissed me on the cheek before getting up. Sounded like he was keeping score.

I heard someone knock on the kitchen door. I quickly adjusted my clothes, ran to the kitchen and opened the door.

It was Selma, her hair deep blue today. "Hi. I'm just on my way to work. Anything urgent?"

Selma's face crumpled into guilt as if she'd just robbed a bank. She clasped and unclasped her hands. "I've been upset all night. Yesterday a woman came up to me outside of the building and asked if I knew you. Said she needed you for something and it was very important. I told her I'd seen you head to the reservoir. Last night I had a premonition that she could be dangerous. Did she find you?"

"She found me. Her name's Nadine Duvet, the murder victim's wife. The cops think she might have killed him. Of course, there are several other suspects. She gave me important information, if it's true."

Selma looked deeply into my eyes as if she was reading tarot cards, which was her hobby. "You shouldn't go to work today. She'll show up there. Call in sick."

I laughed nervously.

"Nadine thinks she's God's gift to buttercream frosting, and she's pushier than an insurance agent, but she's three inches smaller than me. There'll be plenty of people around. She won't do anything." Selma's sigh was heavy with premonition and foreboding. She went back to her apartment.

Selma's dire warnings lingered in the air.

I took DHEA for energy. DHEA is a steroid-like hormone produced by our own adrenal glands but it's sold as a supplement. DHEA, like any steroid, is tricky. It gives energy, but take too much and you can end up in a screaming match, fighting over a cab with a large enraged stockbroker in rainy New York at rush hour. I took less this time, and left for work.

"Hey, Melanie." It was Blanca, the receptionist from the gym, waving and walking toward me on Broadway.

"I didn't see you at the gym yesterday," I said.

"No. They went with a young kid as a receptionist. I was only temporary." She didn't look like she cared. "So, did they ever arrest anyone about the murder of that man in the park?"

"No, not yet. The police don't tell me their plans." Blanca, like Nadine and Carey, assumed I'd have insider information.

"Just a tragedy having that happen in a public playground." Blanca pointed her gold painted nail at me. "You should be extra careful."

"Got my laser sword right here. I patted my bag." I hurried away in the opposite direction, thoroughly spooked. First Selma, now Blanca.

~ * ~

After the class, Louisa and I climbed the hill past fading hedges. There had been a hard rain during the night but the blazing sun rapidly dried the shining pavement. The air was dry and cool. Jackets were on; there was that nip in the air that meant apples were falling off trees in an orchard upstate. A crowd of teenagers from a private school team ran into the park with their coach. Louisa trotted off for the train. When the dust cleared, there was Nadine perched on a bench. She jumped up and raced over to me.

"We get the bus here. I have a map of Riverdale." She shoved it in front of my face. "It will not take more than twenty minutes to get to Andreas Martines' house." She was persistent, I'd give her that much.

"Let's see your map. What's the address?" Nadine's eyes were veiled. She pulled the map away. She couldn't decide whether or not to trust me, like someone dealing with a used car salesman. You wanted the car but you knew the salesman was probably lying. Nadine made a decision.

"265 Grosvenor. Martines lives with his mother. *Le bébé*."

At that moment the bus pulled up. We got on. Despite her small size, Nadine's well-toned arms exuded power. A coiled bobcat, who, when unleashed, kills. She was scheming every moment to put blame on anyone else, including me.

Losing control of Ralph could have led her to do anything, including murder.

I searched on my phone for information about Martines at that address. There was nothing, which was unusual. Everyone has some history online. His was wiped clean.

The bus zipped up the Drive, over a short bridge which spanned an offshoot of the Hudson. The bridge connected Riverdale to Manhattan. Suddenly there were large suburban homes alongside high rises, a suburb for people who didn't like the suburbs. There was a subway, very low taxes on private homes and decent public schools.

"How old is Martines?"

"Twenty-five. That's what the sweet young thing at the gym thought."

"Did she tell you what he looked like? Are we going to follow any man that steps out of the house? Plumbers or Verizon guys, for instance?"

Nadine looked out the window. "I'm not stupid. He has black straight hair, parted on one side. Medium height, muscular squat build. A Spanish Stallone, she said. Olive skin. Works out a lot." I got what I needed. Now I could find him at the gym without Nadine.

The bus entered a wealthy area. Neatly clipped hedges. Large Tudor-style houses, none the same, set back on hilly slopes with long stretches of grass. We were near the Hudson River. We got out at Riverdale Place and Grosvenor. Gardeners' trucks were everywhere, but otherwise few cars were around. It was quiet, the kind of quiet money buys.

There was 265 Grosvenor Place, a house even more imposing than the others on the block. Two story, rambling, heavy wood Spanish-style doors. The fencing in the rear yard looked like it enclosed a pool. If Martines killed Ralph, it wasn't for money.

Being the only people on the street, one black woman and one white, we stuck out like a couple of weedy tomato plants in the gardens of Giverny. I spotted a place to hide in the double hedges that came together between properties. Nadine followed.

I saw something move in a hedge across the street. Suddenly a young spotted deer bounded across a garden into the woods nearby. Right away I felt itchy. Deer carry ticks that carry Lyme disease. I had to get out of here. Lyme disease or finding Martines. Ticks won. I'd never make it as a reporter.

I took a step onto the sidewalk and turned to leave. At that moment the door to 265 Grosvenor opened. Damn. I raced back into the hedge.

Andreas Martines fit his description perfectly. Spanish Stallone, handsome in a tough-guy way. Pug nose but good cheekbones. Dark hair, dark eyes under heavy eyebrows. He wore khaki shorts and a sweatshirt that said Lehigh College. His powerful-looking legs bowed as he walked. I waited for Nadine to make a move but she was frozen, except for her eyes following him. She had lost her nerve. I quickly took a side picture of Martines.

Andreas walked down the slate path to the street and turned onto the sidewalk heading straight toward our hideout. He was close enough to get a good photo. I knew any sound in these bushes would be like a bomb going off. I could hear the scrape and squeak of his rubber soled sneakers on the pavement. The squeaking stopped.

Moving in slow motion, I slid toward the end of the hedge. Martines' butt was only a few feet away as he bent over to tie his laces. He started off again. When he reached the corner and turned left, I stepped out onto the sidewalk. Nadine trudged silently behind. Something changed shockingly since she saw Martines.

Traffic got heavier. Trucks were double-parked making deliveries. Andreas crossed the street. So, did I. By the next block there were enough stores and pedestrians to act as camouflage. I'd use Nadine as bait.

"Speed up," I ordered. "We have to pass Martines. I'm going to that bus stop ahead. Look like you're waiting for a bus. Give me your phone. I saw that it works fine. I'll pretend to take pictures of you."

Nadine was still in frozen mode.

"Give me your phone."

She handed it to me.

I picked up speed and passed Martines, smelling a fruity cologne. Nadine dragged her feet again as if she'd rather forget this. We got to the bus stop. She walked reluctantly into the center of the sidewalk. I snapped pictures.

"That's great. Just a few more." This time Andreas was in the picture, a three-quarter mug- shot. A side shot, then one from the back. Abruptly he stopped, turned around and did a double take. I got one final full-face picture with my own phone. Martines bent his head and scrutinized Nadine with a puzzled expression that became a leer. He strutted toward her.

"Aren't you that girl from the club? Sure, you are." With one step he was inches from her.

Nadine had the look on her face that you get when you see a rat run across the sidewalk almost under your feet. New York has too many rats.

"Yeah, The Red Parrot. You were there with that girlfriend. The one who wouldn't leave us alone. It didn't matter though, did it? We had a good time in that storage closet. Bet we can find another closet. Let's do it again." He reached out to grab her." Nadine's sluggishness vanished, replaced by rage.

"You men are all the same. You think you're a Romeo. It meant nothing to me. How rude to embarrass me in front of people." She was ready to spit on him but stopped herself.

Andreas suddenly looked like someone who could commit murder. He raised his fist prepared to hit Nadine.

"You whore. You're just a tramp in a storage closet. I've had a lot better and can any time I want." He stormed away calling back, "You'll regret this, bitch."

A bus rolled into the stop. I race walked over, fumbling for a bus pass, trying to get away unnoticed. Abruptly, Martines turned in my direction. He stared at me for a full minute. His eyes got even darker and his expression was pure hatred. A cold chill swept over me.

He had to be mistaking me for someone else. I'd never met this guy in a storage closet or anywhere. Martines killed Ralph—why would he be parading around on the street causing a scene with Nadine and glaring at me? I thought murderers usually acted against type, like Mr. Nice Guy. Here he was in public acting crazy angry.

Martines kept walking. I sat down on the bus while it idled in the stop, killing time. Martines walked another block and turned into a store. Nadine jumped on the bus.

"You had sex with a guy you think killed your husband? You didn't know his name?" I was disgusted.

"That's what he said. Men always talk like that. Don't believe everything you hear. Anyway, I was drunk that night. He's the slut." Her words were tough, but her eyes darted around the bus.

"A storage closet? So, you didn't know it was the same guy till he came out of the house. He just threatened you by the way." I shuddered.

"I'm not scared. He doesn't know who I am. I used a different name that night. I was getting back at Ralph."

"I guess you did," I sniped.

So far Martines didn't seem to make a connection between Nadine and Ralph. Maybe this guy hated me because I was with Nadine. I shouldn't have come here with her. I didn't know what I was doing playing investigator. I blamed myself, I blamed Harold for giving me this job.

Martines left the store he'd gone into and stormed past the bus. The driver started to close the bus doors. I jumped up and dashed off, leaving a shocked Nadine.

Chapter Eighteen

I don't want to brag...but...I can still fit into the earrings I wore in high school.
Zazzle.com

I ran across the street. Martines walked out of the Wayward Travel Agency. I scurried in.

The place looked like a time capsule from 1962. Lime green paint peeled off the walls. Dust covered travel posters with the edges curling up advertised crystal blue water and white sand beaches. A lone woman worked there. Her bubble hairdo reminded me of pictures of my grandmother from sixty years ago. Gold bracelets covered her arm practically from wrist to elbow.

"Can I help you?" The sign on the desk said her name was Vicki. Her accent said Bronx.

For a moment I froze. I couldn't just ask her where Martines was going.

"Well you know I wasn't even thinking about a trip till I saw your sign and thought I needed to get away without the kids for a few days." Vicki nodded. Every married woman needs to get away. "Then I met a neighbor's son out on the street just now coming out of your store."

"Oh yes, Andreas. He's such a nice boy, and such a heartbreaker. Do you live on their street?"

Oh no, I needed another street. I should have set up this story before I walked in. What other street had I seen on the bus ride up? Nederlander.

"No, nearby on Nederlander." She nodded. "Andreas told me he was booking a trip and he recommended you."

She said nothing. Those crime shows made getting information look easy. It wasn't. "What would you recommend for me?"

"Well, if you want a guaranteed warm spot and a beach, we have some nice packages to Bermuda or the Bahamas. They're back in shape since the hurricane."

Brilliant sunshine, me in a hammock sipping fruit punch, bright yellow chirping parakeets. Perfect. What about Martines?

"I was just thinking how many choices there are. Like where Andreas is going. There are beaches there, too, right?"

She shook her head. I realized too late he could be going to Cincinnati. Then she said it.

"There are beaches in Colombia, but it's not known as a tourist spot. He only goes to visit his family."

Colombia. He's not visiting family. He's going to disappear. Colombia is known for drug smuggling. Maybe he killed Ralph about drugs.

"It's warm there, right? Andreas mentioned he was going soon."

Vicki came through with flying colors. "Oh yes, it's warm there all year. He's leaving Tuesday because that was the first flight I could get him. He wanted to leave sooner because his grandmother is ill. You must know that." She looked at me suspiciously.

If I was a neighbor, would I know about a grandmother being sick? It was time to get out of here.

"No, he didn't mention it. Do you have some brochures of hotels and places you'd recommend? I'll look them over and get back to you."

"I'll need to get some from the back room. You can look at the books of hotel listings while you wait. They're up front." As soon as she was out of sight, I bolted. I hoped Vicki wouldn't mention my visit to Martines. He'd easily connect me with today's encounter.

~ * ~

I got on the next bus for Manhattan. Devon texted, *Close to more info on Ralph. Let's get dinner. We need to talk.* I called his number.

"I'm really glad to hear from you," he said. "What happened

157

yesterday, Melanie? Why did you leave?"

"Sounded like you were having an important private conversation. I had to get home." Devon's personal life was none of my business.

"We've got a lot to work with now. I just had an encounter with Martines, who allegedly had a fight with Ralph. I was with Nadine. We followed him from his house and got pictures. The big surprise was that he knew Nadine. I mean really knew her, as in having a carnal encounter at a club. She swears neither one knew the other's name. They had a yelling match on the street. He almost hit her."

"Too bad he didn't. He could have been arrested," Devon said.

"Do you have any arrest information from your police contact on Martines?"

"John said he's got nothing so far."

"Martines sure looks like a hot mess. I got away from Nadine and followed Martines to a travel agency. The agent told me he has a ticket to leave for Colombia next Tuesday. First flight he could get. He must be running away, unless he actually has a sick grandmother."

"You know if the writing doesn't pay, you can always become a P.I. That's a lot of information. Pretty impressive." Devon chuckled.

No man had told me I was impressive since forever. That warm feeling hit me again.

"He might be running away," Devon continued. "The grandmother story is so obvious."

"If that's the case, why didn't he leave weeks ago? Someone who would go to all the trouble of making poisoned cupcakes would plan a getaway."

"Maybe the cops are getting closer and he's panicking," Devon said.

I heard a computer boot up.

"I don't think the cops even know he exists. Martines didn't look panicked at all. He lives in a mansion up here with his mother. The mansion and Colombia spells drug money. We need to get more information on him."

"I'm going back to the gym tonight in Brooklyn. See what I can find out about Martines. You sure you won't meet me?" He sounded deliberately casual.

"Evenings don't work for me, Devon."

"Then how about lunch tomorrow? We need to work. We need to eat. And…"

"I'll let you know tomorrow." I interrupted him. Devon telling someone he thought about them too and would send money reminded me this was a work partnership and that was all.

"Martines looked at me like he hated me. I don't have any idea why except guilt by association with Nadine."

"He could just be an angry guy. Next time call me before you go on one of these stakeouts. I'll go instead of you, with you. Don't go alone. We're in this together."

"I hear you but it's hard to remember when suspects come at me unexpectedly." I paused. "I know you're the one with the experience, but I'm gaining on you." Joking helped the butterflies in my stomach.

"Right, I'm a regular Don Juan in partnerships." His laugh sounded bitter.

Did he mean love or work I wondered? Thirty minutes later I was back at my building.

"Ms. Deming, I have a package for you." Anton handed me a bag.

It was Nadine's phone along with a note. "You have all the pictures so bring everything here in the morning. I'll give you the name of an exterminator that I'm sure sold the poison when you get here. Come to 376 West 174th Street at ten a.m."

I laughed out loud. Another lure to pull me in. I could check with exterminators. I didn't need her. The phone she gave me was no help. There were no texts or emails. She just used it as a camera.

~ * ~

Hours later, after Chloe and Daniel were asleep, I felt restless thinking about Martines' angry glare and the day's events. Eleven at night wasn't my preferred time to run, but I had to get these people out of my head. I put on sneakers, leggings, a long-sleeved neon yellow shirt and stepped outside. A half-moon glittered. I'd stay on the sidewalks. No running in the park. Two miles was all. About forty city blocks. I'd be at fourteen thousand steps, near seven miles for the day before midnight.

The streets were nearly empty on a weekday night. Most stores were closed except for an all-night supermarket. Even the liquor store was locking up. It was easy to run with few cars and no kids darting around on kick scooters. I ran up Broadway and turned around near Columbia University's campus at 116th street. I flew back down and was four blocks from home going at a good clip.

"Hey bitch," an angry low voice yelled in my ear and a heavy weight crashed into me.

I landed hard, sprawled flat on the pavement. Knees throbbing, palms scraped. Damn, I guess running tonight was a bad idea.

"Mind your own business," the voice screeched. I raised my head a few inches from the pavement just in time to see a hooded stocky figure in sweats turn the corner, fist pumping the air.

"Screw you," I yelled to the now-empty sidewalk, sounding far tougher than I felt. Everything hurt. One palm and an elbow were scratched and bleeding. I slowly sat up, testing each joint.

"Are you all right?" A kind-faced white-haired gentleman bent down. He held groceries in one hand as he helped me up.

"Just bruises I hope." I tested my legs. "Did you see that guy?"

"I saw what he did. Slammed right into you hard. Could have been a big woman, that kind of run. Couldn't see a face. Came from that corner." He pointed across the street. "Whoever it was aimed for you like a torpedo. Lunatics are all over. I wouldn't run at night if I were you."

If he was me, he wouldn't be up to his neck in a murder investigation either.

"Thanks," I said, surprised he thought this was just a random crazy. The phrase "Mind your own business" had my name written all over it.

Could my attacker be the same person who crashed into me at the park? That runner had on shorts and the legs looked like they belonged to a man. If tonight's was a large woman, that would make seven suspects. It also meant someone was watching our apartment, watching to see when I left. A cold chill and feeling of dread ran through me.

No matter what, no one was going to stop me. I picked up my speed with more determination than I knew I had, and ran the last two blocks. I slowly walked up the steps to the apartment and let myself in silently.

I poured arnica all over my knees, elbows, and palms, took arnica pellets, and an over-the-counter painkiller, and slept badly. It was too late and too much trouble to call the police.

Chapter Nineteen

Murder makes for strange bedfellows.
M. Deming after EB White

Devon's arms reached out to me, but Helene and Nicole jumped in between, laughing and pointing at my stained T-shirt. No! I ripped off the shirt. Clownish faces leered and laughed at my bare breasts until a noise blasted insistently jolting me awake. I bolted upright, shame still lingering, but relieved it was a dream.

In five minutes, I was dressed. Black jeans and a navy Ann Taylor sweater with tiny turtles, picked out by Chloe. We went through the morning routine and ran down the stairs to the bus. I clocked steps at a snail's pace since I ached from being slammed to the ground.

Last night's assailant was too big to be Carey or Nadine. Carey's boyfriend Richard was the right size. Thugs hired by Bennie would likely be men. The elderly man who helped me on the street thought it was a woman. Which woman could that be? His eyesight must have been off.

"Where are my keys?" Daniel teetered near panic in his office. "And where is the hard copy of my review? It was right here. Belinda wants to read it." His boss Belinda always put him in a panic. "Somebody moved my things. How did it get there? I never put anything there."

"Now where's my briefcase?" he yelled.

This was a really bad morning. I wondered if he was stalling, or if there was trouble at work. He had to leave. I couldn't make calls while he was home. A small voice in my head said, *What kind of a marriage is this where you have so many secrets?* Cornelia and Rebecca both said keep Daniel on a need to know basis. Was it that time yet?

162

"Anything I can do to help?" I asked.

"No. I found it." Daniel ran past. "See you tonight."

I quickly dialed Nadine.

"Are you coming?" Nadine sounded out of breath.

"Not happening. Your note said you have the name of the exterminators who can ID the buyer of cyanide. Which company is it?" I asked.

"You have to come up here. I can't leave right now," she whispered.

"Just give me the name of the place. I'll go. The phone will be downstairs here with the doorman."

Nadine whispered, "It's too dangerous for me to leave my building alone. I'll meet you downstairs in my lobby. 340 West 174th Street, Apt 8H. There's a guard. Call me when you're here." With that said, she hung up.

If there was a guard, her situation wasn't dangerous. She wouldn't give me the exterminator's name. But if she found it, so could I. My phone rang.

"Hey Melanie, it's Harold. Glad I caught you. Nice job on the *Playground Hero* piece. You'll see it online tomorrow."

"Great," I muttered, too preoccupied with Nadine to listen to Harold who kept talking. "What did you say?"

"I said it's possible that news services may be interested in your column. I'll try to get payment but the big payoff is the publicity. You'll build readers."

"Fine, as long as they keep my byline." This was great news but I couldn't take it in.

"Of course." He paused dramatically. "We want to ask you to officially join the staff. Do a weekly column. Your columns will be about the real face of crime."

"Sounds fabulous, Harold. Do I get disability benefits?"

"Ha. We have preliminary funds. That's the next good news. Advertisers are coming in. We can start you at two hundred dollars a week as a salary. Plus what we negotiated for the murder columns as a separate fee. That's a column each week. It might go up, depending on how well *Wild Westsider* catches on."

A real job. Real bylines, deadlines, money. "You're the man, Harold." He was now my editor. He should tell me whether I needed to go to Nadine's for this story.

"The victim's wife wants me to come to her apartment uptown to help solve the murder and prove it's not her. Do I go up and see her? She's a real con artist. Add to that problem, last night someone knocked me down on the street. The attacker screamed 'Mind your own business.' This is getting a little creepy." Harold jumped in before I could finish.

"Too bad about last night, but anything for a story. Write it up. Of course, you go. That's exactly what your column is. *The Real Face of Crime*. Now you're a victim too. Better still. You can describe where Ralph Duvet's wife lives, how she's holding up since his murder. It's all perfect for your column. How she feels being considered a suspect."

"What if she's the murderer? Couldn't I be in danger?"

"Nah, I know you're going. You've met before. She trusts you. She has no reason to kill you. You're not her husband." Just like every editor. Anything for a story.

"Can't wait to read it. Readers will eat it up. There'll be a staff meeting next week. I'll be in touch." He was gone.

I was the new Lois Lane. Being paid to write what you want is like having great sex with no strings attached. But crime reporting had danger written all over it, putting my marriage, motherhood, and my life in jeopardy. Excitement and fear bubbled up like twin geysers. I was either having a heart attack or my colon was exploding.

I doused with herbs, meditated badly, and doubled the protein in a smoothie.

I called Devon and got his voicemail.

"It's Melanie. Attacked and warned last night on the street. Going to Nadine now. Meet me there? I'm hoping." I typed the address and texted it.

Rebecca. Another voicemail. "Going to apartment of Nadine Duvet." I gave her the address. "If you don't hear from me by tonight, call Daniel or maybe Detective Levano." She'd be furious at the message. Like saying I was going swimming with man-eating sharks without a cage. Have a good day.

I swung my drawstring bag over my shoulder and locked the door on the way out.

~ * ~

At a copy shop I made pictures of Andreas Martines from Nadine's phone. They were clear. He was easily recognizable. I stepped out the door and suddenly there was Carey Longert, Ralph's ex-fiancé, crossing the street at the far end of the block. Even with large sunglasses, her blonde pixie hair and thin silhouette in black skinny leggings, a gold tank top and draped black jacket, was unmistakable. A cross between Audrey Hepburn and a biker. She hurried east toward Central Park. I followed her. Either I'd gotten really good at this, or she was so intent on getting somewhere she wouldn't have noticed Paul McCartney.

Carey looked around as she arrived at the lower bridle path around the reservoir. She felt in her jacket pocket for something. A taller woman approached, wearing jeans and a white sweater. She carried a beige shoulder bag. The floppy hat and sunglasses said she didn't want to be recognized.

I watched them exchange letter-sized envelopes. No handshake or hugs. This was a business deal, not two friends meeting. Was this woman giving cash to Carey to buy the letter? Or was the woman in the hat the blackmailer Carey mentioned, and Carey was the one with the cash buying back her pictures? If only I had one of those long-range listening devices. I zoomed in and took photos.

~ * ~

On the way to the subway, big billowing clouds chased the sun around the sky. I ran down the stairs to the uptown 96th Street platform. The noise of trains rushing by was deafening. The platform was packed as usual. The train rumbled in.

After a crowded, slow ride I got off at 168th Street. This was Washington Heights, as authentic a melting pot as any place in the city. It had survived Jewish, Black, Spanish, and diverse artistic populations as the rents shot up. The Audubon ballroom on Broadway, where Malcolm X was shot, was a few blocks away. The big mall stores of 125th Street had bypassed Washington Heights. Instead neighborhood small businesses prevailed. At 174th Street I turned left.

174th Street was residential and quiet. I race walked and checked my steps. 5,302. I jogged around the block, stalling. I hadn't heard from Devon. I'd have to go up alone.

"What the hell are you doing?" a voice shouted.

I collided with a small thin man in his sixties with a tweed hat, a cigar in his mouth, and a 1950's style suede and knit cardigan sweater. He yelled and fell backwards. The man was so light, I steadied him with one hand. His face was lined, there were bags under his frightened eyes, dark stubble on his cheeks and chin. The kind of man who needed to shave again by the afternoon. He was sweating and edged away from me, like I was a mugger on the loose.

"Sorry, I'm so sorry," I mumbled.

He walked fast down the block, looking back and talking to himself. I ran another few steps and there was 340 West 174th.

Still no answer from Devon. A partnership meant sharing decisions, not running off to interview on my own. Where was Devon?

Nadine's apartment building was a middle-income housing development put up in the 1970s. These decent cinder block, no frills places had incredibly low rents. Nadine knew how to get through a lot of red tape to get one of these apartments.

Glass doors opened into a green Formica-tiled lobby dotted with fake plants. The guard was a large heavy guy. As I walked in his eyes never left the ball game on a small TV set up on a folding table. Whatever he was guarding, it wasn't the front door.

"I'm here to see Nadine Duvet."

He looked up for one second. "Apartment 8H." He returned to the game. I could have walked right past him.

"She said I should meet her down here. Can you buzz her?"

"Buzz her yourself." He pointed to a panel outside the doors. I trotted back outside and buzzed 8H. No response. I waited and tried again. Three times. No answer. I went back inside. "She's not answering. Is she here?"

"Think she said you should go up."

No, she was to come to the lobby. I called her from my cell and got her voicemail.

"She's not answering."

He reluctantly glanced up. "Maybe she went to a neighbor."

I paced for a while. I could just leave her phone, but Harold said I had to see her. Had Nadine really found the exterminator who sold the cyanide? Her story changed every five minutes. I'd just knock, hang the phone in a plastic bag off her doorknob and leave. I was not going in.

The elevator was small and slow with a round window in the door. I got off and froze. Sunlight glared off the linoleum and the super high gloss wall paint. The ends of the hall disappeared in an eerie supernatural haze. The wall sign pointed right for apartments A-H. Everything about this felt wrong.

With one hand pressed firmly against the cold wall, I placed one foot in front of the other, plodding slowly, I passed E and F. The door to Apartment G was ahead to the left. To the right had to be apartment H. The door to Apartment H was open.

"Nadine," I called out. "Nadine, are you here?"

"Mm, mm, mmaa." A sound like a dog whimpering came from the apartment. I recognized it could be a moan from a woman. I knew it. Nadine was trouble from the first phone call.

I walked backward, keeping an eye on 8H, and rang all the neighbors' buzzers. A small woman came to the door of one apartment. She spoke only Spanish and refused to come with me. I convinced her with a lot of gesturing, to stand at her door in case she heard something.

A force within me that I didn't recognize pushed me on. I suddenly knew this was my life, to be good at this job, to do the right thing. The force propelled me back to 8H. I took a deep breath and stepped through the door and into a tiny foyer.

To the right was a small kitchen, too small for Nadine's grandiose cooking. Straight ahead was a short hallway leading to what must be the living room. My right leg was going numb as if it was asleep. I dragged it as I moved down the hall. Then I saw her lying on the floor in the center of the small square room.

A loud staccato noise startled me. It was a moment before I realized my teeth were chattering. I held my jaw to stop my dancing molars and listened. The apartment was silent except for her labored breathing. I ran to the front door and the intercom. The guard picked up.

"Something's happened to Nadine Duvet. In 8H. Call the police and an ambulance and get up here right away."

"Who is this?"

"Apartment 8H. I just saw you downstairs." My name was not going to be associated with this if I could get out quickly.

"Is she hurt?"

"Badly. I don't know what happened but hurry. I've got to get off." I heard Nadine moan again. She was conscious. I peeked into the living room and burst into tears.

Her eyes fluttered open a crack at the sound of my crying. Blood was caked around her nose and ear. Grey black bruises surrounded both eyes. My teeth wouldn't stop chattering. I held my jaw and shuffled a few steps closer.

"Mmma," Nadine whispered. Then, "Be..." the word was inaudible.

"Help is coming," I said.

I heard voices in the outside hall. Get her phone out of your bag. I wiped the phone with a tissue, and using the tissue, opened a drawer of a table and dropped the phone in. I raced to the front door. The guard and two medics had arrived.

"She's in the living room," I pointed.

They pushed past me. Did I dare leave and run down the eight flights? I stood in the hallway. I heard the guard ask her who did this. There was only her raspy breathing.

"Let's get going," a barrel-chested balding medic bellowed. She was carefully placed onto a stretcher and hooked up to an IV and oxygen. I walked to the elevator with them.

"Will she be all right?" I asked another medic, a skinny gawky kid with a Grateful Dead shirt peeking out from under his uniform.

"We don't know the extent of her injuries, ma'am," he said politely.

Tears welled up in my throat and I dabbed at my eyes with my sweater. The door to the elevator opened and cops got off, a scene from *Law and Order*. Standing in the middle of the crowd were Janet Brown and Rick Levano. I should have taken the stairs and gotten out.

"What the hell is going on here?" growled Levano. It didn't sound like a question so I said nothing. Nadine was put on the first elevator.

"Come with us," Detective Brown barked in a don't mess with me tone.

I obediently followed them. They gave stern orders to the cops and looked around quickly. There wasn't much to see. An overturned lamp. Magazines and papers thrown on the floor. Bloodstains on the area rug which was covered in a pattern of large flowers. A fingerprint team was called. No one could touch anything.

"I promised you a visit to the precinct, remember?" Janet Brown snapped at me.

"Am I under arrest?" I asked.

"Not yet," Levano said.

My stomach turned inside out.

I didn't dare text Devon while the cops watched. I was having a brief glimpse of what it felt like to be in jail. No right to say anything, no one believing your innocence.

I distracted my terrified mind looking at colorful primitive paintings of children in Caribbean island settings hanging on the wall. I remembered the cops took paintings the night they searched Nadine's place. My phone buzzed. A text from Gabby, the West Side Huntley mom, wanting a playdate. No one would want to play with Chloe if they put me in jail.

~ * ~

Neither detective spoke on the trip downtown, which put me in far more of a panic than if they grilled me. I also noticed there were no handles on the inside of the doors or visible locks. I heard locks click into place as we started. I was trapped inside the car and the cops would decide when I could get out. My heart pounded so hard I thought this was it, a fatal coronary in the back of a police car.

I'd been to three crime scenes. That must be the statutory limit. Three strikes and you're automatically thrown in the slammer. Bad thought. Focus on something positive.

I blurted out, "If I hadn't walked in, she might have died, you know."

Silence. They probably had a rule not to talk to suspects in the car. Suddenly my phone vibrated with a call from Devon. For a split second I was happy and forgot where I was. I texted him. *Locked in the back of a police car on way to 24th Precinct. Nadine badly beaten. Don't know if I'm being arrested.* Seconds later he replied.

I'll come to the precinct, which made me tearful.

I texted, *Thanks.*

They didn't use a siren. Was that a good sign? We arrived at 100th Street between Amsterdam and Broadway, headquarters of the 24th Precinct. Levano pulled in. I watched two scared young kids next to us get out of a patrol car in handcuffs. I walked between Levano and Brown up a few steps and through the front doors. Inside it looked like a motor vehicles office, or the waiting room of a public hospital. Plastic chairs were lined up in rows, a cop in uniform sat behind a plastic shield inside a reception area.

We entered a small elevator, got off on the second floor, and walked down a hallway lined with doors, some with frosted glass panes. I heard a woman sobbing, a man yelling curses, then a deeper voice too muffled to make out. Scenes from *Midnight Express*, the '70s horror movie about Turkish jails, flashed in my brain. I sweated under my armpits and forehead as if I was running on a hot summer day. Our threesome entered a small bland room with a table, a few chairs and a telephone. We were the only ones in the room.

"Don't I get to make a phone call?"

"If you need it, you'll get it," Brown answered tersely.

Levano gestured to me I should take a seat. I tried to, but the room swirled violently around me. The lights flickered. My sweaty hands reached out to grab the table. I was falling.

Chapter Twenty

Eat your greens and don't be mean.

M. Deming

Just my luck to faint and wake up in the arms of a female detective.

"Is the room spinning or is it me?"

"Are you diabetic? Can you sit up on your own?" Janet Brown pulled me into a sitting position.

"No and yes." I sat cross-legged on the floor. I had arrived at a new bottom in my life, sitting on the floor of a police interrogation room holding my head. Could my life get worse? I put pressure on the pulse points on my temples, and the room slowed to a rowboat on a lazy river instead of Class Four rapids.

"Sit on this." Brown pulled over a plastic armchair. "And put your head between your knees."

I crawled slowly into the cold, hard, molded plastic chair. Putting your head down is the worst piece of medical advice for dizziness since they told women to gain forty-five pounds during pregnancy. I subtly rolled my eyes. I took out small bottles of passionflower, California poppy, ginkgo biloba and a canister of arnica pellets. My life these days required a portable pharmacy. Levano grabbed these from me like they were ten pounds of cocaine.

"What is this stuff? Do you have a prescription?" The man was a Neanderthal.

"Read the labels. You can buy this anywhere." I yelped.

He picked up the phone.

"Get me a guy in here to test some drugs. This says poppy."

"I'm not a crazed witch who concocts potions. It's not opium. These are healthy. They're sold everywhere." I waved my arms.

A young sergeant came in. "Take these out and test them for restricted drugs."

The sergeant, a young African-American guy with flat abs and weight-lifter muscles, looked at the pellets and laughed. "This is arnica. You can buy it in a supermarket. It's for bruising and sore muscles."

"I told you," I said. Levano ignored me.

"Passionflower and California poppy sound like getting high to me."

The sergeant smiled patiently. "Yeah, but the stuff's harmless. It's sold two blocks from here at a health food store. Ginkgo biloba too. There's a lot of these herbs for calming down. They're legal. Most doctors say they don't do anything. My wife swears by them, but she's a yoga teacher."

I smiled at the sergeant like he was Thurgood Marshall arguing my innocence, except for saying herbs were useless.

"Where does your wife teach? I'd love to meet her."

"That's it, show's over," Levano barked. "Thank you, Sergeant."

He handed me back my herbs. I took some arnica and mixed the three herbs in my water bottle and drank it down. The dizziness abated. I closed my eyes, opened my palms to the universe, and breathed in to the count of six, and released to the same count. Hold and release.

"We'll leave you to your rituals. Don't go anywhere," Brown said.

They left the room. This was my chance. I called Rebecca.

"Thank God it's you. Your message was terrifying. Don't do that again!"

"Next time maybe you'll answer your phone. I'm at the police station on 100th Street with these backward-type detectives. My bad luck I found Ralph's wife badly beaten up in her apartment. They act as if I did it and have no rights. I was there to get information for my column. I called the guard and got her an ambulance. Doesn't that count for something?"

"They're such goons. You're a journalist. Do they blame

Anderson Cooper if people get blown up in Syria while he's covering the war? First amendment. It's still there. You want me to come over?"

"Not yet. I'll call you if I need you. Thanks." She texted immediately, *First amendment. ACLU. Power to the people.* She added a couple of thumbs up emojis. As well as the ACLU phone number.

Devon texted again. *What's happening?* Before I could reply, the detectives walked in.

Levano sat down, his legs man splayed, the blue polyester blend of his suit pulling across his thighs. I got the message. Detective Brown sat across the table, looked at notes, tapped her teeth.

"What were you doing at Nadine Duvet's?" Brown asked.

She had bags under her eyes. I wondered about her marriage. Did she handcuff her husband to the bed?

"Nadine begged me to come see her this morning. She wanted to talk about Andreas Martines. When I got to her apartment the door was open. It was about ten. I saw her lying on the floor."

"Who is Andreas Martines?" Brown asked, sucking in her cheeks.

Why hadn't the cops found out about Martines?

"Nadine said Ralph had been in a fight outside the Kingsley gym about six months ago with this guy Andreas. Not a match, a street fight. Andreas came after him. She didn't know why."

"No idea at all?" Brown looked skeptical.

"Nadine didn't know. Someone at the Kingsley gym gave her Martines' name. A receptionist, I think. Maybe she could help you." Brown wrote this down.

"I still don't get why you had to go to her place this morning." Levano didn't believe a word I was saying. I had to give them more information. And then it came to me. Pretend yesterday was today.

"Nadine wanted me to go with her to take pictures of Andreas Martines who lives in Riverdale. She had the idea that we'd take the pictures to exterminators and see if they recognized anyone as a customer who might have bought the poison. I tried to talk her out of this. My editor insisted I go interview Nadine for my column." It was at least partially true.

As if I had smacked him across the face, Levano's powerful body lunged toward me. I'd seen this before so I didn't jump out of my seat.

"Who the hell do you women think you are?" he yelled. His finger jabbed the air an inch from my face. "I've never seen such a fucked-up case as this. Amateurs doing their own stupid thing." He paced the room.

"Was she conscious when you got there today?" Brown asked quietly.

"Barely."

"Did she tell you anything?"

"She mumbled 'mma,' no idea what she was trying to say. Although I decided it was a 'man.'"

There was something else. I blanked on it.

Brown shifted her tone. "You see what happened to Nadine?" She stood up and stuck her nose nearly into my face across the table. "She may die or be permanently injured. All because she didn't level with us and went around asking asshole questions. Do you understand that the same thing can happen to you?"

Tears started flowing, which was more embarrassing than fainting. They were right. I could have been a bloody pulp by now. The tears were real. They stopped yelling. When you cry, people soften up. They think you're telling the truth. Unfortunately, I'd already met Martines. They'd book me for sure on obstructing justice if they knew about yesterday's encounter in Riverdale.

Nadine told me she was in danger this morning on the phone. I couldn't tell them about that call either.

Levano paced around the table. I stood up and started running in place. "I need to get some oxygen to my brain." Levano's mouth dropped open.

"You think this is a game, like one of those Murder Mystery weekends at some fancy hotel," he yelled. "Sit down. You have a kid, you told us. You probably want to see her grow up." He looked at me with disgust. "Well you won't if you don't stay away from this. Someone out there went after Nadine. It's likely you'll be next. Unless you poisoned Ralph Duvet," he snickered.

I wouldn't take that last threat seriously.

"Nadine is not the murderer?" I asked.

He smacked his head with his hand.

"You jump to dumb conclusions. She's been importing art illegally from Haiti and Jamaica without paying taxes, so she's in trouble with the IRS and now Homeland Security. Her alibi is still up for grabs the morning of the murder. She needed money. She wanted to open a nice art gallery and bake shop in one. She understood she owed too much to Uncle Sam. She was losing her husband to another woman. The insurance money would have been an answer. She'd get rid of her no-good husband and get her own business. Does that sound like enough motive for you?"

Being desperate for money of course was a motive, but it just didn't fit with my picture of Nadine. She reeked of jealousy. Levano took out a stick of Nicorette gum which made me snidely happy. He couldn't smoke in here. Ha.

"My friend, Bruce Salter, said he identified a guy from your pictures as someone he saw the morning of the murder coming out of the park. Could the guy be her attacker?" Harold was right. I was pushy.

"Why the hell do you think we'd tell you?" Levano spit out the words. "Are you some aging hippy who doesn't trust cops to do our job? I'm sick of you West Side artsy liberal types."

Levano's breathing and snorting reminded me of a bull. He might be right about the not trusting cops part, but he didn't have to say "aging" did he? I had to get a better moisturizer. After thirty-five, moisturizers should be thick, not liquid. This was an especially random thought in this moment.

"If we want, we can book you for hindering an investigation," added Brown with an eerie smile.

"Why not first-degree assault.\? We don't know who did this to Nadine." Levano's laugh in this soulless room was too much.

"I want to call a lawyer. My rights are protected by the first amendment. I'm a reporter. I came for an interview."

My hands and feet were shaking, doing an uncontrollable dance together. I wondered if I could have a seizure, not a reassuring thought.

Brown changed her tactics. "Did you see anyone on your way into the building or once you were inside? Anyone suspicious?"

"I bumped into an older man, in his sixties, outside her building on the street. He was wearing a tweed hat, needed a shave, but not a bum. He looked pretty harmless."

"Short, yellow smoker complexion?" Levano looked up from his phone.

"Yes, smoking a cigar. Kind of scrawny. Looked older maybe than he is. Does he sound familiar?" No answer from either of them.

Brown asked, "Do you have anything else to tell us?"

"The guard wouldn't have noticed if King Kong walked in. The address Nadine had for Martines was 265 Grosvenor Place in Riverdale."

Brown scribbled this down. She put her pad down slowly and clasped her hands around the back of her head, stretching her shoulders, arching her back. Her lips tilted up into a half smile, as if she'd heard a mildly entertaining joke.

"What does your husband think about all this playing detective?" she asked.

"Why is that important? I have a job to do, like you. I'm a reporter for the *Wild Westsider* and I was told to go interview Nadine. There are laws that protect freedom of the press. I'm not being charged, so I should be free to leave. Otherwise I want a lawyer."

"You fainted. Call your husband and ask him to pick you up." Levano spat this out and his angular face looked like a devil mask. Janet Brown was busy smiling at a cobweb on the ceiling.

"If you're arresting me and giving me a phone call, I'll decide who to call. If not, I'm fine to leave on my own."

Levano handed me the receiver from the phone on the table. "Call him," he ordered.

I glared at Levano and took the phone. I dialed Food Lovers and Daniel's extension. An angel was watching because he was out.

"Not there. He doesn't pick up a phone if he's at a restaurant. If I can walk a straight line, I should be okay right? Unless you're charging me with something, I have the right to leave."

Brown suddenly turned into a normal human.

"We can't charge you at this time, though probably locking you up would be the best way to get you off this case. The officer affirmed that Nadine responded with a word like man when asked about her assailant. Fingerprints don't show yours except on the intercom. We also found out two different men had been asking about her earlier, but neither one went upstairs according to the guard. We're looking for these men based on your description and others. Until we have the assailant, don't leave your apartment. Whoever did this has been watching and knows you've been around Nadine. You'll be next."

"I understand. Can I go?"

Of course, I had no intention of staying in the apartment. I wasn't under house arrest. I stood up and felt kinder toward these two.

"You know I appreciate what you do, even though it's not reciprocated. I'd like to give you the California poppy. The huge stress here is terrible. It's bad for your immune system, digestion, heart. You probably grind your teeth at night. It's not like taking drugs. Just try it. There are some meditation apps I can suggest." I held the bottles out to Levano.

"I get it. We all sing 'Kumbaya.' Go home." He picked up his phone and waved me out the door.

Brown had her back to me. They had no reason to bring me here except to scare me.

~ * ~

Outside it was still early afternoon. The sunlight blinded me like a flash bulb after the eternal night of a windowless room in a police precinct.

"Finally. I thought you'd been locked up." I blinked a few times before I saw Devon. He was actually here, looking worried and sweet in a lumberjack plaid shirt that fit snugly and called out, I'm strong, let me hold you. A switch that had been in the "on" position pumping adrenaline since this day started, abruptly shut off. My muscles unfroze. I fell, not gracefully, on him. He grabbed my elbow and put his other arm around my waist.

"Whoa. Hold on. Let's find a place to sit."

"Good idea. Food would help too." Devon's arm around my waist was a combination of sweet and sexy that I'd never felt before. I pinched myself hard to make sure this wasn't one of my dreams. "Ouch."

"What are you doing?" Devon's body tense up.

"I wanted to make sure I'm not dreaming. Nice things like this don't usually happen to me."

He relaxed and his arm stayed around my waist. I felt stronger, but why would I tell him?

"Women have called me their worst nightmare, not a dream," he said.

Which made me wonder what he'd done. We passed a bodega, a Spanish market.

"I really need food. My adrenals have been on full alert for hours. I'll be right back." I finished a bag of almonds by the time I came out, as if I've been without food for a week.

"You sure you don't need a few steaks with that?" Devon laughed.

We walked to a bench next to Central Park and sat close together. My leg lightly touched his, causing sudden sparks.

"If I have to be questioned in a police station for every story, I may not be cut out for this." Devon gave a nod of understanding. "They only let me go when they found out Nadine's attacker was likely a man. I asserted the First Amendment. They wanted to scare me. I fainted."

"Do you need a doctor?" he asked. I shook my head. Devon took my hand. He was being a friend but the currents from his hand somehow reached my neck. I wondered if I was turning red, not cool for a journalist.

"What happened to you last night?" he asked.

"I went out running late on Broadway. A guy or a woman knocked me down and told me to mind my own business. We must be getting close."

"We are close. It's not worth getting hurt. How about you take a break? I'll keep looking."

"Never, and let them win? I wrote it all down. It's a good scene." My voice was firm. Devon looked at me with respect and excitement. "I have new information."

"What is it?" My heart raced.

"We wanted to know why Ralph stopped boxing professionally

nineteen years ago? My news should cheer you up. It's great for the story." Devon's excitement was intoxicating.

"Tell me!" I looked into his clear blue eyes and almost swooned, if women still do that. Here was this handsome man helping me.

"I spoke to my friend who owns that gym in Brooklyn. He remembered Ralph Duvet. Said he'd been a very promising fighter twenty years ago. He also said the guy had no luck. Ralph won a match and won it fairly. There was nothing shady about it. The other guy took some blows to the head. Two days later his opponent died from a massive cerebral hemorrhage. Nobody blamed Ralph. No charges were filed or anything. Apparently, there was a clot there waiting to burst. My friend said he'd heard that Ralph took it very hard, blamed himself."

Sadness came over me for Ralph. "So, that was the reason he stopped fighting. Nadine acted like she didn't know anything. I wondered if she'd been lying to everyone, or if Ralph kept it from her too. They met at least eight years after that fight. Did Bennie know? Is that why he set Ralph up to lose?"

I glanced at my watch. I'd screwed up again.

Chapter Twenty-one

I'm a runner because punching people is frowned upon.
Melanie Deming

"I'm due at a meeting at my daughter's school in fifteen minutes. It's the last place I want to go but...Can you walk and talk?"

"Sometimes I even juggle at the same time," Devon retorted.

As we strolled, our hands brushed. In a few minutes we got to the tennis courts in Central Park and the great Victorian Bridge awash in iron curlicues and leaves, spanning the riding path.

We stopped on the bridge that Cary Grant and Audrey Hepburn cantered under in the thriller *Charade*.

"Poor Ralph. Living with the shame he killed a man when he wasn't responsible. Did your friend know the name of the boxer who died?"

Devon shook his head. "No, not yet. He doesn't remember. It'll come to him."

Suddenly, I had a flash of Nadine's bloody face. For someone who hated the sight of blood, I was getting my lifetime's dosage live and in vivid color.

"What's bothering you?" Devon sounded concerned. "Is it Nadine?" He put his arm around my shoulder. Tears burned my eyes, blurring my view of the path, of him. His arm was comforting and enticing.

"What happened to Nadine was horrible. I don't know how she's doing. If she'll live." Devon tightened his arm and pressed me closer to him. He held me like this for a minute, and I let him, my face rested against his chest. The warmth I felt was not friendship. It was much more exciting. One moment more and we'd kiss. Devon took his arm away.

"You know if I wasn't afraid of being fired off the job for harassment, I'd suggest we have something going on between us. I think we both feel it." His eyes were clear and calm.

"I have no idea what you're talking about," I said lightly. I looked at the smooth planes of his cheeks and at his lips. "I'm having a weak moment. "

"So, you're using me." Devon leaned against the bridge. "It's not the first time," he said.

"We're using each other. Didn't we shake on that at Barnes and Noble?" I shrugged as if magnetic guys came onto me every day. "Whatever else I feel, I can't."

"Because you're married." Devon's voice was husky. "This isn't going away."

"You never know. Maybe by the end of the screenplay we'll hate each other. You have complications in your life too."

I waited to see if he'd explain more about that phone call, or tell me about his ex. Instead, he was silent. We walked quickly toward the East Side. Back to work.

"Can you get a medical report on Nadine? Is she able to talk? I'd really like to know whether the detectives brought in the guy who was identified by Bruce Salter. He probably has a criminal background."

"This I can do." Devon took out his phone. He went through an endless number of prompts before reaching John, who said he'd check into it. I admired his hands and long fingers. What was wrong with me?

"John says to give him ten minutes." We continued around the reservoir to the East Side, keeping a careful distance from each other.

"Before they let me go, the detectives did tell me two men asked about Nadine at her building. They also seemed to know a scrawny guy I bumped into on her block. Who was that guy?"

"You can be sure they're not gonna tell you."

"Probably no one connected to this. Nadine told me she was in danger this morning and wouldn't leave her apartment. She had a source for the cyanide but wouldn't tell me. That might have gotten her hurt."

Devon's face clouded. "Glad you never heard what she knew. You've got to be careful. I have another connection in the boxing world. I'll call the guy tonight, see if he knows anything about Bennie hiring someone to attack you and Nadine."

We rounded the bend where the migrating ducks congregated. Mallards in pairs, white-headed tiny black ducks, detouring from the journey south. I suddenly remembered the morning in the park.

"I followed Carey this morning. She met a woman right here on the bridle path. They exchanged envelopes. Could have been money, pictures, or the letter. It was definitely a business transaction. I have pictures." I showed him Carey and the unknown woman.

"Not bad. You could be a pro." Devon chuckled.

"Great. Photos of clandestine meetings, my specialty." I checked my time. "Can you jog a little? I'm pretty late." Devon looked surprised.

We slow jogged shoulder to shoulder for five minutes, which was a turn-on for me, of course. "What about the 1999 death after the boxing match and Ralph's murder?" We went back to a walk.

Devon shrugged. "We don't have enough facts yet, but when the guy died it mattered to Ralph. No matter what the doctors said about a hemorrhage waiting to happen, Ralph still carried the burden around. So much of boxing is confidence. Once a guy is scared to hurt somebody, they're ruined." Devon took out a pad and made notes.

I thought about this as runners passed on either side. "Bennie knew that. He knew he could use Ralph to lose. There's no way I can talk to Bennie now that the detectives have put me on warning."

Devon looked at his watch. "Time to call John back." His contact at the precinct picked up right away. "Is it all right to put you on speaker? My colleague wants to hear the report." He pressed speaker.

"Hi, John. Thanks for your help," I said.

"No problem." John had a strong Bronx accent. "Nadine's still heavily sedated according to the nurse. Seems she'll recover. I gather you knew her."

"Actually, I was the one who found her. Relieved to hear she'll be okay."

"Right. Well she has a broken nose, a hairline fracture in her skull, and a broken arm. She mumbled that a guy in a stocking mask pushed his way into the house and beat her up. No other description yet because of the painkillers. We're hoping to get more as they take her off painkillers."

Devon continued. "Were you able to find out if the cops brought in a known thug for questioning?"

"Yeah. Great story with that one. I don't have a name but it's going around that this goon comes in with a lawyer, Buddy Cohen. Represents all these hoods. They showed him pictures of Ralph. With his lawyer there he said, 'I didn't kill nobody and I'd never do a job like that. I'd never leave a guy lookin' like that for his relatives to see. It's not respectful.' Can you believe these guys?"

"You gotta love this," laughed Devon.

"There's more. He said he was supposed to rough Ralph up. Something about a boxing match. But Ralph was already dead when he got to the playground. He swore he didn't know who hired him. A phone call, money was dropped off. They're bringing him in again about Nadine's beating," John finished.

"Why didn't you arrest him?" I asked.

"No fingerprints or DNA matched at the scene. We're watching him though. See who he talks to."

"I'd bet on Bennie Resor," I said.

"Gotta go." John was off.

I shook my head. "Doesn't anybody get arrested anymore? They threaten me all the time." I was shocked this thug walked out free. He could be after me next.

"Being threatened goes with the job of investigative reporting, not getting killed." Devon added quickly.

"So, I can put 'works well under extreme pressure.' That goon's comments are great for the screenplay." I made light of this to relieve my severe jitters.

Devon nodded. "I'll write the scene. Don't go on any interviews alone. Agreed?"

I was near Chloe's school. "Agreed. This is where I get off. Back to being a mother." Devon reached out as if to take my hand, but stopped himself. I waved and walked away briskly.

My insides churned on the short walk to the school. So, I was addicted to the chase, better than being addicted to the guy. The smell of his pine soap lingered in the air.

~ * ~

The guard at the Huntley School knew me. He buzzed me through two sets of locked doors. This place was safer than a locked cell at the police station except that I was thirty minutes late to a meeting chaired by Buffy Clifford. Which meant trouble.

Right away I knew I should never have come. The women's faces seemed large, menacing, and disapproving, like someone had slipped me a bad drug. New York cops are amateurs at contempt compared to this group.

Buffy Clifford, the chair, who signed every email "Daughter of the American Revolution," was on the board of the Metropolitan Museum and the New York City Opera. Her derisive glance, with a slight lift of her well-sculpted eyebrows, said I was a serf in her kingdom. All around the table were sleeveless Lilly Pulitzer dresses and Prada suits. I took a seat next to Cornelia. Cornelia's daughter was a year younger than Chloe and Cornelia was the reason I was on this committee. "It will be good for you and good for Chloe," she had insisted.

My daughter Chloe was more excited by the detective in our kitchen than my being on this committee. Cornelia passed me a note. "Where were you?" I smiled. Fawn, the Assistant Chair, was presenting.

"'Balloons For Today' said they would make a long arch with one thousand orange and black balloons for the entryway. It will establish just the right scary but fun tone since the lights will be dim."

Balloons were never scary. I could tell them what was scary. My mouth started talking without my brain.

"If you want scary, why don't they make skeletons out of the balloons and we can make cardboard coffins out of boxes. Or headstones." Buffy and Fawn looked aghast at me. My social filter was still on the murder investigation. Balloon skeletons would get a big laugh at the 24th Precinct. Buffy, like a hawk, grabbed me in her talons.

"That seems inappropriate for young children, don't you think? I'm surprised at you, Melanie." Her kids stayed up watching *The Walking Dead* from what I heard. She shook her head, sighed dramatically, and went back to her cohorts.

"We've covered everything and we're just a little over budget?" She addressed Fawn and Bia, who sat together. Their mothers must have loved *Bambi*.

Generically pretty blonde Fawn held a #2 pencil with a very sharp point which seemed like a weapon at this moment with her dangerous long pink nails and glittering three-carat diamond ring with sharp edges.

"We're maybe a little over budget at eighteen thousand dollars, but nothing serious. We've got an inflatable haunted house at three thousand dollars. The master magician who is two thousand. Two face painters who charge five hundred each, but we may need a third. The balloon arch will cost twenty-five hundred. Renting the space is six thousand dollars, with owl cupcakes, popcorn machine, cotton candy maker, soft ice cream machine."

I must have hallucinated the amount of eighteen thousand dollars for a Halloween party for five to eleven-year-olds. They couldn't have actually said that. My brain was too overloaded, the circuits fried. I raised my hand. Cornelia shuddered slightly and kicked me under the table.

"Yes, Melanie?" Buffy said in a furious how dare you ask a question tone.

"Don't you think eighteen thousand dollars is outrageous for a Halloween party for a few hours? Isn't twenty-five hundred for fancy balloons sinful? Children are starving. Families of six could live on that in Africa for a lifetime. I can get you balloons for five hundred over on the slums of the West Side. Give the two thousand to charity."

Buffy, Bia and Fawn exchanged incredulous looks. Bia spoke in a squeaky nasty voice.

"This was decided weeks ago. You should have come to even one meeting. We all give to charity in very large ways all year. Do you?" The three of them gave me one large nasty smile.

I looked around the table. Everyone here was three sizes smaller than I was. They had never liked me. I didn't look the way they looked, dress impeccably, or speak their language. I was poor compared to them and didn't seem to know my place in the hierarchy. Maybe I was a reminder of where they had come from, or where they could be at any moment.

Buffy straightened up in her chair. "This party will be excellent in its appearance because this school's values are about excellence. If the balloon arch is such an issue for you, I'm sure we can find someone in this room willing to help defray the cost." She looked at her coterie of East Side debutantes who nodded affirmatively, checking each other. If they couldn't throw twenty-five hundred dollars out for balloons, their husbands were slipping.

Appearances were everything. Sounded like Chloe would have to balance a book on her head to get an A. I jumped back in.

"How about collecting food to give to a shelter for abused women and children?"

"Melanie." Buffy put her hand on her neck which she extended long and snakelike. "You are clearly unaware of how committees work here." Her eyes looked like a python's, filled with pity and hate. "You don't just walk in here when other parents have been working tirelessly. Her gaze went to her henchwomen. "Put together a plan if you have to, but do it right away. This meeting is adjourned." The group applauded the eighteen-thousand-dollar budget.

No one greeted me on the way out the door. I didn't blame them really. I didn't belong on this side of the park. I shouldn't have come. Gabby, my fellow West Side mom from the playground, whispered, "Good for you."

"Why don't we have tea at the Park Lane Hotel? My treat," Cornelia said as we left the building.

"Sure. Am I dressed okay?" My jeans and sweater had been to a crime scene, a police interrogation, hugs with Devon, Buffy's disastrous meeting, and now high tea.

Cornelia gave me a resigned look. "You won't get kicked out if that's what you mean. You're not interested in my clothing suggestions." She was right about that.

The Park Lane's tea room had cozy tables with layers of white tablecloths, bunches of tea roses on each table and air that reeked of grandmother's perfume. The napkins were huge and pink with PL monograms. There was a six-foot-tall floral arrangement in the center of the room in a four-foot-tall vase that must have come from a tomb in China. The room was a sea of floral pastel Dior dresses with a few modern prints from Rag and Bone, and Intermix on Madison. All sleeveless, thin perfect arms, and mostly blonde hair.

Cornelia slowly shook her immaculate coiffed head with sapphire earrings and looked at me. "What's going on with you, Melanie, butting heads with Buffy like that? Her group will never forget this. You'll have to come up with some shelter that agrees to take food and transport it all."

"Maybe I'll just stand on the street giving it away." I couldn't relax, even sitting back in a pink and gold upholstered armchair. "The amount of money spent gets me unhinged. It's been a long day for me already."

Cornelia ordered tea for us. I asked for herbal. She took off the jacket of her Chanel suit as if she was getting ready for battle.

"I'd like a fruit platter," I said to the waiter after Cornelia ordered pastries. Just because she was paying didn't mean I had to eat the stuff.

"What has happened? Is this still about that sad situation in the park?" She folded her hands together, leaned on them prettily, and stared at me.

I gave her a shortened version of the morning, without mentioning Devon, since her allegiances were just as much with my husband as with me. She added lemon to her tea in a cream-colored Limoges cup rimmed with gold, and delicately lifted it to take a sip.

"Why did you go up there to that awful woman to begin with? I don't understand why you're still involved in this mess. Is there something more that you're not saying? Some other reason?" Cornelia scrutinized me as if she knew about Devon.

"I have a job writing a column for an online paper. That's the main reason I'm involved. I'm covering the murder." I wondered if I could I trust her? I added, "Daniel's not happy about it."

She dabbed at her lips with the huge pink napkin. "Of course not.

Your attention is away from him. All men are like that. With Michael, I just do what I want and don't tell him. It's never a problem. It's harder to get around Daniel since he's home more, but you'll find a way."

Did I hear her right? She said do what you want. Was she talking about work or sex? This was a revelation.

"What is it you do that Michael doesn't like? You seem like the perfect wife," I asked. Maybe there was a passionate artist, or a professor.

"Oh, financial things. Art, jewelry, you know." She brushed off my question and continued. "I mentioned Midge looking for a thrill. I'm not saying that you're frustrated, of course. But if, and I mean if, there are other exciting elements to this pursuit, I might understand your risking your life over this story. He better be worth it. Is this Harold person attractive?"

I burst out laughing. The women nearby turned and stared.

"The opposite of sexy, believe me."

She tilted her head at me and nodded like a wise sage.

"I can tell there is someone. I won't push you for details but I'll give you advice. There are many, many affairs going on in half of the families at Huntley. The women are lonely, the men are not compassionate. There are stud carpenters, gardeners, music teachers, people they meet through art and theatre boards. All the women understand the rules. Do what you want, don't get caught, and be attentive to your husband when you need to be." She paused and looked at me like she could read my mind. "Don't tell Daniel about all this, whatever it is."

I looked at my hands. Could she tell I'd almost kissed Devon, or did she just think no woman would take a job unless there were fringe benefits like hot sex.

"You know you sound like a feminist, and I mean that in the best way." I grinned.

The clinking of teacups on plates, the hushed attentiveness of waiters and murmurs of secrets shared over refined Limoges, was all around us. Maybe I had stumbled on an underground women's support group in the Park Lane Hotel.

"Cornelia, you're one smart, tough woman."

She looked at me expectantly. "And?" she asked.

"And no, I'm not having an affair." A few hugs didn't count. "Now if I could just get this place to serve gluten-free pastry without refined sugar it would be perfect."

She put her hand on her chest. "God preserve us from your eating perversions." Cornelia had a good heart, even if it was gold plated. We gossiped about Sandra Crane's husband's affair, discussed the new principal's hairstyle, and air-kissed goodbye.

I found a text from Daniel which never happened unless someone died.

Chapter Twenty-two

Unhealthy Food, Unhealthy Mood.
Melanie Deming

Saw you called. Tension here bad for Chloe. Have great idea to fix everything. I'll make dinner. See you later.

Why did men always become nicer when they sensed another man was around? Besides, it was our marriage that was the problem, not Chloe.

A text from Devon. *Going to Kingsway Gym in the Bronx to see Bennie Resor now. Join me?* The message was sent fifteen minutes ago.

Can't get there till four. Can you stall till then? I texted. No reply.

I walked back to Huntley, picked up Chloe and took her to the West Side for a playdate.

I wasn't ready to talk to Daniel even though he was having a good husband moment. That was why God made texting.

Can you pick Chloe up at Sara's around five-thirty and make dinner? Have a meeting. Will be home after six.

He responded right away, again unusual. *I can do that. Don't you want to know my idea?*

I wrote back, *Rather hear it in person. See you later.* Heart emoji. Heart emojis were the sweet way to cut off a text. Women used hearts more than men.

Sure, he answered. No heart emoji.

I just lied about where I was going. If we ever got divorced a text could be evidence. To make matters worse, I was ordered, only hours ago, by the detectives to stay home and lock my door. Going to the Kingsway

Gym was for Ralph and my column. I wanted to get an interview, see Bennie in person. Did he hire goons to beat up Nadine and kill Ralph? The rumbling in my stomach, and adrenaline moving through my veins said there was more going on. A research adventure with Devon was too good to pass up.

By the time I got off at Kingsway Plaza, I was ravenous and panicked. There was only one place to get food. I pushed through the doors of a McDonald's, ordered a double fish fillet, and ate the whole thing. Then I ordered another. What had I done? I threw out the bun. This was blackout eating. My stomach bulged. I checked my steps. Over ten thousand after walking around the park and coming up here. Maybe I should run right now. Was I a bulimic exerciser? Maybe I needed a food addiction program. Oh God, breathe. This was all about Devon, Daniel and murder. Breathe. I texted Rebecca.

Meeting Devon for work. Having panic attack.

She replied immediately. *You're in new territory. You're doing great. Keep breathing. Call me later.*

Two small lions guarded the entrance of the Kingsway Gym, left over from when the ornate building was once a public library. Boxing replaced books. I texted Devon. *I'm here.* He didn't reply.

Pacing around outside the gym, the looks I got from people passing by said they thought I was either a City Inspector or a hooker who forgot to dress for work today and who was too old for the job. I went inside. At the desk was a Goth-looking teen, maybe sixteen, with a nose piercing, three diamond earrings in each ear and I'd bet a stud in her tongue. Tattoos covered one arm.

"Can I help you?" she asked. Definitely a pierced tongue.

"I'm waiting for someone. I wonder if you know a guy named Andreas Martines. He works out here, I think." I watched her face.

She bit her lip and refused to look at me. She gave an almost imperceptible shake of her head and went back to her magazine. I'd swear she was scared. Martines could have warned her not to talk to anyone.

I looked out into a cavernous gym. There were three rings with seats around each. A weight training area with three hundred-pound weights being lifted like they were filled with air. Maybe twenty guys in shorts wore gloves in the ring, or waited to fight. Around the outside of it all was a track. Men and women jogged. This was a serious workout place. My own gym looked like a toddler play group next to the Kingsway. Along one wall were some bleachers. Devon sat on a bleacher talking to a small, scrawny man.

I knew that wiry cigar smoker. I almost ran him over on the way to Nadine's apartment. The very same man. Which explained why the detectives were interested in my description. He was Bennie Resor, and he hadn't been arrested yet.

Once he saw me and connected me to this morning on Nadine's block, I could be next on his list. We won't get any information out of him. I sat in the waiting area with my head down praying Devon walked out alone.

"Melanie, is that you? You made it just in time." I peeked out from under my sunglasses and saw that Devon was not alone. "Come on over and meet Bennie."

Of course, Devon didn't know we'd already met. I stood up with my hand covering my mouth. Bennie's one day's growth and old cardigan were this morning's outfit. I stayed a few feet away.

"Sure. Hello." I spoke quietly.

"You all right? Oh, I get it, dark glasses are cool in a boxing gym." He turned to Bennie. "Bennie was telling me about Ralph."

"Not much to say. Bad marriage, bad luck in the ring." Bennie shifted from one foot to the other, like a prizefighter getting ready to fight. He took his cigar out of his mouth only briefly during a coughing fit. His eyes, behind tinted glasses, darted around the room like an edgy lizard, looking for danger. His skin color was definitely closer to yellow than pink. I wasn't a doctor, but not enough oxygen was getting into his lungs. I kept my head down. I'd be okay as long as he didn't recognize me. Devon asked the questions.

"You think it was bad luck that got him killed?" Devon asked.

The bloodshot eyes got teary. "No. I think somebody wanted to teach him a lesson. I don't know why, but somebody. His wife could have hired guys to beat him up so he'd stop fighting."

"Not a great way to get someone to do what you want. I mean, killing them," Devon commented, watching Bennie carefully.

A grimace passed over Bennie's face and he started coughing. Instead of feeling sorry for this sad sack guy, I fumed. He knew men were sent to beat Ralph up because he hired them. I couldn't keep my mouth shut.

"There are plenty of guys right here." I waved my hand at the boxing arenas. "It must be easy to find people to beat other people up if you needed that done."

Bennie stopped coughing and stared at me. "What are you saying, lady? That I would do a thing like that to my own guy?"

I hadn't said that. Bennie was jumpy, racked with guilt. Devon cleared his throat to get my attention. I plowed right on, unstoppable.

"Violence can always get out of hand, right? No one wants to kill anyone, but sometimes it happens."

My own anger exploded. "Why can't you people just get your anger out another way? There are plenty of punching bags here. Or go to therapy. If that's not enough there are herbs that calm you down. And meditation works."

Devon looked at me and shook his head. Too late, Bennie jabbed his finger at me and yelled.

"Are you one of those ban boxing types? What are you doing here? You don't know what the hell you're talking about. This is an elegant ancient sport."

Devon laid his hand gently on Bennie's arm. "She didn't mean anything by it." Bennie pulled away from his hand and peered at me.

"You look familiar. Do I know you from somewhere? That hair and the voice. Yeah, I met you before." He came closer.

I turned away from him quickly and walked out the door. "No. Never been here." I bolted out the door, down the steps and fled toward the subway.

"I am so stupid, stupid," I muttered as I ran. Guns blazing on a soapbox was not the way to interview a suspect.

"Wait up." Devon ran toward me. "What was that all about? Does he know you?"

I couldn't look at Devon. I had blown that whole interview. "Oh

God, when I saw him on the bleachers I knew right away. He's the guy I almost knocked over on Nadine's street this morning. The guy I described to the cops. I should have kept my mouth shut."

Devon shook his head. "He would never have admitted to us anyway that he hired anyone either the day of Ralph's murder or to beat up Nadine. Pretty gutsy for you, though. You knew he could recognize you, but you stayed. That takes some kind of courage, right?"

His deep blue eyes were kind. All I could think was that he was the most supportive man I'd ever met and I was going to tear up. Tears would not be attractive. Just then I saw two guys come out of the gym. They looked around. I pulled Devon into a bodega.

"We've got to get out of here."

I pointed at the gym. Two men with arms like the Hulk stood on the steps.

"Why don't you get a cab and pick me up here. Let's see if they watch you."

"So, I'm the decoy," He peered outside. "Stay here."

He walked out to the street. The two men stared at him. Devon found a cab and waved to me. The men started running toward me the second I left the store. In three steps I was at the cab and jumped in just as the men got to the car. They reached for the door and missed. One of them hit the trunk hard. They screamed curses and threats at me as we drove away.

"Oh my God, oh my God," I was shaking. "They were about to beat me up." Devon tried to hold me, but I pulled away. "At least I never gave Bennie my full name. But he's making the connection to Nadine." My mouth was dry, breathing shallow, I couldn't stop talking.

"What if these thugs find where I live? Maybe Bennie hired that guy last night. I can't even tell the police because I wasn't supposed to be here. They ordered me to stay home. Oh no." I covered my eyes with my hands hoping this was a bad dream.

Devon told the driver to go to The Lenox Lounge at 1285 Lenox Ave. I sat back and waited for the pounding in my head to stop.

"He's not going to send anyone after you. That was just a big show," Devon said calmly. "I don't think he knows who you are. The question is who knocked you down on the street?" Devon's tone was reassuring, but the question scared me.

He continued, "Bennie looks like he's going to die soon from emphysema. He's the one who's in trouble with the thugs he hired. They were hired only to rough up Ralph, not kill him. If you believe them. These goons would want to beat up Bennie, not you. They blame him for getting them in trouble."

My breathing slowed as I listened to Devon. He made sense, although I didn't really believe him.

"After you ran out, I asked Bennie about Nadine. He got even more hyper. He started making calls. I think he's running to Florida." Devon's voice was matter-of-fact but I was panicked.

"Did you see the size of those terrifying guys? They were bigger than the attacker who knocked me down last." My voice squeaked with unattractively. Breathe.

Suddenly I felt embarrassed being in a taxi with Devon acting like a kid.

We pulled up in front of The Lenox Lounge, which had dark-tinted windows and old maroon curtains. The Harlem renaissance hadn't arrived here yet. Since it was just after five o'clock, the place was empty. The booth in the back felt as secluded as a hotel room. We sat next to each other on the rounded seat.

"You don't drink much," Devon said as he looked at a menu, "as I remember from that party. You said it was empty calories?"

"Right. I don't suppose they have herbal tea?"

"Herbal tea wasn't invented when this place opened seventy years ago. You definitely could use something to calm you down. Sangria? It has fruit, might actually be the healthiest choice."

The fruit would probably be seventy years old too and all sugar. Devon's glance was slightly impatient, like I felt with Chloe when she wouldn't eat dinner.

"Sure," I said. "One sip. Can't be worse than wolfing fish fillets at McDonald's."

Devon ordered. I sat back and closed my eyes for a moment. When I opened them, I saw Devon studying me.

"Thanks for getting me a white horse to ride out on." I said.

"Lime-green Honda I think."

"You're a good guy, Devon."

"That seems to be mostly around you." He put his arm around the back of the banquette near where I rested my head. The sangria arrived. "To the screenplay," we toasted.

I swallowed more alcohol, half a glass, than I had in a long time. I'd fall asleep in a minute if I didn't keep talking.

"As awful as this day has been, I feel alive. You're so right there for whatever happens, so uncomplicated."

Devon turned toward me. Maybe it was the sangria, or the danger I'd been through with him, the closeness of his face, but my lips found his in a soft tender kiss. His lips were different but familiar, more yielding. Like the dream kiss. We stayed that way pressed together. My arms were around his neck. He rubbed my back gently. I wanted to do more, go to his apartment, undress each other. I didn't care about anything. I tightened my arms around his neck and...

No, what was I doing and what was he doing? Damn, oh no. He was chocolate fudge and it tasted great, but it was gonna be bad for me. Breathlessly, I unwound my arms from around Devon. He kissed the palm of my hand but I grabbed it away.

"This isn't okay. We have a script to write and now it's definitely more complicated. I don't know why I did that. I'm married and you have an ex-wife or girlfriend or somebody who really cares about you. This is just a bad idea. It's all too much. I led a quiet uneventful life before. Now I'm suddenly Angelina Jolie." My irritation was fraught with panic.

"Could it be we both needed that kiss?" He raised his eyebrows unrepentant.

"Who wouldn't need that." I sighed smirking. "I probably just kissed you because of those twenty grams."

Devon narrowed his eyes. "What? You're on drugs?"

I giggled. The wine was working. "I just remembered sangria has twenty grams of sugar in a glass." Devon laughed, sounding relieved. The waiter smiled.

My phone buzzed with texts from Daniel. *When will you be back?*

I texted back. *Meeting almost over. Home soon.*

A band had set up near the window. Of course, Lenox Lounge had jazz.

"I've got to go home. I love working with you on the case, and the kissing isn't bad either." I slid away from him in this cozy corner banquette, suddenly confronted with the enormity of what I was doing. "Like I keep saying, this is a bigger step for me than it is for you. Not the work. That's perfect." I paused to think of the right words. "I can't handle this right now. Obviously, I want to but I can't..."

Devon interrupted. The spark was gone from his eyes. "I understand. You have more to lose. Like I told you, you're a hot commodity." This time his laughter was forced.

"Sure, but so are you," I retorted. I hoped he'd say more about his life.

"I'll get the names we still need." Devon swiftly changed the topic. "We can't go wrong with the screenplay. If you change your mind about us, you'll know where I am."

Why did I think he said, "*When* you change your mind?"

Outside autumn twilight in Harlem swamped me with melancholy. We got into another cab. I stared out the window. The car stopped across the street from my building. I couldn't look at Devon.

"Talk tomorrow. Thanks for saving that interview." I grabbed the door handle as if it was a life raft, and leaped out of the car. Back to being a wife and a mother.

Cornelia might say everyone played this game, but I didn't think I could. One fact was totally clear. I couldn't handle McDonald's, alcohol, and twenty grams of sugar in one day.

Chapter Twenty-three

You can't make everyone happy, you're not an avocado.

Unknown

I texted Rebecca on the way upstairs. *Can you be my cover? Just getting home. I was with you for an hour, yes?*

She responded right away. *You go girl. No problem. Talk later.* That was a relief. Halloween committees didn't go this late.

"Hi. I'm back," I called out, being careful to sound bored. In the bathroom I checked my face for telltale marks and assumed a contrite being late expression. I washed and rinsed many times with mouthwash. Chloe was still up and she was like a bloodhound. I went in and gave her a hug. She wrinkled her nose.

"You smell funny." I loved my daughter's honesty.

"Rebecca and I ate brussels sprouts cooked with beer."

"That's disgusting, Mom." She scrunched up her angelic face.

Now I had lost my right to complain when she lied to me as a teenager. We looked over her homework, talked about the Halloween party.

"I want to be a detective, like the lady who was here. I need a badge and a gun."

I didn't act as horrified as I felt. "Sure. Not a real gun though."

"Mom don't be silly. Not a real gun."

We took turns reading book seven of *Harry Potter*. Then the telltale "Mom," after lights out which meant something was upsetting her.

"Dad said you might work at his magazine."

A punch to the stomach landed squarely in my abdomen. "Really?

We'll see."

"Would you still pick me up from school?"

"Of course. Sometimes Dad would, like today."

"Next year I'll go myself."

"Next year you're only ten. You might be driving a car by next year, right?" She giggled. I kissed her smooth soft cheek again, found Tic Tacs in her room and took them.

Working for Food Lovers Inc. Maybe it was a joke. I felt sick at the thought of talking to Daniel. I mixed twelve herbs in a glass of spring water, doubled the passionflower, and gulped half the glass. Damn, my head throbbed. Too much alcohol. Herbs had alcohol. Sangria had alcohol. It was as if I'd just had five shots of tequila. I barely managed to get into the bedroom and sprawled on the bed. My eyes were too heavy to stay open.

"What's up? You're asleep already? Was the meeting that bad?" I heard Daniel but I couldn't open my eyes.

"Exhausted. Wine, Rebecca, herbs conked me out," I mumbled.

"I can't wait to tell you my idea," he said with the cheerful voice he used about a new tapas bar.

"Right." I mumbled again.

"Are you awake enough to listen?" The urgency in his voice didn't give me a choice.

"Try. Can't keep my eyes open." Normally he would walk out in a huff without my full attention but he stayed. I opened an eye a slit and saw him perched on the edge of the bed.

"This is going to solve everything."

My stomach clenched despite the herbs. Nothing solved everything. He laid down next to me perched on one elbow.

"I spoke to Belinda after I got to the office. She's willing to have you come work for the magazine. She knows it's been years since your screenplay was optioned, but she's willing to take a chance. You can do copyediting, read submissions, answer letters, maybe even work on a piece for the magazine if it works out. With her supervision."

I opened an eye again and saw he was grinning like a kid who had just given his mom a gift he made in shop. He squeezed my knee.

"What do you think? You get a paycheck and feel worthwhile. You're back into writing. I can stop worrying about something happening so Chloe and I would be left alone."

Dear Belinda was willing to take a chance on giving me a glorified secretary job meant for a new college graduate? I had that job fifteen years ago at *Woman's Magazine* and was promoted to writer. I wrote screenplays. One was optioned. I got a sum of money. Daniel knew this. I was working for the magazine when I met him at a publishing conference. Now he and his boss saw me as a housewife who dabbled and should be available for him and his daughter. Dad getting a job for his screwed-up kid. Thankfully, I was so wiped out I could only mumble.

"You and Chloe left alone?"

"How much did you drink? You missed the point. I thought you'd be jumping up and down."

"Can't jump, too sleepy." Any jumping would be out the door.

"You can call her tomorrow and arrange for an interview with her secretary," Daniel said.

Oh God, I'd rather live in a cardboard box in the tunnel with Shorty.

"So sleepy. Talk tomorrow." I couldn't stay awake. Being comatose was the perfect condition right now. Daniel kissed my cheek saying I smelled like a vineyard. It was the last thing I remembered.

After conking out early, I was up at five. Everyone was still asleep. A new day with zero steps. I used half a bottle of mouthwash and went out and ran three miles, relieved to see other early runners on the street and in Central Park. I got back after six. Now was the time to research exterminators. There were over a hundred in roach and rat-infested New York. I searched the listings from the Bronx near Nadine's apartment, down to Riverdale. The name All-Star Exterminating caught my eye. They had the right area code, 718. I dialed the number. A young guy answered.

"I wonder if you can help me. I'm a writer working on a mystery. The weapon used is cyanide. I need some information about the product. Is there someone I can speak to?"

"Sure, you can speak to me," said a young, cocky voice. "I'm a writer too, by the way, screenplays mostly."

"You're kidding," I laughed. "I thought this only happened in L.A. You know, where everybody has a screenplay in their desk drawer. What are you doing working there?"

"It's a family business, pays the rent. So why use cyanide as the poison? It's illegal. Can't get it much anymore."

"Really?" This was going to be harder than I thought. "It's a lot of trouble to change now. Can you buy cyanide anyway?"

"Sure, under the counter, like anything else. From a shady kind of business, not a PCO concern. The mob is connected with it now. Back in the '70s my dad says you'd see the stuff lying around. It was everywhere, like DDT. They used cyanide for rats. Now we use zinc phosphide in bait form. Does the job."

Mob guys had access to it. "That's really helpful. What's your name?"

"Marty Campbell. I act and direct, too. Gotta be versatile these days."

"I'm with you on that. Any suggestions about shady businesses who sell under the table?"

"Just look for the ones that don't say PCO. That's them. Unlicensed." He hung up.

Now I had two problems. I still had to talk to Daniel. And second, no one would admit they had sold an illegal poison. I changed the plan. Don't mention cyanide, just show pictures of suspects. I skimmed the listings for other companies in the Heights, ones that weren't licensed. Suddenly the name leaped out, wedged in between Banzai Bug and Big Ben Exterminating. Begone Bug Control, 218th Street and Broadway. It was unlicensed, didn't say PCO.

Begone. That had to be the word Nadine tried to say before she passed out, "Be." She was trying to tell me that Begone gave her information. I nearly shouted but clamped a hand over my mouth. Daniel was moving around. It was time to wake Chloe, and I taught this morning.

I walked slowly upstairs from the school bus after Chloe left. I did a three deep breaths meditation.

"Do you remember our conversation before you passed out?"

Daniel asked as soon as I stepped in the door. "Are you going to call Belinda today?" He stood at the stove melting a specialty butter from Denmark. He had three kinds of frozen waffles from France and Belgium to review.

"Sure, I remember," I said as I mixed herbs. "This is a really big surprise." I leaned on really. "You are so sweet to do this for me, and Belinda also, giving me this chance." I forced out the word chance. "But I also have a surprise. I was offered a job writing for a new website started by Harold." I pointed upstairs. "It's a West Side paper, the *Wild Westsider*. He wants me to do a weekly column."

"About what?" Daniel's voice was suspicious. He looked up from the waffles.

"Whatever I want. They do cover crimes related to the neighborhood."

"I don't like this. You're not telling me everything. He just came over and hired you, just like that?"

"Why wouldn't he? That's a little insulting. Actually, it was just like that." My voice had an edge. "Harold knows that I write and work teaching kids in the playground. I started with that."

"Belinda's job will make you more money, since that's been an issue. And it's safer for us as a family. You did sneak in that he covers crime." Daniel flipped the waffles with many tablespoons of butter as if they were pancakes. Everything was better with butter. His motto.

"It's not only about crime. It's a safe reporting job," I lied. "I'm not being sent to Afghanistan. I wouldn't put you and Chloe in any danger. This way I can still pick her up at school. With a full-time job, we'd need a sitter. Our family will be fine."

Daniel and I both looked out the kitchen window. The old couple across from us were in their underwear silently getting breakfast. "I didn't say the job was full-time. Belinda knows you have to be home for Chloe."

How outrageous. A part-time secretarial job? I remembered Cornelia's golden rule. Say nothing and do what you want.

"You ought to think about what's best for us," Daniel continued. He took the giant waffles out of the pan. Five hundred calories each. The butter alone had twenty-five grams of fat.

"What's best for us is high protein, low fat, low carbs, fruit and vegetables. That's what's best for us. I give healthy living my full attention." Daniel shook his head at me, and chewed loudly. He dropped the subject of Belinda and my new job.

I grabbed my supplies for class and a breakfast of yogurt and walnuts. Once again, any work I liked was somehow bad for Daniel and now bad for the "family." If he knew the truth about my column and the screenplay, it might end the marriage.

"Leaving for the gym. Have a good day."

I ran to fencing. I couldn't wait to touché someone, even if it wasn't Daniel.

My column was a job that at last felt right. The screenplay was a dream. I was happy for the first time in years.

~ * ~

Blanca had been rehired once again as a receptionist at the gym. She was on the phone in a low conversation and just waved me in.

I raced into the dressing room, ate yogurt, and wrote notes to myself on my phone. Bennie insisted he didn't hire thugs but they ran after me at the gym. Bennie lied. Bennie was on the street just before Nadine's brutal beating. Ralph's opponent died after their fight nineteen years ago. Was it connected? Martines did seem like one really angry guy and he might have had a fight with Ralph. But Nadine had lied too. Carey exchanged envelopes with a woman and had a weightlifter boyfriend. My interview with the cops. Nadine beaten badly. Was that because of Ralph's murder or art smuggling?

I texted Rebecca. *Daniel wants me to work for his boss. Glorified secretary. Turned it down. Told him about* Westsider *job.*

Yay you. Just wants control. Where were you last night?

Speak later. Took your advice. Fencing emoji.

Chapter Twenty-four

The body achieves what the mind believes and vice versa.

M. Deming

"Why is Devon calling you?" Daniel's voice came at me in a loud, angry tone the second I arrived home from the playground. He stood in the foyer, pretending to look at magazines. My stomach went into a knot.

My bag slipped from my hands onto the kitchen floor. Why did Devon call the house phone? I checked my cell. I missed a call from him, but no text. What would make him call here? From the kitchen I texted Rebecca. *Devon called landline, asked for me. Daniel wants to know what's going on.*

Rebecca replied quickly, *Always deny. You don't know why he called. Can't go wrong.*

Why didn't I think of that? I stepped into the foyer.

"I don't know why Devon called. Maybe it's about writing a screenplay? I pitched the idea for the mystery to the agent. He heard me. What did he say?" My face was as bland as Detective Janet Brown's.

"He asked you to call him back." Daniel's eyes were suspicious but his hands and shoulders relaxed slightly.

"Did he leave a number? Oh yes, I think he gave me a number. I'll look for it." This innocent thing was not that hard.

"I have his number." Daniel's voice was even louder this time. "I don't like that he even called. He always has one thing on his mind and it's sex. Especially with married women. I've known a few who got involved. Big problems. He's known for breaking up marriages. He lives with a woman, too."

Oh, that hurt. So, I've been played. I kept my face neutral. "You never mentioned his Don Juan problem before. Just that he was a freelancer who hustled for money." I stopped and pretended to think for a minute. "I remember we talked about boxing because the character I described was like Ralph, a boxer. Devon said he knew people in that world." I paused and casually looked through my bag. "You don't have to worry. I'm not going to have sex with him." Which was true.

"I'm not worried," Daniel insisted.

I didn't believe him. He waited for me to return home. He never changed his schedule because of me.

"Good to be warned," I said offhandedly.

Of course, I wanted to sleep with Devon. Most women would. I kissed him, but I didn't sleep with him. There was a huge difference. Okay, maybe just a big difference. But I didn't sleep with him. Daniel went into his office, satisfied that all was secured.

I exhaled and collapsed on the couch.

"I have a meeting." Daniel stopped in the living room and kissed me on the cheek. A rare occurrence. I was a fire hydrant; a dog was lifting his leg.

As soon as he left, I called Devon.

"Why'd you call the house phone? You almost caused a disaster."

"I had information. Doesn't Daniel know we're working on something?"

"Do you tell your girlfriend when we get together?" He didn't answer. "Besides you play around a lot from what I hear. Especially with married women."

"My former girlfriend and I are separated. I don't think one time is a lot. It was after we split up." Devon sounded annoyed. "By the way, you're married." There was a pause. "Sounds like Daniel told you to stay away from me. I hope you don't."

Who was I to accuse him when I was married? He was right about that. He sounded as if he was telling the truth. Could I work with this man? Lots of women worked with guys and wanted to have affairs with them but didn't. I barely managed to stop last night.

"This has got to be strictly work. I don't want to be a marital disaster. I'm out of here when we stray off the screenplay." No more cozy banquettes and wine.

"What did you find out?" I finally asked with a sigh.

"A week before Ralph got killed, Bennie asked my contact at the Brooklyn Gym to get him some big guys for a job. My contact refused. He's sure the job was to beat someone up. Bennie definitely hired the guy the cops brought in."

"Your unnamed contact ought to tell the cops. Of course, he won't, right? You can't, or you'll lose your source." I paused. "Is this really the reason you called the house? Do you want Daniel to know we're working together?"

"I thought Daniel knew already. Why wouldn't he?" Devon's voice was rising.

"I told you Daniel doesn't like crime reporting. Anyway, you haven't been exactly all about the work."

I should let this go. If we just worked together, there was nothing to hide. Besides, we had a screenplay to finish.

All at once a strong wave of loneliness and a hopeless feeling swept over me. Devon wasn't perfect. I starkly saw how the joy and light had seeped out of my marriage. Daniel didn't support my work, and I didn't know what I wanted. My drive to find Ralph's killer drained out like I'd cut a vein.

"Maybe it's not that good a story. Maybe I should let this go." What if Chloe heard me sounding so pitiful?

Devon came back so fast and intensely it was like an oxygen mask had been slapped on me. "Don't lose it now. This is a good New York story by the woman who knew Ralph. The scenes are set up. Except for the ending. We're almost there. You check out exterminators, I'll track down information about the boxer who died after the fight with Ralph twenty years ago. I have one more source for a name. I'll call you when I get any information. On your cell phone. Check your phone and be careful. Don't give up now."

Could he be this supportive, irresistible guy and a phony at the same time? He was saying exactly what I needed.

"Thanks for the pep talk, coach. I like to hear your voice too, but never on the house phone." There was silence. "Are you still there?"

"I'm here. Just have a lot on my mind." He cleared his throat.

"What's wrong?"

"I have a lot of bills recently. I have to look for more work."

"I get it. Sure. Money's a problem for me, too."

"Yeah, but I'm the one paying my ex's bills and my father's." His laugh had a bitter edge to it. "My life has complications, that's all," he said.

"Well so does mine, like because you called here today." I went on.

"If we're going to see this through, I think Nadine tried to give me the name Begone Exterminators. I found it in a phone book. I'll leave soon to go there and show pictures of the suspects. We can't mention cyanide. It's illegal."

"I'll meet you there. Let me know when you're ready to leave. It's getting too risky." He was talking about the case, but he was also talking about us. We hung up.

The emptiness inside returned. I took DHEA and ten herbs. I wouldn't stop because of Devon or Daniel or anyone. Ralph deserved the truth. This was not going to be another one of many unfinished projects strung throughout my life.

I slowly washed my face in the master bath, a term that should be banned, which was inside the master bedroom. I put on blush. Suddenly there was a sound.

A click. Just a small quick metallic-sounding click. Suddenly, another click.

Old buildings have lots of clicking and banging noises. Ancient pipes wheeze, bringing up heat and hot water. This click was different. I knew this particular sound well. It was the metal lock mechanism of the front door, which in this apartment was loud. The sound brought back Chloe as a toddler who woke up when she heard the click. I learned to close the door in slow motion. Daniel must be back.

"Hello," I called out.

There was no response. He was pissed off. I listened for Daniel's usual loud footsteps. There was a rare silent moment in NYC. Not a car alarm or a siren or a footstep. My hands were stuck out in space where I held the blush and waited for the next sound. Goddamn, I was having a really, really bad day. I heard a thump, like someone knocked into furniture. What the heck? What was going on now?

"Hello," I called again.

No reply. Did I imagine those sounds? I heard another muffled thump. Someone was in the apartment...and it wasn't Daniel.

Was this the burglar who robbed Gertie? In my gut I knew the answer. I'd been warned. I hadn't listened. Instead I'd found Nadine and been recognized by Bennie at the gym. The attacker, and probably murderer, was here. I didn't need to put on makeup for this scene.

I was in the far end of the apartment. The only way out from here was through the window, and it was too high to jump. I could pull the king-sized mattress out the window and land on that. No, it was too big for the window. For a second, I regretted not buying the two twin mattresses for the bed, which guaranteed better separate sleep according to the salesman, but were more expensive. Really? My life could be over and I'm thinking about mattresses.

Tie sheets together? I wasn't good at knots. The window was out.

Feeling stupid, I got down low and crept into the bedroom from the bathroom. In an uncharacteristic decorating moment, I overpaid for a five-foot-high mirror with paint rubbed off the frame in ways that the saleswoman convinced me was country chic. It hung opposite the door to the bedroom. I saw the thinnest dark silhouette appear and disappear in a blink along the edge of the frame. My heart stopped. My life was over.

Forever. I thought I'd live forever. All that high protein and low fat just to be killed by a crazed murderer. I should at least be able to eat a final blowout meal, lasagna and a huge piece of chocolate mousse cake.

I dropped to the floor, grabbed the phone next to the bed and the Mace out of the drawer of the nightstand where I'd left it. Like a pro I dialed 911. I gave the address in a whisper and said send cops. They told me to stay put and stay on with them. Both were bad ideas.

I dragged my bag on the floor with me. Nadine's knife was in there. It was so dull it couldn't slice an apple. I saw a heavy metal curtain rod that Daniel stashed under the bed. I could use that like a sword. He had finally done something right. The feel of the rigid steel in my hand was the familiar foil I needed.

Should I lie here in the back of the apartment just waiting for a murderer to find me, or was I going to get myself out of this mess? It was like a lifetime of waiting for something to happen reared up and said no, not anymore, no more waiting.

Mace in one hand, metal curtain rod in the other, I jumped up shrieking wildly hoping someone in the building heard me and came to help. Where were Devon, Daniel, Levano and Brown with their stupid games now?

I ran out of the bedroom into the foyer and stopped short at the sight of a black-clothed figure with a ski mask. The figure rushed toward me. He held something shiny up high. The clear bulbs in the ceiling fixture reflected light off a large knife.

A voice I didn't recognize started screaming. "I hate you, get out of my house, you bastard." It was me. I brought my curtain rod up high. My fencing instructor's voice was there. "Beat, touché, beat, touché. Fast tempo. Don't wait. Keep it fast, beat touché." The rod came down hard on the hand that held the knife. The knife fell to the floor. I moved my right leg forward, bent at the knee, and lunged with the rod straight at the black clothed figure with a fury that was shocking. There was a sharp cry of pain and it was not from me.

The figure dropped to the floor.

"Are you all right?" I bent down to help him.

What? No, don't do that. What the hell was I thinking? Stop! In that second of stupidity, the attacker grabbed my ankle. The hands were strong and a muffled voice said, "Got you, you stupid bitch."

"Never," I screeched. I sprayed so much Mace that he let go. I took off for the kitchen back door and the stairs that would take me to the lobby and safety. The murderer was too quickly up and after me. I was almost at the door. He was very close again. I still had my foil. Bend at the knee. Go for the hit. I lunged again at his abdomen and jumped away. He wavered for a second, long enough for me to spray Mace. Crap, it was empty. His hand with the knife flailed toward me and I felt a pain sear my arm.

"*En garde*," I shouted. I used the curtain rod foil again, this time as a bar and pushed hard. The black hooded figure fell back but stayed on his feet. He was trained, he knew how to win.

"No," I screamed so loud my throat clenched. A can of DermaMag, a magnesium oxide spray, came into my sight. It was inside the door on the counter. I grabbed the spray and jumped outside the back door. The attacker grabbed my arm in a painful grip.

With strength and aim I didn't know I had, his mask and wild dark eyes close enough to see, I sprayed him full in the face with magnesium oxide. His hold on my arm loosened. "Aah, aaah!" a gravelly voice screamed.

I jumped out the door, pulling him with me since his hand still clutched my arm. I pushed one final time with the rod. We both fell, he slipping down the stairs, me falling back onto Selma's mat. I heard the thumping of the body on the stairs. I looked and saw his arms and legs bent like a rag doll. The eyes were shut. Had I just killed another human being?

"No, no, miss, we can't have this," Anton shouted, running up the stairs. "Who is this?"

"How would I know? You're the one who let him in." My heart pounded wildly. My breathing came in short gasps. "Call the police. He tried to kill me."

"You called already. We're here." Levano, his hefty shoulders and blue suit walked up the stairs. For the first time, the sight of him was comforting. Following him was what looked like a platoon of cops. They couldn't all fit on the landing so they arranged themselves on the stairs like a color guard waiting for a debutante to emerge for the ball.

Selma rushed out of her apartment. "Oh my God, Melanie, what happened? I told you to lock your door." She tried to hold me back, but I walked down the steps to the moaning, not dead figure.

"By the way, this is what happens when I stay home," I said in a snide voice to the detectives.

Janet Brown glared at me and bent down. She ripped away the mask from the fallen figure. Everyone, including me, gasped as we saw not a man, but a blonde middle-aged woman with dark roots. A woman I knew. It was Blanca, the receptionist from the gym. One crazy fierce woman. Blanca who just happened to meet me on Broadway. Who kept asking me about the case? I had a fleeting thought. She was the right height. Could she be the same woman from the park who exchanged envelopes with Carey? Did she attack me two nights ago on the street?

"Blanca? Why?"

"Who is this?" asked Levano.

Even in pain, Blanca's eyes were filled with desperate hatred. She spoke in her deep gravelly voice. "You should have left it alone, Melanie. He deserved it. I did it for Jorge, Jorge the Great."

"Who is Jorge to you Blanca? Why kill Ralph and try to kill me?"

"What the hell is going on? So now you know this woman too?" Levano yelled, impatient as ever.

"Yes, I know her. She works as a receptionist at West Side Fitness. I saw her there this morning. She's probably on a lunch break and planned to ditch the costume and go back to work. She might have done the same routine the day of Ralph's murder."

This time when I said Ralph's name, Blanca's pained face got contorted with rage. She weakly raised a fist and tried to spit which ended up all over her face. "*Asesino*," she said. It meant "murderer" in Spanish.

"Why was he a murderer, Blanca? Who did Ralph kill?"

Blanca narrowed her eyes and stayed silent. Perhaps she realized she was confessing.

I tried another approach. "Do you have a husband or someone to call?"

The look of pure terror on her face was my answer. She began to sob hysterically and screamed, "Don't call my son. He did nothing."

I looked at Levano. "I don't know for sure if she was the one who killed Ralph, but she tried to kill me back there with a knife. It should be in the kitchen, or outside the door where she dropped it." I pointed up the stairs.

The paramedics emerged from the freight elevator with a stretcher. I moved out of the way. From the way she fought them, I didn't think Blanca had any broken bones.

"Hey Charlie, she needs to get that cleaned up." Levano pointed to my arm which was grazed by the knife. I was in shock. I didn't feel anything. Charlie swabbed it and put on a butterfly bandage. My phone rang. It was Devon.

"Are you giving up on the exterminator trip?"

"No need to. I've been busy fighting off the murderer, I think."

He paused. "Jesus, I don't think you're joking. Are you all right?"

"I'm alive enough to hope you're calling with new information." I held my breath.

"We have a name." He said with excitement. "The guy who died nineteen years ago is called George Martines, also known as Jorge the Great when he was alive. His son is Andreas. Am I good or what?"

"More than good, you're almost perfect, Devon. The woman who just tried to kill me is Jorge's widow and Andreas Martines' mother, I think. I can't talk now. I'm with the police."

"Goddamn, you did it," he cheered. I hung up.

I turned to Levano who was a step below.

"I think this woman is Andreas Martines' mother. Her husband was Jorge Martines, a boxer who died after a match with Ralph Duvet almost twenty years ago."

I realized it was Tuesday. "You'd better round up Andreas Martines fast because he has a ticket to Colombia for today."

I had a lot of satisfaction when I saw Levano's mouth drop open. "We've been looking for him," he said.

Levano got out his phone and called his chief. Two cops went up to the landing outside the kitchen door and with rubber gloves took the knife and the curtain rod. Levano turned to me.

"I don't know how you know all this, but come down to the precinct and let's go over the facts. You oughta get a tetanus shot, by the way." It was the first time he had spoken to me with any respect. It was about time. I was giving him this case. To say nothing about the fact I could have been killed.

"You used this to get away from Martines, if that's her name?" Janet Brown held the Mace that fell down the stairs.

"Only partially," I said.

"What's this?" Levano pointed at the magnesium oxide.

"The Mace ran out. Magnesium is an essential mineral, supposed to be sprayed on arms, just not in the face. It really works. All-natural Mace, if you don't want to put chemicals on your attacker." I spoke fast and laughed which almost became a sob. "Mainly I used the curtain rod as a foil, disarmed her and got a direct hit. Twice by the way. She was tough." I almost did a victory dance like football players do in the end zone.

Detective Brown, for the first time, regarded me with approval. "So, you know self- defense."

"I take fencing classes for a better butt and thighs. Guess it's useful to stay alive too."

Brown laughed.

Suddenly I couldn't talk anymore, the adrenaline was gone, I wobbled.

"You feeling it now?" Levano's voice sounded strangely kind.

I nodded. My body started shaking. A medic put a blanket around me. Selma sat me down on the step. She held my hand.

"I'll make sure she gets to the precinct when she's up to it," Selma announced in a voice you didn't argue with. Her hair was a midnight blue that made me smile.

"Might try some brandy," said Levano.

"Twenty grams of sugar? I don't think so."

He was right but I refused to tell him.

The platoon of cops left. "I'm coming with you," said Selma. I squeezed her hand, glad she was here with me.

We slowly stood and walked up the stairs. Rebecca called.

"What happened with Daniel? Did you convince him you didn't have sex with Devon?" I rewound one hour. All this happened since then?

"I'm alive with just a scratch so I'm fabulous."

"Alive with a scratch? Knowing you is like watching a Tom Cruise movie. Tell me you're not hurt. I'm coming over."

"I think I'm in shock. Can you meet me at the precinct? The detectives are waiting. I could use a posse."

"On my way," Rebecca said.

I texted Devon and told him to come to the precinct and be prepared to tell the cops what he knew. I changed into a loose sweater that hadn't been sliced and didn't have dried blood on it. My hands trembled. I took out herbs, then put them away. If I could save my own life, I didn't need herbs. I could handle this. I took propolis for infection and applied liquid arnica around the bandage. Selma and I headed for the precinct.

~ * ~

This time I was in a big conference room with windows with gates. I had Rebecca, Selma, and Devon with me. We all drank fresh-squeezed organic carrot and celery juice which I insisted we get to flush the violent toxins.

"His mother came after you with a knife?" Devon was astounded.

I soaked in his admiration. Fortunately, Selma sat between us like the Great Wall. Rebecca next to me, slammed my leg under the table and chortled.

"Melanie can perform amazing feats in any position." Now I jabbed her leg.

Levano, Brown and a uniformed stenographer came in. Levano was the calmest I had ever seen him.

"We have Andreas Martines. The airport police took him off a plane at Newark Airport. We also stopped at the Fitness Club and got Blanca's bag," he said.

"She is Blanca Martines, mother of Andreas as you thought, Melanie. She's under police guard at Bellevue. She has a badly twisted ankle, dislocated shoulder, blurred vision and high blood pressure. That's all. She talked non-stop once we said we had her son. She says she did it all. The cupcakes and the bat. She doesn't want her son to get charged. Andreas is not talking. His stepfather hired a lawyer who's now told them both to shut up."

"Blanca really raises the bar on being an overprotective mother," I muttered to Rebecca, who laughed. "You have her confession. Do you believe her?" I asked Levano.

"I think she was responsible for part one of this murder. We have a team out there now to do tests on her pots and pans and to see if there's any cyanide traces. They'll check the arsenic level in the water. We're hoping to find cyanide at the house. Her lawyer will say she was confused when she confessed. We can get a conviction, just not sure on which murder charge. Will you testify against her? Assault with intent to kill with a deadly weapon."

Were there enough herbs to get me through court? Daniel would be outraged. I hadn't even called him.

"Yes, of course I'll testify. As long as I get police protection on a Caribbean Island," I said, only half joking.

Levano looked as if he wanted to call me a spoiled liberal West Side type but stopped.

"Unnecessary. They'll be away for a long time and too old for vendettas if they ever get out."

Devon was taking notes. "What about Nadine? Can she identify either of them as assaulting her?"

"She's completely alert, annoying the hospital staff complaining about the hospital food. She thinks she remembers a tattoo under the glove on the wrist of her attacker. Andreas has a tattoo that matches her description," said Brown. She turned to me.

"Melanie, we need your whole story now, under oath." Brown's tone was polite, but deadly serious. Nadine and I were their star witnesses. I gave them Begone exterminators and the rest of what I remembered. Most of it anyway.

Chapter Twenty-five

All's well that eat well.

Melanie Deming and Shakespeare

"You're bringing that into my house? Do you know how many grams of fat and pounds of cholesterol you have there?" I was horrified. Nadine had arrived with trays of pastries and cakes. Daniel was in ecstasy. He was throwing a party a month after the arrests.

"You know nothing about food. You only have a passion for solving murders," Nadine said with her nose in the air. "Just do what you know and leave the rest to us, the gourmet chef and the food writer."

Daniel furiously waved me over.

"Would you cut it out? She's going to be famous soon. Besides, you're making me look bad again," he hissed, not softly enough.

"That's ridiculous. Pounds of butter and sugar make you and your heart look bad, not me," I snarled back. I sauntered out of the kitchen relieved not to be in charge. Rebecca handed me some very strong punch.

"Why did Daniel do this party? Is he announcing your divorce?" Rebecca had had a few glasses already.

"Divorce by dessert?"

Rebecca wore a black dress with a deep plunge almost to her navel. She stared at Devon. "He's so adorable. I don't understand why you haven't slept with him. If you don't do it soon, I may." She wasn't kidding. Yes, Devon was here catching looks from every woman. Detectives Levano and Brown had arrived. Daniel had even invited Susan the agent from the party, who was now the agent for *Playground Hero*. Belinda, Daniel's boss, was resplendent in flowing emerald green.

Harold, of course, was talking to everyone, taking credit for hiring me and making my column a success. Solving Ralph's murder was really what made my column a must-read, at least on the Upper West Side.

The week before the party, Rebecca gave me an ultimatum. "If you don't buy new clothes I'm not coming." So, everything I wore was new. Faux leather leggings and a low-cut maroon silk blouse that was destined to have a spot on it before the evening was over. My shoes were chunky and high. Judging from Devon's expression, I guessed the clothes were a success.

Paul, Rebecca's husband, was here. Everything about him screamed scientist, from the pipe in the pocket of his brown vest to his corduroy pants. Everything except for his black eye. Paul said he walked into a swinging door in the lab. Rebecca heard that the secretary's irate husband came to work and punched him. I was sworn off any future revenge phone calls for Rebecca.

I whispered to Rebecca. "I can't handle affairs Rebecca, you can."

She raised her glass to me. "Here's to self-control, abstinence and safe sex. Boring." With that she went for a refill.

"Did I hear safe sex?" Devon appeared on cue at my elbow.

"Actually, what you heard was no sex is safe sex." I smiled at him, feeling light as I did recently when I was with him.

"I heard today that Bennie moved to Florida," he said. "He'll be lucky to live a year. He has lung cancer." So that was why Bennie looked yellow.

"We can add his illness to the screenplay. Maybe he'll be willing to talk if he's that sick. Might be worth a trip South." The words were out of my mouth before I realized what I had said.

"Really." Devon moved closer. "Both of us could go."

Daniel tapped a glass at that moment to get the group's attention, especially mine.

"Welcome everyone." Daniel beamed a special warmth, which he reserved for parties and food. "We're celebrating a few terrific events tonight. First, Melanie has a weekly column called *Aftermath* in an up and coming online paper, *wildwestsider.com*. We hope she'll read part of her series *Murder of a Playground Hero*.

"Yes, you must," from friends and detectives.

My stomach churned.

Daniel continued. "The second announcement is that I have a new column debuting in Food Lovers called *Meat Your Way to Good Health*, which will give recipes for low fat meat recipes galore that can save your life." Applause and cheers. "Third, with us tonight, just out of the hospital and already baking, is Nadine Duvet, widow of the deceased hero. I have recently named Nadine the next Best Pastry and Dessert Chef in the city. You'll get a chance to sample her desserts tonight."

Loud cheers. The detectives and I were the only ones that knew Nadine was up for tax evasion and smuggling art. The Feds would be easier on her as long as she testified to help the murder convictions.

"Everything you eat tonight will be in my new book, *Ooh La La Dessert* with many recipes by Nadine. The book will be out next year." More applause. "Let's toast to success, desserts and a long life." Daniel winked at me.

I got first billing ahead of meat and dessert. For Daniel that was a big step. He was tolerating Devon as my co-writer on the screenplay. Susan already had two companies interested. I had a few thousand online readers now. This was all way beyond my wildest dreams.

Cornelia, stunning in a red clinging knit dress, though a large Chanel scarf proclaimed she was all business, tapped her glass, "Melanie, read your column about the murder. We want to know the details."

Levano nodded. "Absolutely." He had become one of my online readers and commented frequently, often acting as a fact checker. Murder made for strange friendships.

I felt like throwing up. Reading aloud to a crowd was more terrifying than fighting off an attacker. Thank goodness I'd had alcohol, and L-Theanine. I took out my new iPad.

"Wait. Don't start. I'm here." Selma strode in, her hair a shocking orange, wearing what looked like a black lace and velvet workout suit. She took the spotlight. "First, I have news. Gertie found her necklace. Back in the freezer. She has no idea how it got there."

"How about the super put it back after he found it in a porter's locker?" I said.

Levano nodded in agreement.

"Such a cynic," Selma retorted.

I cleared my throat and read.

"Ralph Duvet was once a brilliant welterweight. No one at the 91st Street Playground had any knowledge of that fact. He kept it hidden because he was filled with shame. Jorge the Great, also known as George Martines, had been his rival twenty years ago. Their rivalry was highly promoted. Finally, a fight took place in the lower boxing circuit. Jorge went down after five rounds. Ralph was declared the winner. That night Jorge developed a severe headache. By the next day he was in a coma, and died a day later from a ruptured aneurism in the brain. The officials said the aneurism had been there a long while. No charges were brought." Devon broke in here.

"If today's boxing regulations were followed back then, the fight wouldn't have happened at all. A mandatory physical and CAT scan or MRI would catch the aneurism and Jorge would be in surgery, not in a ring. Ralph was not responsible for his death. But Jorge's wife and son thought differently. Back to you, Melanie."

"Jorge's widow, Blanca Martines, remarried a year later. By then Jorge's son was almost four. The new husband, Ramon, was a successful contractor and they lived a luxurious lifestyle. Ramon could be controlling and explosive. Andreas dreamed about his deceased father, Jorge the Great. He covered the walls of his room with publicity posters of Jorge. The police also found a letter threatening Ralph in papers in the basement which they think Andreas wrote." I looked up and continued the story without reading.

"Blanca bought that letter from Carey in the park. I gave the police the picture of the two women exchanging envelopes. Carey left for England the night after the exchange with the money Blanca gave her. When confronted by the police through her lawyer, with the evidence of my photo, Carey admitted the other woman was Blanca Martines. My guess was that her boyfriend Richard had the threatening letter in his apartment the whole time. The robbery I witnessed was staged to make it look like it had been stolen so she could sell the letter. Her lawyer was insisting on immunity to get her to testify." I continued reading.

"Ramon wanted Andreas to work for him. Andreas refused. There were fights, the mother was always in the middle. Tension was constant at home, fanning revenge. Andreas decided his life was falling apart because Ralph killed his father. It was at that time Ramon gave him an ultimatum. Andreas had to work for him, get a job, or move out. Ramon was finished supporting him. Andreas' hatred for Ralph became even more irrational. His mother was terrified. After he came home with a cut lip, black eye and bruises, she knew he'd been fighting Ralph. Blanca Martines got more and more desperate about her son."

"I am the one who found out Martines beat up Ralph," boasted Nadine.

Levano took up the story. "We allege that Blanca decided to kill Ralph herself so that her son wouldn't commit murder. Melanie, why don't you keep going."

"Blanca used poisoned cupcakes to get the murder blamed on Nadine, who is a well-known chef. She was sure no one could trace it back to her. But Andreas followed his mother. He watched Blanca leave the box with a note saying it was a gift for Ralph. She left the scene quickly."

"Andreas watched Ralph eat a cupcake, and become violently ill. Ralph was strong and didn't die fast enough for Andreas. What if the teachers or parents arrived? We might have saved him. Andreas picked up the bat and finished him off. The police don't think the mother could have delivered a blow with that much force, although Blanca insisted she did it all."

"The next day, a homeless man became the second victim of the poisoned cupcakes. The remains of the box of cupcakes were found with him. Blanca Martines has been charged with two homicides. She's under a suicide watch since she found out about the second death by cupcake." I saw Daniel edge toward the kitchen.

I rushed to a big improvised finish. "Blanca assaulted me on the street at least once, and broke in here with a plan to murder me. As you can see, she clearly failed which is why we're all here. I highly recommend fencing lessons." The crowd applauded. I turned to Janet Brown.

"Detective, why don't you tell us where the case is now?"

"The District Attorney feels they have enough to charge them both with first degree homicide. Blanca has charges of manslaughter against her for the death of Junior, the young homeless guy. And, of course, the assault on Melanie with a deadly weapon," said Janet Brown.

At what had to be the worst moment to show off desserts, Daniel and Nadine walked in loaded with platters of pastries, and chocolate and vanilla buttercream cakes covered with lavender and green flowers. Gorgeous. There were whistles and applause. Was I the only one thinking about poison and sugar? I went to the kitchen and returned with a platter.

"Gluten-free raspberry walnut muffins with maple syrup," I announced.

Devon stepped up, took one bite and looked relieved. "Hey, this is terrific. Maybe I'll go gluten-free, after I get back." He looked everywhere but at me. What did he say?

"Get back? What are you talking about?"

"I got an assignment today to go to Romania and Russia with Brian on his book tour. The magazine is sending me to cover restaurants and general culture in Romania."

I was shocked and suspicious. Why now? "For how long? When did this happen?" I had a lot of questions that weren't going to make any difference.

"The assignment is for at least a month. Belinda may want me to continue on to Estonia and Slovenia. She called me into the office yesterday. I don't want to go, but the money's good. I need the money." I noticed for the first time that he had dark rings under his eyes.

"Money problems are getting worse with Alice, my ex-wife. Also, my father has health issues and has stopped working in the last month."

He quickly added, "I think if we put in the hours in the next week or so, we'll be close to having a first draft."

I nodded, but I was thinking about my argument with Daniel last week.

"You're going to keep writing about murders and work with Devon. Where do I come in here?" Daniel had asked.

"This is the first time I've been excited about a project, and I have a platform. This is a great chance. I've got to take it. You work with plenty of women. Nothing will change for us."

"I hope that's true." That was all Daniel had said.

I thought this meant he accepted Devon, the job, the screenplay. Maybe he hadn't accepted anything. Instead, he may have asked Belinda to give this job to Devon. Or maybe this overseas assignment was just a coincidence. Devon needed the money so it was good for him.

"Let's do it." The words were out before I realized what I was saying.

Devon had a quizzical smile. "Are you thinking what I am?"

"The screenplay. Let's get it finished before you go. Louisa can teach for a few weeks. After you leave, I'll go to Miami to talk to Bennie. We can add the interview by Skype and email." Devon looked disappointed. That wasn't the plan he had in mind.

~ * ~

Nine days later, I was in Miami ping ponging from straight-up fear about interviewing Bennie to pure excitement at a few days to myself. I was out for a run on the beach. Vicki, the travel agent in Riverdale, would be thrilled. The sand was packed hard and the ocean was a sparkling green. The stars had aligned, my karma somehow improved to get me my dream. Susan received a decent offer for the screenplay, making a trip affordable. As I argued to Daniel, it was all tax deductible. *Playground Hero* was nearly finished. I was checked into a small hotel on Collins Avenue in Miami.

Tomorrow, I had a meeting with Bennie at a Cuban restaurant in Old Havana. Devon set this up. It turned out Bennie was anxious to talk since he was dying, which probably meant he'd never serve time for hiring those thugs who hadn't killed Ralph anyway. Devon left today for Russia.

The beach was perfect for a run. The air was slightly cool as the sun went down like an orange fireball.

My cell phone rang. It could be Chloe. I stopped and answered it, panting, not checking the number.

"Do you want company?" I heard the voice, stared at the phone, saw the name displayed, and still couldn't believe it. We said goodbye yesterday.

"What? You mean now? Where are you?"

"In about five minutes."

"How about ten? I'm out running on the beach, but I suppose I can turn around."

"See you in five," he insisted. I hung up and called Rebecca, breathing hard. "He's here."

"Of course, he is," she said with her know-it-all tone. "He's not stupid, even if you are. What are you going to do?"

"I don't know."

"Well, do the right thing for you, just you. Just this once. Call me after." She hung up. What did she mean after? What was the right thing for me? I got back to the room and only had time to take California poppy, passionflower, and a few drops of valerian to take the edge off my total panic.

There was his knock at the door. I never asked him why he was here. I guessed we both knew the answer. I took a deep breath and opened it. He was in a T-shirt and chinos, his shoulders seemed wider, his eyes seemed more green than blue today. He had his suitcase.

"I couldn't let you do the interview alone after the Kingsway fiasco." Devon chuckled standing in the doorway.

I looked at him wide eyed.

"I thought you were on a plane. Where are you staying? Am I supposed to invite you in? I'm a little sweaty." My questions tumbled over each other. Devon raised his eyebrows and looked at me with those seductive, caressing eyes.

"Planes fly to Moscow from Miami it turns out. Believe me, a little sweat never bothered a guy. I have a hotel room down the block, but your place has a certain appeal. The inviting in is up to you." He stood there and waited. He tried to seem casual.

I looked at Devon clearly, probably for the first time.

I gestured around the fairly small hotel room with a queen-size bed, two chairs, small tables and the usual unusable desk against a wall.

There was a narrow balcony with canvas chairs.

"Not a lot of space for getting work done, right? We could sit on the balcony and chat or go downstairs and I could watch you have a drink." I crossed my arms to calm myself.

"I'm not unhappy you're here for the interview," I said. "Bennie and I were never best friends. Since you didn't give me any advance notice till five minutes ago, I think I have the right to ask you, is Bennie really why you're here?" I waited but smiled at him in a way I hadn't before.

"I could tell you why I'm really here, but I'd rather show you." He picked up his suitcase, set it down inside the room, and closed the door. I didn't stop him. Devon reached out and put his arms around me. He pressed my body against his. We kissed deeply in many exciting ways for a really long time. I came up for air and pulled away from him reluctantly.

"You know this is one time only."

He nodded.

"Like the time I ate a piece of decadent cherry chocolate cheesecake. I mean maybe it was two pieces. At a Christmas party. I'd had too much eggnog. Never again. Just that one night."

I rambled on and Devon's laughter filled the room. His laugh had warmed me from the first moment I'd met him on the street with the speed demon biker. He gently kissed my mouth and moved down my neck. I was having trouble focusing. In another minute I'd be lost in him. I pulled away again. "You know I gave up my run for you and I'll have to exercise at night and you know what happens when I run at night..."

He peered at me.

"I'll race you through one hundred push-ups right now, but I can think of so many better ways to burn calories." His mouth returned to my body which suddenly felt totally alive, pulsed with the electricity I felt from the moment I saw this man.

"We can skip the push-ups," I gasped. "I'll try it your way."

He laughed delightedly again. Now I was too breathless to talk anymore. His hands were warm and his touch was knowing and just the way I thought it would be. He took off my shirt. I took off his. I felt a moment of panic about my marriage, and whether I even knew how to be with another man and for one brief second I worried about those meager 5,275 steps. Could I just do it his way? Just this once...Oh no, those hands, those lips. After that I blissfully didn't think again for a very long while.

Acknowledgements

This book could never have been written without the support and expertise of many people. A huge thanks to my writing coach, Sonia Pilcer, and the other talented writing group members Naomi, Shannon, Clem and Lisa. Sonia told me years ago the main character wanted to be funner.

I am extremely grateful to Aimee Levy who read it first and cheered me on. Aimee and my sister-in-law JoEllen, I thank them both for their artistic assessments.

To the generous writers at the New York City chapter of Sisters in Crime, who laughed in all the right places and provided a safe place to read aloud and a warm home in which to grow. And thanks to all the guppies.

Gratitude to Peggy and Michelle who told me that everything is possible.

Thanks to Kiersten Armstrong for her technical support.

And to my husband, thank you for putting up with the mess, and thanks to my daughter for always showing me a better, quicker way.

About the Author
ngood@nancygood.com

Nancy Good is passionate about mysteries and New York City, where she has lived since graduating from Columbia University. She is a member of Sisters in Crime nationally and the NYC chapter, and is a past member of the Authors Guild. Nancy is the bestselling author of *How to Love a Difficult Man* (nonfiction) and has appeared on numerous TV shows including Oprah and CNN.

She lives in NYC with her husband and her cat. She's a student of herbal medicines, bikes on the trails in NYC, and hikes in the National Parks. Since she sings in choruses in Manhattan, she thinks a murder in a concert choir may be in the future for this series.

Killer Calories is the first in the Melanie Deming Manhattan Mystery series. *Killer Condo* will be next, a murder on Park Avenue.

VISIT OUR WEBSITE
FOR THE FULL INVENTORY
OF QUALITY BOOKS:

http://www.roguephoenixpress.com

Rogue Phoenix Press

Representing Excellence in Publishing

**Quality trade paperbacks and downloads
in multiple formats,
in genres ranging from historical to contemporary romance,
mystery and science fiction.
Visit the website then bookmark it.
We add new titles each month!**